The Elemental Coven

Witch's Ambitions Trilogy Book Two

Kayla Krantz

This is a work of fiction. All of the characters and events portrayed in this novel are either products of the author's imagination or are used fictitiously.

The Elemental Coven

Cover by Laura Callender and James Price
Edited by Kat Hutson

ISBN: 978-1-7324230-3-9
First Edition: August 2018
Library of Congress Control Number: 2018903574

https://authorkaylakrantz.com/

Never be afraid to stand up for yourself or those you love.

Witch's Ambitions Trilogy

Book One: The Council

Book Two: The Elemental Coven

Chapter One

Prisoner

MOST PEOPLE ASSUME that life is like a game of chess, each decision cold, calculating, and ultimately leading toward one large goal—our purpose in life, whatever that may be. I've never agreed with that idea. To me, life is more like Jenga; we stack decisions on top of one another without a guide or any real idea of what we're doing. One wrong move causes it to all come crashing down, leaving you to deal with the ruins your life has become.

And the worst part of it all? There's no precision, no warning that you're reaching that point until it becomes too much. Then it's too late. There's no way to stop it.

Shit happens. Plain and simple.

And that's the vague version of how I've ended up here ... wherever *here* actually is. It's the silence that wakes me, jolting my senses like a burst of electricity. After the chaos on the battlefield, it's unsettling how loud nothing can be. Have I gone deaf? Have I *died*? There's no way to tell.

1

My mind is a hazy web of confusion that proves violent the longer the moment stretches on. I try to wiggle my fingers, but it's hard. Considering I had been completely paralyzed the last time I was conscious, I'm already making remarkable progress. I strain harder, trying to sit up and open my eyes, when razor-like pain shoots through my ribs where I had sustained the most damage. Memories flood my mind at the realization of my consciousness, and I cry out, though I'm not sure if it's from pain or shock.

Can I call it luck that I'm still alive, or is it more of a curse at this point?

My face hurts from lying on the hard surface for so long—agony courses down my neck every time I move—but as my memories return, I hardly notice. I'm a prisoner of war, and it doesn't take much wisdom to know things will only go downhill from here. Maybe it would have been better to just let the darkness swallow me whole. For all the effort the Elemental Coven had gone through to get their hands on me, I don't see them simply letting me go.

I force my eyes open, suddenly fearing the idea of not being alone in this place. Wherever I am, it's *dark*. I can't see no matter where I try to look. I blink and open my eyes again, but the darkness remains unchanged. It's probably for the best. If my situation is as dire as I imagine, I most likely won't *want* to see what's waiting for me. I strain to pick up the smallest sound, but all I hear is the blood pounding in my ears and the steady thumping of my heart in my chest.

Only slightly relieved, I try to move again, but my wrists are firmly bound in front of me. I struggle to remove the bonds, sending fresh waves of pain through my body whenever my sharp elbow grazes my side, and grit my teeth to keep from crying out again. I may be alone for the moment, but as it stands, I have no idea *where* my captors are or when they'll be back.

They could be watching me through magical surveillance, for all I know, waiting for me to wake up so the torture can

2

begin. Images of bleeding and burned witches flash through my head, switching me to panic mode, but I manage to reel my mind in long enough to untie the ropes on my wrists with the telekinesis I've honed over the course of the past month. A sigh of relief passes my lips when they thump to the floor, and I rub at the tender skin, wincing at a particularly raw patch at the base of my palm.

I try to stand, but my weak leg has absolutely no interest in responding to me. I slam back to the floor, on the verge of either screaming or crying … I'm not sure which. Mind racing to form any two-bit plan, my hand accidentally grazes my side, and I feel the cuts—every single one. Oddly enough, it's not physical pain overwhelming me in that moment; it's emotional.

My wounds are nothing. If I live long enough, they'll heal just fine. Only one pain truly matters, a scar I never see healing—Helena's death. My best friend, murdered in the Battle of Ignis by the same witch who left me mutilated.

Why aren't I dead, too? I let out a slow wail of agony that sounds more animalistic than human.

I wish I were dead, that I had died beside Helena, that I wouldn't have to live a moment longer knowing she no longer breathes the same air as me—or *any* air, for that matter. I stop struggling, then. That horrible existence is the one I'm trying to go back to, isn't it? The one without my best friend. Without my parents. Without *anyone*. I chomp my teeth into my bottom lip to stop it from quivering. Crying has never helped me before, and it certainly won't do the trick now.

But how can I do anything else? Everyone's gone besides Clio, but as far as he's concerned… I'm not sure. He abandoned me in the middle of the war, leaving my anxiety to try to guess *why*. The Clio I know would never do such a thing. I trust him with my *life,* so the thought he might've left me for dead is too much to bear.

Is he dead, too? It's the only answer that makes sense.

That reminds me once again that it's nothing short of a miracle that I'm alive, I guess, but my death was never really part of the Elemental's plan. They need me for something, though what that something is, I haven't the foggiest. I'm the most useless of all the witches on the Council. I'm confident in that. I can hardly control my powers—hell, I can barely *walk*—and yet, I'm the one they want for my *potential*. The word has been used on me so much, it's all but lost its meaning. Now, I'm here to stay, even without their pathetic restraints. My leg makes sure of that.

And where are they, my captors?

Eyes the color of a violent thunderstorm fill my mind as I wrack my brain—a desperate attempt to pull out my last memory before unconsciousness claimed me. I can picture the boy who brought me here, and it doesn't help to remember— not much, anyway. I know I'm only doing it because I don't want to *forget* how I messed up, how I doomed myself to this fate, and how it had been *me* who had doomed others in the same way.

I had been so ready to fight tooth and nail for my freedom just a few minutes ago, but I can't now. My will is gone, defeated by my own self-esteem. The more I try, the more I feel the confines of my cage. It isn't a good feeling, being completely and utterly helpless, but here I am. It hurts to admit I'm weak, that I can't save myself, but there's no way around it.

Not anymore.

As I sit in the dark, I contemplate my options. Do I call for help or try to make a break for it? What would a sane person do in this situation? I have no idea, not even a faint inkling, because sanity left me a long time ago. I sit up, cracking the light scabs across my ribs to serve as an instant answer to my dilemma. Between my leg and the injuries sustained in battle, I'm in no shape to go *anywhere*. Even a boost of terror won't get me far in this condition.

Despite it, something within me doesn't want to back down, can't give up. I struggle to stand again, pain erupting in all my damaged areas. Before their death, I had thought my parents' betrayal was the worst pain I could face. It's ridiculous how wrong I had been. I collapse back to the floor with an audible thump, fight completely gone. I ball my hands into fists and whack my knuckles against the hard floor until they bleed. What's the point of going on? If everyone I love is dead, where can I go even if I do happen to escape?

Nowhere.

And for some reason, nowhere is the only place I want to be. I *want* to disconnect, to be away from it all and not think about how I messed up, about how things went wrong so fast. With the walls closing in, death seems my best option, and I'm ready to accept it with open arms. When that thought fades back into the void from which it emerged, I digest it. I had been the brightest witch in my Coven. How did it come to this?

I'm not a bad person. That thought makes me burst into a fit of giggles. I don't even believe it myself.

Chastity's body on the pyre reminds me what kind of person I actually am. *I* was the one who took her life. She was younger than me, and now she's dead. When I get right down to it, I'm not much better than the ones who kidnapped me. So why do I feel like I am?

It's ironic, really.

When I thought I was going to die, I fought to *live*. I *chose* to live, no matter the cost. Now, I'm regretting it. I'm not sure why I ever tried to change my fate. This has always been it. I don't have to be clairvoyant to know that. Alive for the moment, I'm dying on the inside, and the whole process is agonizingly slow. A flash of Helena's lifeless eyes fills my brain again, and a short, sorrowful chuckle passes my lips. It's probably better not to fight, to shorten my endless march to the grave and all the years of pain that might accompany it, but how can I just give up now, after everything?

After the price Helena paid?

I'm lost. Not in the temporary sense, not anymore. It's become part of my persona, the very fabric of my being, and it's absolutely terrifying.

Time has no meaning in this dark pit. I can rock myself to madness in the span of five minutes here. When the door finally opens, it could be two hours later or two days. I have no idea. I groan at the light slowly trickling into my personal Hell as the moment drags on. I blink, and the light strengthens but still doesn't seem right. It's watery, as if I'm seeing through a filter. No matter how many times I open and close my eyes, that doesn't change. I must've been out longer than I realized.

If my captors are coming to kill me, I wish they'd get it over with already. I can't run, I can't fight, and now, to make matters worse, I can't even *see*. The light proves too much for me when I hear the door creak open to its full extent. I lift a hand to block some of the brightness, but it doesn't help. Even worse, I know someone is standing there, *watching* me, but my vision won't cooperate. They're a shadowy outline, a mass of nothingness.

"Finally come to torture me?" I sneer, hoping my captor has no idea that I'm temporarily blind.

Whoever it is remains silent for a long moment, and I wish I could see them more than ever. What are they doing? Watching me? Brandishing a knife or some other primitive weapon, searching for new ways the Council hasn't even thought of to strip me of my dignity?

The possibilities are endless.

"At least you're not in shock anymore," a deep voice finally says. "That's good."

My jaw sets. Even without sight, I know who it is. That voice belongs to my kidnapper—the one with the silver eyes who snatched me from the battle that most likely destroyed my entire Coven.

"You," I snarl, trying to move away from the light and grimacing in pain. If he's watching me, there's no way he didn't notice it.

"Tensions are high, I understand that, but you must listen to me when I tell you we won't hurt you."

That's the opposite of what I expect. I scoff, softly at first, but within a minute, the sound turns to a chaotic stream of laughter. I shuffle, trying again to better see him, and my foot kicks aside the abandoned rope. "You won't?" I lift my arm to reveal the myriad of bleeding wounds down my ribs. Even if I can't see them, *he* can, and I hope they look as bad as I imagine they do. "You *killed* my best friend... my parents... everything's *gone* because of you."

"We're in the middle of a war," he states, as if that answer justifies every tragedy his people have inflicted. So many people are hurting right now, and he doesn't give them a second thought because *he's* still okay.

Typical asshole.

"How can you be so cold?" I whisper. "How can you not care?"

"Think what you will. I can't say I blame you, but everything we do has reason. A purpose."

If that's the truth, I already know why I'm here. I'm the Council's pride and joy. Or I was, anyway. What better way to strike a nerve than by destroying me? "Just kill me, then. I have no information for you. Hell, I barely know anything about my own life. You're wasting both our time."

"I knew you were stubborn, but I didn't realize you downright *ignore* people. I just told you *we aren't going to hurt you*, and I'm not here for information, either." His voice is louder when he speaks, and I realize he's closer.

"Then go away."

"I can't do that, Lilith," he replies. "I have orders."

That can't be good. "Leave me alone," I growl, swiping out blindly, though I have no idea if he's close enough to hit.

"Relax. You're hurt, Lilith. I need to take you to our Healer."

I have no way to respond to that. Words fail me. After everything my loved ones have suffered, why in the world do their executioners care if I live or die? Why am I so important that I'm still alive and they're gone forever?

That's what the whole thing has been about, remember? I freeze at the voice. *Chastity warned you in Mentis that this would happen.*

I have heard this other voice only once before, at Chastity's execution, but I have no idea to whom it belongs. Swallowing heavily, I push away my unease. The voice most likely belongs to another Elemental, but who? And why contact me now when things already look so dire? Are they in the room too? I pause at the idea that I don't know how many of them *are* here. I want to believe there's just my kidnapper, but why would it be so simple?

Nothing else in my life has been.

A hand grasps my elbow, and a scream leaves my lips. In the confusion of hearing the voice, I had forgotten about my kidnapper. "Get away!" I bark, but he doesn't stop.

He pulls me up with ease, and as soon as my feet hit the floor, I forget about my fear. The pain in my ribs is all I *can* feel. It jolts through my body like a handful of jagged razors pumping through my blood, and I scream out in pain, ready to collapse again.

"I'm sorry, Lilith. I know this hurts," he says, but I pay him no mind as he pulls me across the room in what he probably imagines to be as gentle a manner as possible.

My mind shuts down, too overwhelmed by the mix of pain and fear to function properly, and my world turns black.

***

WHEN MY EYELIDS flutter open again, I'm lying on a table with my bare shoulders digging into cold metal. My eyesight is still faulty, so I depend on my other senses to give me a picture of my new and current danger. A light breeze tickles the skin on my shoulders, and I sit up, realizing how much of me is bare under the light blanket draped across my torso.

I screech at the fresh wave of pain shooting into me, and that's met with instant protest. "Don't move too much, Lilith."

My pain disappears at the familiarity of the voice—it's Ambrossi.

Chapter Two

Old Friends, New Enemies

IT'S A NEW sensation, being so confused that I'm at a loss for words. The shock of hearing *Ambrossi* after everything sends my system into a state of disrepair. He's my friend, my Healer... the smartest person I know in all of Ignis when it comes to healing. He's watched over me like a goofy older brother for as long as I can remember. Hell, I've literally put my life in his hands on more than one occasion. My mind can't comprehend the fact that it's *him* sitting before me. That he's here in the pit of my tragedy, *sharing* this moment with me. I had suspected him once of having ties to the Elemental Coven but never put much more thought into the idea.

I guess I should have.

I blink stupidly, so caught off guard that I don't pay attention to the fact that the cloth has slipped away from my more intimate areas. For a moment, I feel as if I've left my body—that I'm merely *watching* this scene and not part of it. Is it a dream? Is it possible I'm in some kind of coma and this is my mind's way of processing it all? My brain swirls with information, grasping at anything to try to comprehend the situation unveiling before my eyes.

Where am I?

Am I still in the bowels of the Elemental's prison, or did the Council somehow save me during my blackout? Am I back in Ignis with whatever's left of my Coven? Or am I dead, and the afterlife is a real thing?

The light from the room fills my vision in a way it hadn't during my last spout of consciousness. I can see again, and I'm quick to take advantage of it. The space around us is white and bare, but when I look past Ambrossi to see a boy with silver eyes smiling at me, I hardly notice a thing about my environment. My kidnapper is here, and Ambrossi seems less than concerned.

The hair on the back of my neck stands on end, and my fingers dig into the edge of the table. "What's going on?" I demand and wince as my words burn all the way up my dry throat. Apparently, I've been unconscious for some time, and it's hard to tell whether or not that's a good thing.

Ambrossi once again ignores my protests and somehow gets me to lie back down on the cold, metal table, carefully rearranging the cloth as he does so. At the gesture, the rest of the scene sinks in, and I realize just how fragile I am in such a dangerous situation. I glance down at my side to see a few drops of red have soaked through the blanket. I shiver, and it inches the fabric aside just enough to see the complete sum of devastation on my side. It's even worse than I pictured it would be.

Ambrossi catches the expression. "You were hurt in the battle," he says, studying me with the intensity of his emerald-colored eyes. "But you're going to be okay."

"Y-yeah… I know," I say, my face twitching in irritation.

Despite how it looks, my new wounds are the least of my problems. I might've trusted Ambrossi before, but I don't now. Everything's upside-down; I'm so deathly confused about the situation I've ended up in, and the last thing I want is for these people to know I'm anything less than confident. "And then I was kidnapped. Don't forget that…" I say with a pointed look at Silver-Eyes. "But that doesn't explain why *you're* here."

"Come on, Lilith, you're a smart girl."

Ambrossi isn't one to beat around the bush. He's open, *honest*… so much so that I had been prepared for him to say three words in response—*I'm an Elemental*. But he didn't. He won't, and that makes me sick in a completely different way. I don't know him. Not really. He's been living a double life of darkness and secrets—as much of a stranger as Silver-Eyes.

"You're one of them?" I say at last.

"It's my understanding that you're one too," he replies calmly, as if that statement doesn't carry all the weight in the world. "Hold on. This will sting." A pinch of his magic jabs through the deepest gash in my side.

I grit my teeth, determined not to show just how much it hurts. "You knew them… Iris and Chastity… didn't you?"

Ambrossi nods once, setting his fingers to the laceration he had just sealed over. He's going out of his way to avoid eye contact, and I can't tell if I'm angry at him for it or relieved. I don't think I could handle the unfamiliar personality coming from a person I thought I had loved.

"You helped Iris attack the Ceremony," I mutter, piecing it all together.

"I had help," he says, mouth set in a grim line as he finally brings himself to meet my eye. "Stop moving." Another piercing pain sears through my flesh, and I reach out, grasping the metal bar of the bed for support.

"Who? Are they still in Ignis, waiting to hurt more innocent witches?" He pretends not to hear me, eyes on the next cut down my side. Frowning, I tack on, "When were you planning on telling me the truth?" The pain makes my voice sound much rougher and stronger than I would've been able to manage on my own. I don't like to show my emotions, but part of me hopes he'll *hear* the pain, that he'll *know* it's not me and that will be enough to bring him back—the Ambrossi I *do* know.

Instead, he says in a cold voice, "I wasn't." I stare down at the floor, blinking just once to keep the tears in the corners of my eyes. He takes that as encouragement to continue. "There were plans, and I had orders. Everyone had their roles to play. You'll learn soon enough."

"Is that right? Do I have a *role* too?" I hiss.

Ambrossi shrugs, drumming his finger on the newly formed scab on my side to test its strength.

My nostrils flare, and I have to resist the urge to sit up again. "How are you so *calm?* Did you not hear the part where I said I was *kidnapped?* Is that my role?"

"In time, it'll come to feel like home," he replies, focused on healing the last two gaping wounds.

I don't respond to that; I *can't.* I go limp on the table, and Ambrossi passes me a small smile, probably with the assumption that I'm cooperating when really I don't know what to do. Things are surreal.

This isn't Ambrossi. I stare up at the stark white ceiling. He has to be brainwashed. That happens, right?

I lift a hand to wave it in my face, checking to see how well my body will respond. I pray for some kind of delay, anything that can give more fuel to my dream theory, but I eventually reach the conclusion that I'm awake. Except things are wrong—backwards, even. If I'm awake, how can I possibly explain this feeling of living outside my body? It's crazy. *I'm* crazy. I have no idea what's right or wrong here, who I can trust and who wants to kill me. The Elementals have already taken so much from me, but then again, so has the Council. Things aren't as black and white as they used to be. They're twisted, with me right in the middle of it all, just a grey line of defiance.

Before the Battle of Ignis, I had thought maybe the Elementals were right. But now, staring at the ugly wounds they've caused with the pain of Helena's death in my heart, I can't decide. Both sides stand in darkness. A darkness so thick, it's impossible to see who's in the wrong—if either of them can make claims of ever being right.

Emotions are very unlike me, but in the moment, I'm a bundle of them. Everything I've held in since my Arcane Ceremony decides to rear its ugly head, and tears burn in the corners of my eyes. My goal had been to save my loved ones. I never actually considered the idea that all the people I want to protect may not be on the same side of the fight.

I can't save everyone. That thought is accompanied by the image of Helena collapsing in the battle, at the light dancing in her soulless eyes as Clio dragged me away from her dead body. Every little thing I had hoped would die deep in the depths of my subconscious has surfaced. One sob passes my lips, and after that, there's no stopping it.

Want it or not, I'm here, and for all my thinking, I can't figure a way out.

Ambrossi's fingers prod at the tender flesh on my side, but I don't look at him. I can't bear the thought of risking eye contact when I'm like this. I'm too vulnerable, and this situation is still too uncertain. I blink a few times and resolve to force every scrap of emotion away from my mind. When the tears finally dry and I'm inevitably embarrassed for letting my fears out on display, Ambrossi senses I'm in no mood to talk. He remains silent and goes to work healing me as tenderly as I had seen Lynx heal Callista after the river poisoning. I know he could've finished it much quicker, but he's taking his time, dragging things out to give me time to breathe.

As much as I hate him right now, I appreciate his thought-fulness. It's the little things that count after all, right?

I keep my eyes on my hands, both embarrassed and surprised by my own emotional outburst. This has been long overdue—I foresee many more in my future—but I hate that it had to happen *here,* in front of my kidnapper and a turncoat, in the midst of this nasty war of which I somehow keep finding myself smack dab in the middle.

From time to time, my eyes stray over to Silver-Eyes, but he doesn't say anything. He's quiet, watching the scene with a lack of emotion on his face. I'm sure I glare every time I glance at him, but he doesn't speak and neither do I. It's like the tension between us has us bonded to an oath of silence I don't remember taking. Finally, Ambrossi's magic recedes from my skin, and he sits back in his chair. Just like his face, his thoughts are impossible to read.

"How do you feel?" Silver-Eyes asks.

"What do you care?" I snarl, glad that he's the one to break the odd silence.

He gives an indifferent shrug. "I don't, really, but I thought I'd attempt being nice. I need to make sure you're almost back to your full strength before you meet Willow."

Of everything that's happened to me over the course of the last twenty-four hours, his words strike me the most.

Willow, the girl of whom everyone refused to speak. The girl who was just like me, who had been *executed* for her abilities.

"But she's—"

"Dead?" he guesses.

I nod weakly—the only movement I can manage. If I

had been confused before, it's nothing to what I feel now.

"Well, things change," Silver-Eyes says and turns to grab a cloth from the table beside him. "Get dressed."

He tosses it to me, and I blush, once again reminded of the fact that I'm essentially naked. I make quick work of pulling the clothing in place. The slim-fitting black dress clings to me in ways I'm not used to. I pick at the fabric as it drags across the new scabs on my side and notice Ambrossi's eyes on me again.

"You'll come back if you have any issues, right?"

I smile and look him full in the face. "No."

He blinks at me, and I see just a hint of concern, but he doesn't push the topic. That's also unlike him.

Pushing away the irritation, I dip my head and jump from the table, gathering what little manners I have left. "Thank you."

It's been a decent while since I've stood on my own two feet without any support—so long, in fact, that I've forgotten just how bad my crippled leg really hurts. It hurts more with the memory that my adopted parents did this to me, that they *wanted* me to suffer like this just to lessen their own anguish. The anger proves too distracting, and I stumble, lurching toward the floor with the sudden rush of agony. I squeeze my eyes shut, but the pain of hitting the floor doesn't come.

I open my eyes and realize Silver-Eyes caught me. He kneels beside me, holding my chest against his, my bad leg trailing behind me mid-fall. His hands on me only serve to further push the anger through my blood, and I gather myself before shoving him away. All I can think of is Clio and how he would knock this boy out if he were here.

But he's not. I'm alone.

My anger slightly put out but not completely distinguished, I glare at him. How can they even pretend to care about me after everything they've put me through? It isn't right.

16

Healing my injuries is the *least* they can do. I shouldn't be grateful for it. I should demand more. A wiggle of power moves inside me, then bursts without further warning into a wave of energy, slamming Silver-Eyes into the wall.

A hint of a smile plays on my lips, then my attention turns to Ambrossi. I try my best to seem intimidating, though I know my appearance is too far off the mark. This is hard. A real stuck-between-a-rock-and-a-hard-place situation. I don't want to hurt Ambrossi—I've *never* wanted to hurt him—but in the moment, I'm not sure I have a choice. He admitted to being one of the Elementals, one of the people who have systematically worked to tear my life apart. After everything I've been through with Ambrossi, I take the betrayal personally.

"Lilith, I'm sorry," he says.

Before I can ask what for, his eyes shift to my leg, and that burning anger is back. Did he know the truth the entire time? Did he also have a role in what my parents had done? I try to throw him in the same manner I had Silver-Eyes, but my powers freeze in place. I *feel* them retreating into my core, content to never return. Turning on my heels, I see Silver-Eyes has gotten back on his feet, gray eyes illuminating with the force of his powers.

Tingling starts in my fingertips, and I start to panic. If he knocks me out this time, how do I know he won't just kill me? The thought of Willow being alive, of her being one of *them*, gives me the sudden energy and courage to fight through the despair that had been so ready to consume me ten minutes ago.

"Lilith! Relax!" Silver-Eyes demands.

I don't acknowledge him. With the tingle spreading through my limbs, I *can't.*

"I'm not going to paralyze you again, okay?" he says.

His words mean nothing to me, but I'm starting to find it difficult to stand, let alone argue.

"I just need to lock up your powers for now. You can't go to Willow like this. Hell, you can't leave this *building* like this."

"You're too unstable," Ambrossi adds in a much nicer tone.

As if that'll make a difference.

I try again to push my powers out, but they won't budge, and the attempt proves too much on my already limited energy supply. This time, I *do* collapse, and neither of them try to save me. I hit the floor with a thud and see stars. The metallic gleam in my kidnapper's eyes disappears, and he lets out a heavy sigh. With the tingle of his magic receding, I take a moment to see myself through his eyes, and I look pathetic. I really do. I can't deny that, but at the same time, I don't pity myself and I don't understand why he pities me, either.

For me to still fight after what I've just endured takes strength, if I do say so myself, even if I am bloody and on the verge of an exhaustion I have no idea how to cure.

"Lilith, I really think we've gotten off on the wrong foot."

I lift my head enough to glare at him, spit a mouthful of blood from the fresh wounds in my tongue, and wait for him to continue.

"I never even told you my name," he says. "I'm Maverick."

I blink at him, unsure what to do with the new information. In no way, shape, or form do I see it ever being useful.

Then he says, "Are you ready to meet Willow?"

Chapter Three

The Land of New Life

ANXIETY. EAGERNESS. WONDER.

My heart can't make up its mind about what I should feel in the moment.

Willow, the girl of a thousand mysteries.

Am I really about to meet my doppelganger? The girl whose life I've essentially shadowed? Can it be this easy after people having avoided the topic like the plague for so long? If it suddenly *is* this easy, maybe I should be concerned. My gut tells me meeting Willow will be good. Surely, the leader of the Elementals will be reasonable, logical … and will tell me why in the hell her people have been willing to risk life and limb to capture me.

It's remarkable in a strange way, like I'm meeting my idol. But she's more than that. Our paths in life have been too similar to be mere coincidence. Somehow, someway, I'm connected to her. Maybe she feels it too. Ending up on this side of the war with her makes me sure of that. No matter what twisted thoughts my brain creates, there's one screaming difference between me and her—she's here by *choice*.

I purse my lips at the thought. Like Chastity, Willow had made the decision at some point in her life to be an Elemental, to *die* for her beliefs. I can't imagine what drives so many witches to willingly take this path, but I know she isn't an average witch. The bit of information I had learned of her was enough to know she had power—*has* power.

She isn't even supposed to be *alive* let alone still in this war.

My head swims with so many unanswered questions, I feel like I'm about to hurl. Did she really die when the Council executed her? If she did, how did she come back, and why does her Coven seem unamazed by such a miracle? My head throbs with the beginning of a migraine, but I hardly notice. Time passes remarkably quickly with me trapped in the bowels of my own mind. I don't even mind the fact that Maverick has had to help me across the building when normally I would've scratched his eyes out just for *thinking* about it.

His strong arm is wrapped across my lower back, and his easy stride carries my own. Anyone catching a glimpse of us in this moment might assume we're friends, though we're anything but. I've hardly noticed his supposed kindness, and it's freeing in a way.

When we exit the building, I'm finally brought back to the present. I don't know what I had expected beyond my prison, but this is not it. For land housing such evil, this place is magnificent, unlike anything I've ever seen before. Eerie, crystal-purple, leafy plants taller than me have sprouted up everywhere, and the air beyond the odd, enchanted forest of plants is of a darker purple. I don't have a clue where we are, but I'm willing to bet it's far from The Land of Five.

Maverick smacks quite a few of the plants away as he leads me through them. Being a good foot shorter than him means I don't even have to bother. I follow with ease, with *wonder*, as if we're close friends and he's about to show me something amazing. I should be panicking. After all, I have no idea where Maverick's taking me, but I'm calm. I could wander through these beautiful plants for days without a care in the world. That's not like me. I suspect that whatever magic lies behind this scenery is responsible for my mood as well.

Maverick smirks once, and I know it's because of the look on my face, but I can't help it. For a moment, just one fraction of a second, the world slips away and I'm a kid again, seeing the beauty in everything without the pain, fear, and anger to accompany it. This place is so different from my old home in the desert-Coven Ignis, it's almost like a fairytale land, and I'm in love.

Do they have fairies here too?

The place just seems too perfect for there *not* to be. That thought reminds me of my friend Fern. Just like Clio, I have no idea if she's alive or dead. I hadn't seen her in that final battle, but suddenly, I wish I had. It's next to impossible to remember the last thing I said to her. If I had known it'd be the last time I'd see her, I would've worked harder to memorize the conversation—or better yet, keep her safe.

The smile leaves my face at that, and I dip my head, no longer as amazed by the world around me. The dirt beneath our feet becomes a smooth gray pavement, making it easier to balance on my bad side. When the maze of plants comes to an end, I push Maverick away, and my jaw drops at the sight of the Victorian-style mansion—similar to the home Crowe, my old mentor, owned in Aquais—sitting on the top of the hill. It's enormous, and I easily imagine it's as large as my entire Coven combined.

"That's Willow's," Maverick says, pausing to catch his breath, and puts his hands in his pockets.

And here I am thinking the Council had been immoral for their lush lifestyle. "Why is it so big for one witch?"

Maverick sucks air through his teeth. "Willow's... *special*. You'll see."

I've already been told she's dangerous. Do they have to keep her tucked away from the rest of the Coven because she's a risk for them as well as me? Maverick's hesitation certainly makes me wonder.

People thought the same of me, too.

I frown. I'm right, of course, but I can't shake the feeling that I'd be better off knowing what I'm up against. "Why can't you tell me?"

"It's hard to explain," he says quickly.

I had expected that answer, so I don't push the topic further. But now I'm curious. If my answers don't lie inside the mansion, then there are none. I follow Maverick into the extravagant building without a single complaint. For me, that's saying something. The foyer is large and beautiful, bronze statues stashed in each corner. Red curtains and tapestries run along parts of the wall, and I clasp my hands together, wary of touching anything. Each piece of fabric is worth more than my life, I'm sure.

When I step farther into the room, a smell washes over me, steady and acrid. I've smelled it before a number of times, but still I freeze and slip my hand over my nose. I turn to Maverick, my eyes streaming water. "What is that smell?"

"Death," he says, his tone unchanging. He doesn't cover his nose, either.

I'm not so careless. How can I willingly venture into a place reeking so strongly of corpses? Either Maverick is madder than I guessed, or there's more to this story than anyone's bothered to tell me. For all I know, this could be the Elementals' dumping ground and I've done them a favor by waltzing here myself rather than forcing them to carry my dead body. The whole Willow thing could've been a ruse to lure me here. Honestly, it's the only way it makes sense.

And look at that. It works.

Maverick walks on, and other than glaring at the back of his head, there's not much else I can do … even if this is a trap. My magic is still locked in my core, and my scars are far too fresh for a physical confrontation. I push away the chills running down my spine and follow him. The smell of rotting flesh only grows stronger, and I consider breathing through my mouth before I realize that's not much better.

The last thing I want to do is *taste* it.

We turn a corner, and a growl catches my attention. Maverick stops, putting a hand out to block my path, and I stop too, though more out of surprise than obedience. I glance around, but through the shadows, I don't see anything capable of making that noise.

"Careful," he warns.

Whatever it is dodges past me. Its growl again echoes down the empty corridor, but I can't place the source for all my trying. Heart pounding, I look desperately to Maverick for answers, but he only offers a smirk. Anger mixes with a rush of surprise, and I take a step forward to see the beast materialize from the shadows in the wall. A tiger stalks toward us, ears flat against its head and teeth exposed, looking as real as Maverick and me despite having appeared from *thin air*. My senses sharpen with a hint of fight-or-flight, but there's something different about this creature. Stitches cross the front of its face and run down its sleek side to a patch of missing fur, revealing bloody flesh beside its shoulder. I breathe in and realize this cat reeks of death.

"It's a work of art, isn't it?" Maverick asks.

The cat pauses to sniff the air, and its ears flick upward again. The growling stops, and I realize now how loud the silence had been without it. The creature swoops down to lick its paw, and my shoulders sag. It seems to have reconsidered us a non-threat, and I'm relieved—if it can be called that. I don't know how to kill something that looks as bad as I feel. The massive cat gives us another once-over before dematerializing back into the shadows.

"What the Hell is wrong with it?" I ask, staring at Maverick through wide eyes streaming water. I don't know how much longer I can tolerate this smell. I already feel as if it's burning the inside of my nose all the way up to my brain.

"It's dead," he says simply, as if it's the most normal thing in the world, and continues walking, passing the spot in the shadows where the tiger had disappeared.

"Oh," is all I can manage. I eye the spot warily before following Maverick deeper into the mansion.

There's another concept I need to wrap my head around. If Ignis is the Land of Fire, this place must be the Land of New Life. First Willow and now animals too? Something about this place must make death a temporary condition. A shiver runs down my spine at the idea.

I glance nervously into every shadowy corner after that. If there's one tiger, who knows how many more there are. And who's to say it's just tigers? There could be grizzly bears or lions—anything waiting to rip me limb from limb. Maverick walks the same way he did before the tiger incident, and I know it hasn't shaken him a bit. What I don't know is *how*.

"How does an undead tiger not chill you down to your bones?" I finally ask.

He shrugs. "Just doesn't."

He's seen it before. He has to have. If he's as close to Willow as I imagine, he's seen it a hundred times over at least.

"Are there others?"

"You ask a lot of questions."

I push my lips into a straight line. "Yeah, that happens when I'm *kidnapped*."

"Oh, get off it, will ya?" Maverick rolls his eyes before putting in the effort to walk faster than I can.

I don't bother to try matching his pace, instead falling back a few steps. What can I expect of my life anymore? This place has me completely upside-down, and studying the blank walls leaves me with the feeling it won't be righted anytime soon. Despite being a mansion, this place doesn't seem glamorous; a person of luxury surely wouldn't be able to stand living in such *emptiness*. It says a lot about the owner.

And I'm not sure I like everything it says.

Crowe's mansion had boasted paintings, photographs, and tapestries on every possible inch of wall—things that show some shred of the owner's humanity, or even *existence*. This place has nothing of the sort. It could be a stage or a theater; I would never believe someone *lives* here even though Maverick claims otherwise.

This mansion, filled only with shadows and silence, is a tribute to Willow's mysterious legacy.

Chapter Four

Willow

IT SEEMS LIKE we've been walking for an eternity, but I'm sure it's only been ten minutes, tops. While Maverick's words still fuel the anger inside me, there's not much I can do about it. So instead, I think of Willow. I can't imagine what she's like in person, but the thought of her pet makes me cringe. At the very least, I can take comfort in the idea that she'll be as disturbed as I am.

The inside of the mansion is a labyrinth. I realize now that the blank walls are a sign, but I hadn't put two and two together. With the walls and corridors looking so similar, I don't know how Maverick walks through with ease. My head pounds with the attempt to map out my surroundings. I can't make heads or tails of it, but I know that if I somehow lose contact with Maverick, I'll be lost.

What a great way to thwart invasion.

Somewhere in my mind, I realize Maverick's talking to me, but I can't understand his words, let alone reply. My mind flits between memories, shown like a compilation of my recent Hell. This place ... I have no words left to describe it or the way I *feel* about it. It was crafted out of war *for* war, and it shows. I've always considered myself tough, resilient—but these witches? They take that idea to the next level.

We come to a Gothic archway barred by a set of red imperial doors, and my mind empties at the sight. I know without knowing that she's somewhere behind them. Suddenly, it's not a fantasy anymore; it's real.

When Maverick turns to look at me, the question in his metallic eyes convinces me I'm right. Despite my situation, I'd been confident until now. The thought of Willow being so close makes my mouth run dry. It was easy to think up a speech when part of me wasn't entirely sure Maverick was being honest, when I was imagining a scene so far-fetched it may as well have been called fiction. Now that I know he's not lying, I'm suddenly at a loss for words.

He doesn't give me much of a chance to prepare before he pushes us inside. On a bookshelf near the door sits a cat with three legs, stitched in the same manner as the tiger. It's hard to look at, but it doesn't seem offended by my cringe. It blinks at us with its one remaining eye and pointedly turns away its nose. This one doesn't blend into the shadows, and I frown at Maverick. Did only the tiger have that ability, or does this cat just happen to be the only creature around *without* them?

"They can't all disappear," he offers. "I think it depends on how long they've been dead."

"Oh." I bob my head. It doesn't make me feel better to think some of these creatures might be as powerful as witches, but it's something I can understand despite the horde of

27

questions it presents.

"Miss? Are you here?" Maverick calls into the seemingly empty room as we step deeper into it.

It's so silent that once again I'm paranoid it's some kind of trap. No one can live in conditions like these, right? We turn the corner into a throne room, and I blink stupidly at the red-carpeted steps leading up to a matching throne. Perched there is a girl—a *woman*, I remind myself brusquely—sitting sideways in the lavish chair so her legs drape over the armrest. Despite being at least a decade older than me, she looks young, nothing like the way I pictured her. Her long, curly hair flows down her back, a few strands falling into her face to obscure her sharp cheekbones and black eyes. She's striking but not in a beautiful way. Her appeal is more otherworldly; she looks stranger than any witch I've ever seen, made even more so by the array of undead tigers and lions lurking in the giant pit in the floor before her.

Some of them eye us suspiciously, but for the most part, they seem to mind their own business. I have a feeling that if we move any closer, they won't be as calm. These cats aren't here to be cute, cuddly pets. They're protectors, warriors, and they're already dead, so they have nothing to lose in a fight.

"Hello, Maverick. Is this the prisoner?" the girl asks, sliding her legs to the floor to prop herself on the edge of the cushion.

Maverick dips his head, fingers laced in front of him as he stares at the ground. "Yes, ma'am."

My face scrunches at his tone. He sounds nervous despite being nearly twice Willow's size. That's power.

"There was a brief confrontation in Ambrossi's chambers," he adds, "but I was able to subdue her. She hasn't said much since. I would think a witch in her position would be more vocal." Maverick raises an eyebrow and looks my way. "She loves your pets, though."

I shrug, knowing the comment is meant as a sting to get a rise from me, but I don't want to play his game. I *don't* mind her pets much. As long as they keep their distance, of course.

"See? She's the Queen of this game."

I force down a smirk at that. He knows exactly what I'm doing. I might not like Maverick, but seeing his relationship with Ambrossi offered me a better opinion of him than I would have had otherwise, though it's still hard to forget he's the reason I'm here.

"The Queen, huh? Can that be my official title?" I ask, lifting my chin. This is the first thing I've said in Willow's presence, the first time she hears my voice. I want her to sense my strength, if not from my physical appearance than through my confidence.

Willow frowns and swipes her long brown hair over her shoulder. "No. The only Queen around here is me. And I hope you didn't spook my pets with all your stomping around. They're a little excitable."

"*Me* spook *them?*" I ask, jaw hanging open in disbelief. "Look at them! They're not pets, they're *monsters*. *Maybe* try hanging some kind of warning sign outside the door."

Willow smiles coyly at Maverick. "She's talking now."

My shoulders sag as I realize I fell for her game. Maverick raises his eyebrows but decides not to say anything else.

"You've done well, Maverick. I'll let you know when I need you." Willow gives him a dismissive wave, and all signs of playfulness are gone, just like that.

He doesn't waste a second in leaving the room, slamming the door for emphasis. The dead felines seem the same for his absence, but I eye where he'd just stood in envy. I'd rush away from the smell of this place too if I could. Once Maverick is out of earshot, Willow turns her odd black eyes on me, and I shiver when our gazes meet. Suddenly, I remember she's as dead as her pets, and I feel more than uncomfortable being here alone.

"You must be wondering why you're here."

I scan the undead felines around her before meeting her gaze once more. "Among many things." I find that the more my eyes meet hers, the easier it is to look at her. I wonder exactly how her magic works ... and to what extent it affects the witches she encounters.

"You'll get your answers in time," she promises.

I want to believe her, but I don't. I *can't.* I scoff and roll my eyes. "Yeah, that's what the Sage tried to feed me, too."

"I bet you were told many lies over there," Willow says, cupping her chin in her hand.

"As I'm sure will be the case here." I'm a captive of *war,* for crying out loud. Lies are the least of my concerns, but she brings up a good point. I've been given the short end of the stick for too long. When does it end?

"The lies end here, Lilith. I mean it when I say we want to help you."

I narrow my eyes. Can she read minds like me, or was that just a fortunate guess on her part? "You do? Really? And why should I believe that? After everything your people have done, you want me to believe you care about me?"

Willow breathes deeply through her nose and looks down at me, an absence of emotion on her face. I can tell she's processing what I said while trying to keep the lid on her own emotions. It's a face I'm sure I make a lot, but she seems better at it.

"I understand why you're hesitant," she says. "If I were in your position, I'd feel the same. You've been through many trials in the past few weeks, but we're not the bad guys."

Tears bubble in the corners of my eyes. So maybe I'm

not as good at composing myself as she is. Her voice is so calm, like everything hasn't changed in the past twenty-four hours, and I know it's because *her* world has not. She didn't care about Helena or my parents. She didn't know them, so their deaths are nothing but another casualty.

"How dare you lie to me?" I spit, clenching my hands into fists. "How dare you face me with your good-for-nothing promise like it wipes everything away... like it'll fix everything you've destroyed?"

Willow blinks and drops her hand to her side, apparently waiting for me to finish my rant.

I gladly oblige. "You killed my best friend. You killed my parents. You destroyed my home Coven. You don't give a damn about me or my people. You've set out to destroy me for curbing your attack on the Arcane Ceremony. Am I right?"

Willow sighs. "I'm sorry you feel that way, but you're wrong. I never wanted to hurt you for that. In fact, I love hearing the story of how you rushed in like a lioness to protect your friend." She pauses to tap her forefinger against her lip. "You'd be surprised by just how complicated a situation this is all around."

"But *you* destroyed my Coven. Not them. You," I spit.

Willow shakes her head. "On the contrary. We *saved* it."

I can only blink for a minute, shocked by her statement. "The survivors... if there *are* any... will be sick. They have no hospital to care for them."

"*We* didn't burn it," Willow says, eyes locked onto mine.

I search into the depths of her eyes for some sign of a lie, but I don't see one, and it angers me. "Then who *did?*"

"The Council."

"Bullshit. I was with Crowe and Tarj when it happened."

"Mm-hmm, and where were Rayna and Hyacinth?"

"The... the Sage sent them to Aens for... for a special

mission."

"Uh-huh. Are you sure?"

No. No, I'm not. I realize that despite being skeptical, I had taken the Council's word at face value, no grain of salt anywhere. When they blamed the Elementals for all the death and destruction, I had been quick to believe them. Even worse, I helped them.

I'm a pawn too. A *stupid* one. "Why would they do this?" I demand.

"What better way to not only draw out the Elementals but unite the witches capable of rebellion by destroying an entire Coven?"

I feel like the floor is about to disappear underneath me. Could she be right? Could it be that this entire time, I've been fighting on the wrong side of the war?

"You're wrong," I say, unwilling to admit defeat.

Willow puffs out her cheeks and looks up at the ceiling for so long that I look too, just to see what she's looking at. There's nothing there, but finally, she turns back to me and says, "This conversation is best saved for another time, one in which you're more comfortable. If it means earning your trust, how about a peace offering?"

I fold my arms across my chest, trying my best to hide all the pain, both emotional and physical. My leg feels ready to buckle at the knee, and despite Ambrossi's magic, my side throbs like I've been stabbed with hot metal. The tiger closest to me sniffs the air and licks its muzzle. It smells that I'm weak, that I'm injured. It probably knows more about me than I do by my scent alone.

If it knows how worthless I am, surely Willow does too. So why does the leader of the *Elementals* care to make peace with *me*? For the life of me, I can't think of anything she could earn from the effort. I don't even know if there's anything she *can* do earn my trust at this point, but I'm certainly not about to discourage her from trying.

"What do you have to offer me?"

"I think you'll like it. Consider it a token of goodwill," she says and claps once.

A set of doors, similar to those I entered with Maverick, open from the wall behind her. They move in slow motion, but the next passing moment is very real. A girl with bright red hair walks through the archway, and the world spins around me when her black and green eyes meet mine.

It's Helena.

Chapter Five

Helena

'VE FAINTED BEFORE, but it's nothing like my reaction to Helena's reappearance. My legs collapse under me, but I have no strength to stop it. I feel my mind disconnect from the rest of my body, and everything moves so slowly again.

I'm thankful I passed out before I hit the floor, because I'm sure the impact was rough.

When I come to again, I blink to clear my eyes, grateful to still be able to see. Silky fur brushes my arm, and I jolt away from it in reflex. An undead tiger passes me, not even bothering to look at me as it stalks away. It takes a moment to remember where I am, then all at once, everything comes screaming back in a whirlwind of thoughts that refuse to focus.

I shut them *all* down, focusing instead on the physical

situation of my hands. My fingers clench at my side, feeling the stones beneath my body, and I know where I am—in the shallow pit. I must've fallen right in. A loud breath fills my ear, and I turn to see the tiger beside my head. He'd snuck back in the fraction of a second I'd looked away, and the thought startles me. *Magical* animals are apparently not my cup of tea. I lock eyes with the beast for just a moment, and the same shiver that ran through me when I looked into Willow's eyes returns. If eyes are the windows to the soul, are these undead creatures so unsettling because they no longer *have* one?

The tiger blinks its massive eyes and watches me, as if I'm the most interesting thing it's ever seen. Groaning, I struggle to sit up, and the cat jerks its head away like I struck it, pausing its sniffing to watch me through glowing, black and amber eyes. Its head remains bowed to study me, and I wonder if I should be concerned. I ignore the reaction instead and raise my hand to my head. Only then do I realize Willow kneels beside me with her hand on my knee—the reason for the cats' watchful eyes.

"Lilith, are you okay?" she asks evenly, black eyes boring into mine. Can she see into my soul? I feel like she can. "You hit your head pretty good."

I dig my fingers through my hair until I find a lump. She's not lying about that. "I-I'm really not sure anymore," I say, dropping my hand before my eyes dart to the place Helena had stood before my fainting spell.

I want to verify it hadn't been just a dream, but the sight of her again doesn't strike me as real. She hasn't moved from the place beside Willow's throne. Like with Willow, an ethereal white glow surrounds her, like she's my own personal savior from the agony my life has become.

I don't know how I manage to pick myself up off the ground without magic, or how I do it so *fast*, but the next thing I know, I'm holding my dead best friend in my arms. I never want to let her go despite the potent smell of decay wafting from her body. I ignore it, burying my face in her orange curls and knotting my hands together in the small of her back.

Nothing can tear us apart right now.

"Helena, when he killed you…" I stare at the wall behind her. I have absolutely no idea how to finish that statement. I can't make eye contact; the emotions in me are too raw, too *unstable*, as they were in Ambrossi's chambers. Letting anyone, even Helena, know how much pain I'm really in leaves me feeling suddenly vulnerable, *weak*, and I can't risk that here when I still have no idea what they want from me. Even though Willow chooses to be silent, I feel her watching us and know she's listening just as intently.

It's not important. All that matters is Helena. Even though I kept breathing, my world ended the same moment hers did, and I can't imagine the perfect way to get her to understand that. It's hard to believe she's back, that at least one wrong in my life has been made right.

She pulls back to smile at me, and I don't stop to wonder if I'd squeezed her too tight to breathe—or if she even needs to anymore. She's so pale, I can see all the bluish lines of the veins in her face, but it doesn't seem important because there's *life* in her eyes. In the back of my mind flashes the all-too-vivid image of what they looked like dead, and I wish more than anything that someone would wipe that image from existence. As long as she's breathing, or at least *seems* to be, she can have two heads and I won't care. No words pass her lips, but they don't need to. Somehow, I know by the gesture alone that she understands what I want to say—what I *feel*.

"Now that that's out of the way, do you accept my gift?" Willow says behind me.

She sounds closer, but I don't turn to check. I nod slowly without taking my eyes off Helena. I've never been more grateful for anything in my life. I don't want to think about what Willow might do if I refuse. Willow sets her hand on my shoulder, and very hesitantly, I pull my hands off Helena, as if I'm scared she'll disappear completely once I do.

Willow smiles. "Your friend will be here later."

"Mm-hmm," I mumble, too wrapped up in the moment to realize that's her way of politely returning to business, of pulling me away from this rare bliss.

"We have much to discuss then, Lilith. Helena, you're dismissed."

I swallow roughly. Bringing Helena back to life was most likely *not* an easy task on Willow's part. If I were her, I'd expect something in return. But I have no idea what that is.

More importantly, I'm not sure I can afford it.

Helena dips her head before turning to leave the room. It hurts that she doesn't try to argue—that she doesn't try to stay by my side. '*Your friend will be here later,*' Willow had said. I need to focus, I know I do, but it's hard now that my mind is split. Maybe that was the point of this. What better way to win than by lowering your enemy's guard?

When the stately doors swing shut behind Helena, I wonder about her not having spoken a word. How badly had she been damaged by the battle that had ultimately killed her? And more importantly, how much of that had Willow fixed when she brought Helena back?

"It takes time to adjust," Willow says.

"Huh?" I ask, tearing my eyes away from the now closed door.

"You're worried about your friend, but you don't need to be. She'll be okay." She reaches out an eerily white hand to pet the head of the massive feline beside her. It had climbed out of the pit, so ready to protect her from any potential threat that it stuck as close to her hip as it could manage. The beast purrs and inches toward her before licking the palm of her hand.

I press my lips together. I want to believe Willow, but that skeptical voice in the back of my mind doesn't cooperate. What if this is all a trick just to get me to agree to her terms, whatever they may be? Elemental powers are unconventional. I wouldn't be surprised if Willow has a witch somewhere who can make people see things that aren't there.

"I was the same way when I first came back," Willow adds.

My concern for Helena turns to wonder. I may have been through a lot, but I've never *died*. Not yet, anyway. Willow knows what it's like on the other side, or if there is one at all. She's seen it firsthand, and Helena has too.

No wonder her gaze is so chilling.

I look at her for a long moment, but I'm not sure what kind of expression I should wear. "The Council... *killed* you, right?"

Willow nods, a hint of a smile playing on her thin lips. The reaction is as unsettling as her eyes. "I have the power of resurgence, Lilith. I can bring just about anything back to life."

"Even yourself," I murmur with a new sense of awe. For all the power I possess, I can't imagine a stranger feeling than bringing myself back from the dead. Or anyone else, for that matter.

"The comfort I find in death, other creatures could never understand. Eventually, we all die. It's our ultimate destination in life, but it doesn't have to be terrifying. It's beautiful. Every aspect of life is beautiful. After all, it's not a matter of *if* we die but rather *when*."

She's right in a way. We're all promised death, or at least, we're *supposed* to be.

"That's what I used to think," she admits, dipping her chin to cast a shadow over her eyes. "Now? I'm not so sure."

Neither am I. Before the Elemental Coven, there had only been one thing I was ever certain of—death—and now I can't even guarantee that.

"Still. Whatever *this* is"—she says, gesturing to her body and the massive cat beside her—"it's easier than living. Without having to eat or go to the bathroom, it's a very low-maintenance existence."

I stare at her for a long moment. On the battlefield, when I thought I was minutes away from death, I hadn't been scared—I was *calm*. Peaceful, even, with the resigned thought of my death at the front of my mind.

Maybe she's right about that too.

Despite everything I've heard, she looks so normal—so *sweet*. I'm confused about how I should feel for her, but that's the danger. If the story Crowe told me is true, she led an all-out war against the Council once. It was *why* she had died, or at least the reason the Council had chosen to give. Not that they have a record for truth-telling. "Why did they do it?" I ask.

"Kill me? I'm sure you've heard theories."

"Yeah, well, the third side to every story is what actually happened. That's the one I'm most interested in," I reply.

"That's a tale for another time," she says, turning away. The tiger she had been so intent on petting looks up at me with what may be sneer on its dead face.

I frown, on the verge of a pout. Willow had promised my experience with her would be different than what I went through with the Council, but so far, it's the same. I'm being given bits and pieces—not enough to complete the story but just enough to entirely change the way I see it.

My impatience gets the best of me, and I try without success to probe her mind. The wall surrounding her thoughts is the thickest I've ever experienced, and I'm disappointed for believing the result could be any different. You don't become the leader of anything by letting anyone and everyone traipse through your thoughts.

"So, what happens now? Are you forcing me to stay?" I call after her.

"Do you not want to?" she asks, looking at me over her shoulder.

Her voice is so soft, lilting, as if my answer to that question won't change *everything*. Of course I don't want to be here, but how can I leave, knowing Helena's here too? That Willow is *alive?* That the Elemental Coven is thriving?

"Will the Council look for me?" I ask. "Do... do they want me back, or have they already labeled me a traitor?"

"It doesn't much matter. Either way, they'll find a replacement... they have to," Willow says, moving back to her throne at the top of the tiger pit. She watches her cat curl into a ball at her feet.

But I know I'm not so easy to replace. Doesn't she?

I'd been the Sage's apprentice, next in line to take the most powerful position in the Land of Five. My results in the Arcane Ceremony weren't close to being matched by anyone, and if that's not bad enough, they let everyone know how special I really am. I'm prone to develop five powers at the least, and that's not something *anyone* can do. Something tells me they won't just forget.

Not that easily, anyway.

"I don't think you've told me what it is I'm doing here," I say, clenching my hands into fists.

Willow plops down in the throne, making it a point to meet my gaze. "You're my sister."

Chapter Six

Blood, Bonds, and Breaks

*M*Y EARS FILL with a blasting ring that blocks out everything else, and spots dance in my vision. I brace myself, convinced I'm on the verge of fainting again, but I don't. I collapse to my knees and stretch my hand toward the ground, closing my eyes to try ridding myself of the swirling motion. The sensation passes, but I still hate myself for it. Willow's haunting word echo in my mind. How can she be my sister? How can I be related to *her*, this ghost of a girl, the leader of the rebellion?

I feel someone's arm propped underneath me a second before cold liquid runs down my throat. I splutter, not at all gracefully, and struggle to regain myself. When the water makes it to my stomach, I have the strength to open my eyes. They focus on Willow's eerie black irises before I break free of her grip. She pulls away a few feet, a glass of water clutched in her hands, but over my rising tide of nausea, it's hard to be sure of anything.

It can't be true. It just can't.

"Did I hear you right?" I force myself to ask.

"Yes," she says, setting down the glass before gathering her white gown to sit on the edge of the tiger pit. By the way her clenched jaw moves, I have a hard time telling if she's angry or hurt. Either way, the expression leads me to believe she's telling the truth.

And that somehow makes me feel even worse about the whole thing. So instead of doing something, I do nothing. I sit on the floor, staring down at my hands as if I've never seen them before. The undead cats leave a wide circle of space around me, as if even they sense something in me is off kilter. I don't know how to respond to Willow, just as I don't know how much time passes in silence. Willow gives me time to absorb the news, and I'm grateful, though not as grateful as I'd be if I never knew the truth at all.

My real parents are most likely dead, and my adopted parents definitely are. But now a sister I didn't know I had is alive—in a strict manner of speaking—and she's less than five feet away, waiting for my *opinion* of her.

"Where have you been all this time? Why…" I find myself as tongue-tied as I'd been when face to face with Helena. There are so many holes in the story of my past that I don't know where to start trying to make sense of the few pieces I have. What questions should I ask? Or better yet, which questions *can* I ask without upsetting her?

I know just one thing about my childhood—Regina and Howard, my adopted parents, had gotten me from my real parents somehow. All I know about them was they'd been Mentis witches and crippled me for life in an attempt to hide my real powers. I don't know why they took me or how they got me in the first place.

I run my tongue along my teeth, casting another glance at Willow from the corner of my eye. Can it be possible that other members of my family are out there somewhere, hiding until the war blows over?

"I understand this must be distressing," she says as she catches me eyeing her.

A flash of indignation crosses through my confusion, and I narrow my eyes at her. "You *think*?" Distress doesn't seem a strong enough word to describe the chaos in my heart and mind. She's had *years* to deal with this, knowing who she was the entire time. She had never been left to wonder, never abandoned in the web of lies and darkness like I have.

"Take a breath," Willow says, and I obey, but it doesn't stop the world from spinning around me.

After Regina told me the truth of my accident, minutes before her death, I thought I had my life figured out. No more secrets, no more surprises, but I've barely scratched the surface. I don't know how deep the truth goes, and the thought that I might *never* know hits me like a sucker punch to the gut. Who *were* my real parents? And how did I get torn away from them?

Frowning, I finally ask, "What happened to them? Our parents?"

Willow's face remains expressionless, but I can see a thousand memories in her eyes. I'm not the only one this conversation pains, and I almost regret my topic of choice. "If you think they abandoned you, they didn't," she said. "They're dead. Both of them."

I hadn't known that for sure, but it didn't surprise me. I press my lips together and wonder if she thought that news would've been better received than my assumption. I'm handling them both the same. "I figured that. Tell me the truth. They were Elementals too, weren't they?"

She glances down at her hands, pressing her palms together as if deep in thought. "Powerful ones."

"So, you've kept up the family legacy," I say, unable to hide the venom in my voice. I don't know what's a lower blow—learning that I'll never meet my real parents or learning that they're the reason I'm in this mess in the first place.

"Lilith, you must understand it's not as if they planned this. Any of this."

I raise an eyebrow. For her to still be so trusting after everything she's gone through really says something about her character. I wonder how she does it. "But they did," I say. "Even if it wasn't intentional. They knew what joining this war would mean for them... for their family. They *sacrificed* us. Don't you see that?"

"No. What I see are two people who gave it their all for the sake of the greater good." Willow pauses for a moment. "You're too young to remember them, but I do. They loved us *so* much. They never wanted anything bad to happen to us."

"Then what happened? Both of us have had terrible lives, and we have them to thank for it," I say and force myself to stand, using the jolt of pain in my leg to further fuel my anger.

"Life is just a series of events, not all of them planned. They were wonderful people, Lilith. And as such, they fought for what they believed in. Don't you see they did this *for* us?"

"Clarify," I say, my body rigid with fury.

"They fought in the war to try to make the world a better place for *us,* even though they knew it could and probably *would* cost them their lives."

I snort, but the longer her words hang in the air, the more my resolve fades. "They died with you, didn't they?"

Willow shakes her head, a tear caressing her cheek. I didn't know she was capable of that; apparently, her existence isn't as low-maintenance as she believes. "They died in battle. Dad died saving me, and Mom died for you."

Now it's my turn to cry. I'm tired of that—people *dying* for me. To think my own mother valued my life more than her own and I've done nothing but hate her. "If we were born into this, as enemies of the Council, why aren't we dead too?"

Willow simpers and jumps to her feet before taking two steps along the edge of the tiger pit. "You forget, I *did* die."

"If not with them, then when?"

"I was executed... not too long after the battle that claimed them. In all honesty, I don't know how I brought myself back, but here I am, and one thing's certain. I will never let them do that to me again."

I remember watching Iris and Chastity's executions. They had been burned to ash, impossible to distinguish from a handful of dirt. It's hard to imagine Willow taking the pile of nothingness to which her body had been reduced and building herself back cell by cell.

"I don't remember any of this," I say, staring blankly at the floor.

"As I said, you were young."

I pause to let the information sinks in. "If I was just a baby when you were executed... that was less than twenty years ago," I say, uncertain if I should scream that fact or whisper it. When Fern told me about her—even when Tarj, Ignis' representative in the Council, mentioned Willow later—the stories had made it seem as if Willow's death had happened *centuries* ago, so far in the past that the information had no hope of existing now in the Land of Five.

How had people forgotten about her so quickly?

Willow reads the question on my face. "The Council has a witch who can make others think certain thoughts... or forget them. Her name is Tabitha. She's the Council's lifeline, for obvious reasons. If people think things are fine, there's no reason for them to rebel."

I knit my eyebrows together. "If that's true, if she has such a huge role to play in the Land of Five, then how come I've never met her?"

"No one has but the Sage."

"Then how do you know she even exists?"

"We've seen encounters with her inside the Sage's memories. You know it's impossible for the human mind to *create* images of a face it's never seen."

I consider this. "So… Tabitha's erased your story from every mind in the Land of Five. But not ours. And she couldn't keep it from the people who told me about you. Why?"

"At one point," Willow says, "every single one of us was affected by her power. But with the truth, she becomes even easier to tune out. To deny. Plus, there's something to be said for dying. Mentis magic just seems to have a weaker effect on us."

I glance up at her, trying to gauge the emotion in her words. "What's it like? To die?" I ask, reaching out to skim my fingers down the nearest tiger's back. The skin beneath the fur is cold and stiff, but a low purr rumbles up its throat, as if it were very much alive.

"I don't remember much about it. I doubt Helena does, either. When the brain dies, it also stops making memories. One moment I was burning alive, and the next, I was lying in the mud, gasping for air. There's a big black gap of nothingness in between."

I try not to do it, but her emotions create an opening in the barrier around her thoughts. Through the hole, I see it—her demise and her rebirth. I don't know which one is more haunting, but I don't envy her. When the memories fade from my own mind, a chill runs down my spine, and I meet her gaze.

It's good to know I'm not the only one with a painful past.

"You're powerful, clearly," I say. "You brought Helena back... But what about my parents? Are they here?"

Willow raises an eyebrow.

"My *adopted* parents."

She sighs and sets her hand on the golden armrest of her throne. "No. No, they're not."

I tilt my head, avoiding Willow's gaze. I don't know how to feel about her statement. It's true I didn't have the best relationship with Regina and Howard toward the end, but the thought that they're still dead leaves me cold. They did raise me, after all, and for that, I owe them *something*.

"Why? Why bring back some people and not everyone?"

"Think of what a horrible place this world would be if I brought back *everyone*, Lilith. In order for there to be life, there must be death."

"I wasn't asking you to bring back everyone. Just my parents."

Willow sighs again and swipes her hair out of her face. "This is difficult for me to say, but if you must know, I could've brought one of them back."

My eyes drift in turn to each of the undead felines around us; there are at least ten here. It's hard to keep the suspicion out of my voice. "Just one?"

"I... it exhausts me... using this gift. Have you ever used your magic until your reserves ran out?"

I don't want to sympathize with her, but I've felt that before just once—empty and hollow, a generally terrible feeling.

"Bringing back one life, whether animal or human, does that to me," she says.

"But your pets—"

"Are all in varying stages of decomposition," she

continues.

When I study the cats, I see she's right. Her power isn't as straightforward as I'd thought. With any miracle comes a catch, and Willow's ability is no exception.

"I had so many of my warriors to help, and I thought you'd be over the moon with Helena. You have to believe me when I say I wish I could've brought them both back, but I couldn't. It would've been too much. I tried what I could, but when we went back for them, the Council had already taken possession of the bodies."

I give her a curt nod, careful to keep my face angled toward the floor so she can't see my emotions.

"And… wouldn't it have been more painful for me to bring back just one, knowing I *chose* which one got to live? At least this way, they're together."

I swallow once, rough and jagged as her words settle. I can understand where she's coming from—really, I can—but that doesn't stop the pain. In a way, she's right. I would have preferred my mother, and if she had chosen my cold-as-ice father, I might've grown to resent her for it. Who knows?

"Why was I spared, then?" I ask, trying to change the subject and the train wreck of my thoughts with it.

Willow draws her eyebrows together. "I told my fighters not to hurt you."

"No, not that battle. The one that killed our parents… that killed *you*."

Willow shrugs. "The Grace of the Gods, I'd imagine."

I snort. If the Gods have any role in this, I'd hate to think what he has planned for me in the future. "They wouldn't talk about you, you know. You're taboo. *Everything* about my past is," I say, clenching my hands into fists at my sides.

"Because what they did to me… to our *family*… was wrong, and they know it."

The room falls silent as the three-legged cat on the bookshelf jumps to the floor. Tail held high, it makes its way to Willow, and she scoops it up without an ounce of hesitation.

"Why did no one tell me the truth?" I ask as she goes to work scratching it behind the ears.

"*They* probably didn't even know. Honey, if there's one thing the Council is good at, it's lying."

A chuckle rumbles up my throat, and before I know it, I'm full-out laughing like a psychopath, so forceful and sharp that the scabs on my side crack open and bleed again.

Willow eyes me in concern. "Are you okay?" When a drop of my blood hits the floor beside me, she looks at it and blinks. "I think you need to go lie down for a bit."

"No. Forget that. What I *need* is to figure out how to get back at these people... to finally stop them."

Willow smiles wide enough to show the gap in her teeth. "That's what sisters are for."

Chapter Seven

Settling In

I GENUINELY LIKE WILLOW.

This emotion comes as a surprise even to me. After first hearing the hushed whispers of Willow's existence back in Ignis, I had built up my own image of what she would be like. I was wrong, but oddly enough, that's a *good* thing.

She's strong. Stronger than I'll ever be. Like a phoenix, she rose from her ashes and took charge of her life. She rallied others to follow her, to get back at the people who ruined her. I can learn a lot from that example. Despite all I've ever been through, I'm still just a fragile creature. She's experienced *death,* and yet her outlook on people, on life in general, is far better than mine will ever be. It took being here for me to realize how much I'm lacking as a person. With everyone telling me how powerful I am, it had been too easy to forget that I'm *not.*

For the rest of the day, Willow doesn't bother to go much more in depth about how we'll get back at the Council, but the gleam in her eyes comforts me. I like that twinkle; it shows promise. I saw the same in Helena's eyes at one point before life had stolen away her hope.

Thinking of her rips the joy from my body. I'm relieved that she's alive, that she doesn't blame me for her death—I think—and that Willow's my true-to-life, flesh-and-blood sister, but it all seems too perfect. Something is bound to take a turn for the worst, right?

I'm still a prisoner of war.

But am I really?

I ponder the question for a long time. When Willow asked, I hadn't answered her because I have no answer to give. If physically I'm free, my mind will never leave. While I might not care for Maverick, he hasn't physically harmed me, even when he could have in Ambrossi's chambers. Willow said I'm safe from her hunters, and I trust her word on the issue. Wandering around the manor full of undead 'pets,' however, gives me the distinct feeling that I'll be met with opposition if I try to leave.

Willow turns her attention to me. "Are you hungry?"

I've been so wrapped up in my thoughts that biological necessities like food and sleep are easy to forget. For not needing either, she sure keeps track better than I do. With the moment of rest from my hellish anxiety, my body seems to remember that even though I've been tasked with a superhuman mission, I myself am sadly mortal.

"Yes, I am," I reply as we step into the grand hall.

It's lusher than the Council's quarters had been. A long dining table with an embroidered white tablecloth takes up the center of the room, surrounded by blue, gothic-style chairs. A glass chandelier hangs above the table. The walls, like the rest of the manor, are blank.

"I'll get you something," Willow murmurs. "Wait here."

I plop down gratefully into the nearest chair and rest my head on the table as Willow makes a very regal exit. When she returns, she's carrying a plate of the most amazing food I've ever eaten in my life. Midway through my meal, one of her tigers wanders up to me, sniffing for a bite. I pause, eyes darting between the chicken and the tiger before flicking to Willow. She nods, and I slip the rest of my chicken to the cat, who happily accepts with a crunch of its jaws.

"You can pet him if you want. Despite what they look like, they're sweethearts," Willow says.

I've already touched a handful of them, but the fact that this one holds my gaze makes it more intense. Does it feel threatened by me? It's impossible to tell *what* it thinks. My hand shakes as I move it toward the cat's face, but it accepts the gesture with a bow of its head.

"I didn't think they needed to eat... anymore," I say, stroking the soft fur along the side of its face.

"Some of us do, some of us don't. Depends on how long we've been dead," she says with a shrug.

I translate that to mean it depends on if their internal organs have rotted away or not. The tiger licks its mouth and plods away, tail swishing happily with each step. It doesn't have a care in the world, and I wish I can say the same. Watching Willow's pets only adds questions to the pile I already have. Can these creatures die again? Do they keep rotting away until they're nothing, or does Willow's magic actually make them immortal? Her tiger had eaten, and to me, that suggest *something*.

"Will they... will you... *die* someday?" I ask.

Willow shrugs and shrinks in on herself. "I don't know," she admits. "And that's a scary thought."

"You've never seen one of your pets die?"

She shakes her head. "They've disappeared. Runaways,

I've always believed."

"Maybe," I reply, but part of me isn't convinced. Maybe they did die and she wasn't aware. That still doesn't explain their missing bodies. "So why tigers and lions?" I ask to lighten the mood.

She shrugs, seeming grateful for the attempt. "They're my favorite. What's your favorite animal, Lilith?"

I blink, and my mind plunges into memories. My first thought is a cat as I remember the silver ball of fur that used to belong to Helena. "Something I can depend on," I begin to say before I realize I'm even speaking. "A dog."

Willow nods and watches me take another bite of chicken. "Good choice."

***

WILLOW TRIES A handful more times to send me to bed. The more I fight it, the more my resolve crumbles. Even if I don't want to sleep, I can't deny how tired I am. The wounds on my ribs are still in bad shape, maybe even worse since I've given them no chance to heal, and I know they'll only go downhill from here if I continue to push myself.

At the end of the tour, Willow has me stay in a room alone. It looks like it had been a bedroom once, but now it contains a handful of bookshelves, a desk, and a chair. It's oddly quiet inside, and even though I don't hear her lock the doors on her way out, I'm paranoid she did, just as I'm convinced Maverick will appear at any moment to take me to my holding cell.

It unnerves me that she didn't tell me where she had to go. When she comes back, she's alone. "Sorry about that. Had some business to take care of," she says and pauses as if she spots the question on my face. "You're not getting put back there," she informs me matter-of-factly. "There's no need for it."

"So, I'm *not* a prisoner anymore," I state, unsure whether or not I mean it as a question as I search the room behind her, expecting another witch to enter at any moment.

"Do you feel like you are?" she asks, propping her chin on her hand.

I shake my head.

"Good. You'll come to like it here, I promise."

I nod without emotion. It's too soon for me to guess either way.

My response seems to relax her. "Let me show you to your room."

There's a phrase that gets my attention. In my time spent on the Council, I had been promised a room but had never actually been given one, instead being forced to bunk with other Council members. I follow without protest from the splendor of the odd room down the empty hall. It seems to be the farthest from the main portion of the manor, and I wonder if there's a specific reason she chose it. The farther we go, the more piqued my interest. When Willow finally selects a door to push open, I freeze. There's a dog sitting in the middle of the room. White fur covers it from its head down its shoulders, making the ugly lengthwise scar down its side more visible. I shiver, immediately guessing it had been completely cut in half at one point. It doesn't seem bothered by the fact as it stands, letting out a little yap to make my bones rattle.

"How do you like him?" Willow asks from behind me.

I blink, trying to regain myself the same way I had after my first encounter with the undead cats. "How long has this dog been dead?" I ask, staring at its shimmering outline. I expect it to jump into the shadows like Willow's tiger, but it doesn't. Its stumpy tail thumps on the floor as it anticipates my next move.

"Not long enough to have any powers."

"So, he's just a regular notdead dog, then? Fantastic." My comment doesn't damper his energy, either. He walks right toward me to lick my hand. His back rises to the middle of my thigh, but I don't feel uneasy with him like I do with the tigers. There's something endearing about his personality—sweet, even. A smile lines my lips. Will I get to a point where seeing undead creatures is my norm? One look at my sister answers that question.

"What's his name?" I ask, petting his ear.

Willow smiles. "I was hoping you'd tell me."

"You want me to name him?" I ask, letting my fingers sink into the soft white fur on the top of the dog's head.

"Well, yeah. He's *your* dog now, after all."

The dog looks up at me, and I feel the ice melt on my heart just a bit. How can I possibly say no? "How about Kado?"

"It's a strong name," she says, holding her finger to her chin. "I like it."

Kado yips again, and I pretend he's adding his approval.

"Well, I'll leave you two to get acquainted," Willow says and departs with little more than a dip of her head.

Then I'm left alone with Kado. He seems just as happy as he had a moment ago. I pet him again as I pass him to wiggle into the clothes Willow had left on my dresser. I lie in the bed, and Kado's quick to join me, lying in the curve of my legs.

It seems like a lot of time passes, but sleep is hard to come by. I can hear the undead tigers moving through the shadows and the lions patrolling the halls. It's safe here. It's odd to be comforted by so much death, but I am. I feel comfortable despite having all the reasons in the world not to be.

Maybe Willow's right. There *is* peace in death.

Kado noses a bit closer to me, and I hug him tight like a stuffed animal. He doesn't smell like death—or maybe I'm already more used to the scent than I thought. It doesn't take long for my warm thoughts of death to turn against me. Regina and Howard are still dead, and possibly Clio and Fern. Tears steak down my face when I remember Clio saving me from Helena's fate, his promise of getting help still echoing in my mind.

My brain doesn't want to accept the possibility of his demise.

Surely Willow would bring him back too. I try to assure myself with that thought, but then the hope fades. She hadn't been able to bring back my parents. Of course, there's a chance she doesn't know who Clio is—how *important* to me he is. Or, even worse, she might've thought he'd sided with the Council as the Ignis Adept and left him for dead.

I can't keep doing this to myself. I force my eyes to remain closed. Enough things are fighting me without my mind joining the fray.

Maybe when I wake in the morning, things will make sense again. For now, focus on the positives.

At the very least, Helena is alive. That gives me more reason to live than I had this morning.

When I feel as if I'm on the verge of sleep, light knocking sounds at the door. Kado's head pops up instantly. I groan, considering ignoring it completely, then the knocking grows louder.

"Come in," I call sleepily, face pushed into the pillow.

I hear the pop of the door, and *Ambrossi* steps in. Now, *I* pop up on the bed. "Ambrossi?"

A sheepish smile crests his face. "Is this a bad time, Lilith?"

I glance at Kado as if he'll answer for me. "No, I guess not. What do you want?"

"We got off on the wrong foot," Ambrossi says.

My lip quirks up, though I'm not sure if it's the beginning of a smile or a sneer. "You could say that again."

"If it's any comfort, I'm glad you're here."

"*Are you?*" I ask. "That wasn't the impression I had."

"Yeah, I am."

My lip quivers. "Then why the evasiveness? Why the—"

"I never lied to you, Lilith," he interrupts.

"You haven't told the truth either, though, have you?"

He tries to smile, but it comes out more of a grimace. "It's complicated."

"What isn't?" I stifle a yawn and look longingly at my pillow. The initial shock and curiosity at Ambrossi's appearance has already faded. All I can think of now is how much I wish I were asleep. "What happened?"

Ambrossi sighs and tugs at the black band around his throat. I think the question was too much before he stops to stand in the center of my room, his back to me.

"Ambrossi?"

"I'm sorry. I can't look at you when I say this."

I realize he's *ashamed*, which fills me with a sickening mixture of sadness and disbelief.

"The week before your Arcane Ceremony, the same week you started developing powers, I received a message from Alchemy... that my mother was sick. *Really* sick. My father wanted me to come home, to see if I could help her. And I *wanted* to, but..."

"The treaty," I say.

His hair shuffles as he bobs his head. "I was heartbroken, thinking there was an illness even *Lazarus* couldn't cure. But I didn't know what to do. Then your fairy friend—"

"Fern?" I ask in surprise.

"*Fern* came to me. She said... she said she could help me. And I was so desperate, Li, so ready to try *anything*, that I listened to her. She introduced me to a witch who helped me sneak into Alchemy, and I saved her. I saved my mother," he says, finally meeting my gaze with that last sentence. "She would be dead without Willow and the Elementals."

I silently digest his words. I feel like such an awful person—a truly despicable being. When I had woken up to see Ambrossi here, I had immediately assumed it was for some selfish reason. Not everyone makes decisions based on their own need.

I wobble unsteadily and stand up, pulling Ambrossi into an awkward embrace, resting my face on his back. "I understand," I assure him, and it feels good to know that not *everyone* loses the battle against their personal demons.

Chapter Eight

Hopes and Expectations

ON THE MORNING, I expect to see Willow as soon as I open my eyes, so I can't deny my disappointment when I realize I'm alone. The room is silent. Kado is still tucked into the rut of my legs, and I groan at the stiffness in my joints. I haven't moved all night. The dog's fuzzy head pops up as I nudge him gently with my heel and sit up, gritting my teeth against the pain in my side. The skin feels too tight, tender, and I know it's freshly infected. I can only imagine what kind of bacteria has gotten into it during the multiple times I've broken it open.

I poke at the wounds once, grimace, and listen to the thump of my hand on the mattress as I send another useless glare around my room. Willow isn't here. There isn't even a note saying where she's gone or a hint of what I'm supposed to do with myself. I run through my memories of last night, but she hadn't given me a clue then, either. It dawns on me now that I should've asked.

Too little too late.

Sighing, I contemplate my possible plans of action. Kado lets out his little happy yelp and watches me, paw set on my knee.

I envy his optimism.

"Are you hungry?" I ask him, running my hand across the scar on his side.

He jumps off the bed at the contact, and I can't tell if he's excited by the prospect of breakfast or upset that I paid so much attention to his old wounds. Either way, he holds his ground beside my bed, watching me through shining eyes. I'm not as enthusiastic as he is about my next move. My nose twitches at the thought. No one said I *have* to get up. I can simply lie back down until someone comes to get me for whatever it is they have planned. I don't have to do a damn thing until then. *Thinking* of that choice is enough for me to crinkle my nose in disgust. It reeks of pathetic—not the vibe I want to give. I'm still not convinced I can trust them, and part of me imagines Willow feels the same way. Why else would she stick me in the room farthest from everyone else?

That gives me one option—leave the room and risk the labyrinthine halls in the hopes of finding my sister.

I don't see that I have a choice.

When I think I've made up my mind, Kado jumps back on the bed, his massive paws barely avoiding the scars on my side. He bares his teeth, and my eyes grow wide. I lift my arm on reflex to protect my face a moment before I realize his attention centers on something *behind* me.

I look up and see it—a snake as thick as my arm, coiled around the bedpost. I scream and scramble to the other end of the bed, Kado yipping at the beast like he's ready to dive into combat while I struggle to untangle the blanket from my legs. The snake watches us with an expression dangerously close to amusement on its scaly face. Much more composed with the distance, I study the snake and note the subtle, ethereal glow above its dark emerald back.

It's another one of Willow's pets.

Does she have an entire zoo?

I pick my bangs out of my eyes and give the snake another glare before patting Kado on his side. He's not happy with my new roommate, but I'm not about to move it. I don't think it's a threat, either, or it would've made its move while we were asleep. Kado is nowhere near relaxed but stops barking to look at me, and I tilt my head. He growls once more at the snake but obliges and jumps down. I sigh through my teeth, snake forgotten as I prepare myself for the pain of stepping onto my bad leg. Like my side, it's tightened up, making progress to the door considerably difficult. I stop a few times, worried I'll collapse, but Kado offers his support to help me across the room. I pet him appreciatively, already glad for his companionship. When I go to open the door, he pads away to growl at the snake again, and I'm left to stare at Maverick on the other side.

"You're not Willow," I say, folding my arms across my chest as petulantly as possible.

Maverick smiles. "Your observation skills are remarkable."

"Oh, yeah? How are yours?" I ask, stepping aside to reveal the snake and Kado. "See anything wrong with this picture?"

Maverick glances over my shoulder toward the bed before grinning. "Gave you a fright?"

My lip twitches, and I barely manage to bite back my rage. "You guys could've warned me about the snake."

"But then it would've taken the joy out of the meet and greet!"

"I could've killed it. Willow would be upset," I say, then glance at Kado. "*He* still might."

Maverick rolls his eyes. "They'll be fine. Trust me."

Now there's sound advice.

"Go get dressed," he says, eyes on the spot of my dress clumped with dried blood. "We don't have all day." He points to the bathroom. "Willow left you a fresh outfit."

"Wonderful," I retort, not mentioning the fact that I *do* have all day to waste. Instead, I make quick work of going to the bathroom and dressing. I don't even look in the mirror. In every one, my reflection changes anyway. Not for the lighting or the mirror's composition but for no reason other than my changing perspective of myself. So I avoid it completely and return to the door. "Good enough?" I spit, swiping a knotted black lock out of my eyes.

Maverick raises an eyebrow. "Can't brush your own hair?"

I narrow my eyes. "My hair is none of your concern, thank you. Where's Willow?"

"If you want to walk around looking like you've got a mop on your head, be my guest. And Willow's busy. She sent me."

"For what?"

Kado stops barking, and I realize he's come back to my side. For the first time since I've met him, he seems stiff and cold, and I realize he's feeding off my emotions for Maverick, unsure whether to perceive him as a threat or not.

I'm liking this dog more and more.

"To keep you busy. Or, if you want the honest answer, to keep you out of *trouble*." His eyes shift toward the snake again.

I frown. "That is *not* on me."

Maverick shrugs. "I suppose not, but it's a good example just the same."

"Where's my sister?" I try one more time. I think of shoving him aside, but even I'm not cocky enough to assume myself physically capable of it.

"She's busy. Remember, she runs this *entire* place. That isn't done with magic. It takes hard work. A lot of people depend on her, and just because you're her sister doesn't make you any more important than the rest of her Coven."

"So I've learned," I state, thinking of the trip my old mentor, Crowe, had taken me on through the Land of Five. So many people had been missing from their Covens, and if our guess is correct, they had all come here to join the Elementals.

Willow really has her work cut out for her. I'll have my work too, I'm sure. Helena's recovery alone will make sure of that, and if Clio comes back the same way… I cut that thought off almost instantly. It's too much.

"Fine. Then can I see Helena?"

"Later," he says, turning to walk into the hallway.

I ball my hands into fists at my sides and follow him. He doesn't have to like me, but a bit of civility would be nice. "So, mind telling me where we *are* going?"

"Willow wanted me to take you back to Ambrossi, first of all," he says, eyeing the spot on my side where the clothing sticks already with fresh blood. "Then I need to introduce you to a few people."

"Afterward, can I see Helena?"

Maverick shrugs again. "Afterward is not my problem."

My lip twitches in a mixture of amusement and annoyance. The longer I stare at him, the more I realize I can relate to him. It's nice meeting someone else who doesn't take any bullshit for an answer.

***

"YOU DIDN'T GIVE them a chance to heal, did you?" Ambrossi asks, frowning at the array of ugly scars down my ribs. I don't look at them. I don't have to in order to know they're bad. Ambrossi's expressions are enough.

I consider lying but don't see much point in it. "You really think I had the opportunity?"

"You used to be such a sweet little girl, Lilith. I never would've guessed you'd grow up to have such… *bite.*"

I narrow my eyes at Ambrossi, knowing that wasn't what he really wanted to say about me. I might've been sweet at one point in my life. Hell, I might've been innocent too, but it doesn't matter. Just as it doesn't matter how many times he reminds me of that person, who I used to be before my life changed. She's not me, not anymore. I'm far too gone, and shoving the past down my throat only serves to further cement the change.

For better or worse, only the Gods know.

"That's not me anymore."

Ambrossi scrunches his face, and I recognize that look, that need to argue. I'm sure I've worn it quite a few times myself in the past, but the expression passes as he decides I'm right. "From now on, take it easy, please. I'll be sure to pass the message to Willow too, so no more excuses."

I sigh and give in. It doesn't seem worth it to further push the topic. "Sure." I peer at Maverick over Ambrossi's shoulder. "Are we good to go now?"

Ambrossi and Maverick exchange a look before the healer nods and steps away from the table. I jump to my feet—well, *try* to jump to my feet—and make my way to Maverick's side.

"Who are these people I need to meet?"

"Higher-ups. Your sister's top-ranked people," Maverick explains and leads the way out of Ambrossi's chambers.

I nod. Let's hope this ends better.

Once outside, we cross through the eerie plants and purple sky. I wonder if this is the heart of the Elementals' land or just the edge. The path we take seems familiar, and I realize it's because it leads the way back to the building in which they'd held me prisoner.

The building is large—Romanesque. The door looks like it came from someone's home—the window, too—but I know better. The sturdy pillars and decorative towers give it a completely different feeling—this place is all business.

I freeze, digging my heels into the dirt in case Maverick decides to start dragging me. "I thought I *wasn't* a prisoner anymore."

Maverick laughs. "My, my, aren't we a little self-centered? You do realize this building has more functions than what you've seen? This is the Community Villa. It's got the cafeteria, meeting room, hospital wing—"

"And prisons?" A blush lines my cheeks, and the fire that had blazed so strong only a moment ago dies out. I don't know why I didn't consider that myself. "That's friendly," I quip, to hide my own embarrassment.

Maverick shrugs. "All part of the community. Not everyone has sunshine in their hearts."

I glare at him, and he smiles. Thankfully, he doesn't comment on my outburst as we enter the opposite side of the building from where they keep the prisons. He takes the lead down the length of the hallway, passing kitchens, living rooms, even a laboratory. This building doesn't seem to hold out on any luxury. The longer we walk, the more my anxiety eases. The place is much homier than I would've guessed for a prison. When Maverick finally picks a room to enter, he pauses, placing a hand in my path.

"What?" I ask, tilting my head.

"You don't want to be rude, do you?" Maverick asks, smiling at me as if he's just told the funniest joke.

I must be the punchline, because I don't get it, and my confusion has to show.

"Lilith, I'd like you to meet Grief," he says, gesturing to the empty room before us.

I blink once, twice, three times, trying anything to stall as I process the situation. Is he crazy? Or does he just really want to piss me off? I can't decide. "Is this a trick?"

'In a way,' a voice replies.

I frown, glancing around. It's not Maverick's; it's the disembodied voice in my brain, the one I hadn't been able to connect to anyone.

A few feet away, the air shimmers, and I stare in hesitant fascination. Maverick folds his arms across his chest, looking bored by the abnormality, but I can't tear my eyes away from it. The shimmer takes shape, and before I know it, there's another boy in the room. He shakes out his sleeves, and after a minute of complete silence, he doesn't introduce himself, going so far as to avoid even a moment of eye contact.

I glance at Maverick, but that annoying smirk has returned to his face. "This is Grief," he says. "Grief, I'd like you to meet Lilith."

Grief nods but makes no effort to communicate beyond that. A moment later, he disappears back into the air.

"What the *hell*?" I ask.

"Grief's shy. Spends most of his time hiding. He's the champion of hide-and-seek."

"Why doesn't Willow make him show himself?"

Maverick shrugs. "Hard to make a witch do things when he can literally disappear at will."

My lip quirks, but I'm not nearly as amused by Maverick's statement as he is. "Is that right?"

"He'll come around eventually. He cares for Helena's pets and performs surveillance. They take to him more than the rest of the Coven, but he's a real great guy when you get to know him."

That hadn't been my first thought. All I can think of is how I've heard his voice before, but I can't tell Maverick. A witch with the power of *invisibility*—it seems surreal, but then again, so does Willow's power.

"Where did he go?" I ask.

Maverick glances around the room before his gaze returns to me. "Impossible to know if he doesn't want you to."

I stifle my sigh. "So where to, now?"

"Breakfast," he says simply.

The response catches me off guard, so all I can manage is a surprised, "Oh."

I want to keep exploring, to see what other places this new land has to offer, but I can't argue. I have no choice but to follow, and I do. Maverick easily leads me to a beautiful room with elegant dining furniture. It's not as beautiful as the kitchen in Willow's mansion, but it's far more beautiful than the kitchen in my Ignis home. Willow, Ambrossi, and Helena are already there, empty plates in front of them. I pause when I see them.

"What's this?" I ask warily. I've learned to not like crowds; they usually mean trouble. Of course, this gathering isn't big enough to be considered a "crowd", but it unnerves me just the same.

"We just want to welcome you into the Coven properly," Willow says.

Maverick helps me into a chair and sits in the one beside me. The witch circling the table, filling our cups with a sweet juice that's a mix of citrus and tropical, makes me uneasy. Willow's smile is huge despite the heavy silence. She begins to talk, then Maverick and Ambrossi chime in. Helena and I exchange a glance, and before I know it, the tension is gone completely. For a bit of time, I let myself believe the war has never happened, that I'm home in Ignis with Ambrossi and Helena. I don't focus on Clio's absence—on *any* of my recent losses. For the first time since my life first tipped downhill, I'm happy.

Maybe I fit in here, after all.

Chapter Nine

The Truth Hurts

*J*UST AS THAT thought fades, footsteps announce someone else's arrival. I pull myself from my thoughts and catch sight of the person standing in the doorway. With his wavy blond hair and chocolate-brown eyes, he could pass for innocent. If I didn't know better, I might've believed just that.

"You," I snarl, stalking toward him.

He might have smiled, but all I see now is the image of him covered in blood and grinning. He killed Helena in the Battle of Ignis. My stare doesn't falter when I grab his shirt, curling my fingers as tightly into the fabric as possible. "How dare you show your face to me after what you did to her?"

"Lilith! No!" Maverick yells, and I feel him grasping my shoulders, trying to separate us, but I'm a pawn to my anger now. The harder he tries to pull me away, the tighter I grip.

68

"I'm sorry about your friend," the boy says, voice dripping with contempt. "I am. But the UnEquipped have no place in battle. You know that. It was just as much her fault as it was mine."

I see red, and before I know it, I've hit him so hard in the face that it's red as well. I raise my hand, ready to strike him again, when the anger drains completely; I've felt this sensation only once before. I know instantly that it's the work of another Elemental, specifically the girl who had poisoned Callista.

By the time her magic fades and I regain control of myself, Maverick has taken me far from Helena's killer and right out into the purple plants. He storms through them, hands on my upper arm to stop me from returning to fight, and I let him pull me, feeling my sanity slowly return. Grudgingly, I find myself glad Maverick stepped in before I had the chance to hurt the boy again—I might've killed him.

"You can't do that again," he tells me at last.

I shrug. "Why not?"

"Because Sabre's one of our best fighters. He deserves respect," Maverick spat, voice thundering with anger.

"No, he doesn't. He killed Helena... I won't *forgive* him for that."

Maverick raises his hands in surrender. "Fine. You don't have to be his best friend, but you *do* have to be civil. Willow expects it of you." I roll my eyes, and Maverick lets out a breath before glancing over his shoulder. "Look, I have work to do, and if you're intent on knives and fire, this isn't going to be easy for either of us. I can't risk you going off on anyone else like you did with Sabre... like you did with *me*."

"So what are you saying?" I ask, raising my eyebrow.

Maverick lets out a loud sigh and stares at me for a long time, as if I've just said something profound. Finally, he rolls his eyes and with a wave of his hand says, "You're free to go for the day."

I take him up on the offer, watching him depart through

the plants, and suddenly, I'm alone, wondering if that was a smart choice on Maverick's part. I don't know what to think of what's just happened, of *everything* that's happened since I arrived. Somehow, with my mind focused on Grief, my feet take me through the entrance of the building before I've decided whether or not I actually want to go back inside. My awe of him goes beyond his ability; he's been *following* me. He has to have followed me if I heard him all the way in the Land of Five.

If Maverick had never taken the time to introduce us, I would've never known he existed, and the handful of times I've heard his voice would be nothing more than another uncertainty within the mystery of my life. Now that I know what he sounds like, he's so much easier to find. Even *through* the labyrinthine halls of Willow's mansion, I locate him.

When I round the corner into the room he occupies, I can't see him. But I know he hasn't spotted me, because his train of thought hasn't changed. He's thinking through a to-do list. So I keep my pace, using my telekinesis to muffle the sounds of my awkward footsteps. When I'm close enough to feel the heat of his skin, I lunge and grab the back of his shoulders.

In his surprise, he drops his focus on remaining invisible and turns to me with wide brown eyes. "Lilith! You just about… gave me… a heart attack." He clutches his chest, and for a moment, I almost feel bad.

Almost.

"You have a lot of explaining to do," I snap, releasing him to fold my arms across my chest.

"I can't do that if you kill me first," he retorts and finally drops his hand, standing straight to glare at me.

"You were at Chastity's execution."

He blinks at me, his silence answer enough.

"*Why?*"

"That's… complicated," he muses, fingers tugging at the dark hairs of his short goatee.

"Try me."

"Well, it depended on you, I guess," he says. "If Chastity had successfully captured you, I was supposed to help bring you back."

"And if she failed?" I demand, staring at him with so much contempt that he wiggles under my gaze.

The air shimmers, and I recognize his effort to disappear again. I grab him with such ferocity that the undead cat in the room growls in protest, as if even it knows I'm serious. It lifts a threatening paw, and I glance at it before dropping Grief's arm.

"What were your plans if she failed?" I ask again, overly calm.

He rubs his arm where I grabbed him. "To help you," he says at last, looking up from the ring of red, fingerprint bruises.

I pause at that, frowning. "Help... *me*?"

Grief doesn't say anything, his gaze trained on the floor.

Then everything clicks. "*You* lit the fire... Chastity. I—"

He looks up, eyes both haunted and swimming with tears. "Yeah."

That one word is enough to overwhelm us both in our own emotions and memories. He helped me when I didn't know it. He was there as an enemy and a friend, and I don't know what to do.

"But... if you were there, have *always* been there, why wouldn't *you* just grab me? I would've never seen it coming."

Grief shakes his head. "Willow didn't want you to know I existed. We had... an advantage before you learned the truth."

"All this time, I thought I killed her." I nearly choke on the words.

"Now you know."

One last, haunting look, and he disappears from sight. I let him, glad for it. I can't look at him anymore, and he must feel the same. His thoughts soften when he leaves the room and quickly crosses the mansion. I don't move. I stare at the floor so long, the undead cat who growled at me paces to my side, butting its head against my hip for attention. Its big amber eyes look concerned, and my fingers unconsciously stroke the fur between its ears, though it hardly breaks me from my trance.

Then I hear Maverick's voice behind me. "What trouble are you getting yourself into now?"

I turn to look at him, barely blinking back tears. "Nothing."

I can tell he doesn't believe me, but he has to have seen the tears in my eyes, because he doesn't press further.

"What do you want?" I ask, voice stiff as I try to get my emotions under control.

"Just wanted to see if you were okay," he says, "and that you were staying out of trouble. Took me a minute to find you. You know, for being crippled, you move fast."

I smirk at that but can't manage a real response. I envy Grief. More than anything, I wish I could turn invisible and slip away from this conversation, from my entire *life,* and never have to worry about being found ever again.

Chapter Ten

Witch Warriors and Fairy Friends

*D*ESPITE IT BEING clear as day that Maverick wants to be far away from me, I somehow convince him to take me to see Helena. He groans about it—I'd expected it—but it doesn't take much to wear him down. He glares at me as he turns on his heels to lead the way, but I don't let it get to me; attitude or not, I got my way. He probably obliged because he's worried about what I'll do if left alone again. I imagine he feels personally responsible for me the way most people feel for their pets. If I maul somebody, it's on him. Maybe that's not such a bad thing if it means making him just a bit more malleable.

I don't want him to see it, but after facing Helena's killer, I'm on edge and filled with so much self-doubt, I'm convinced everyone can see it radiating off me in waves. What if everything that's happened has been just a dream, the resurgence incident with Willow just another figment of my overactive imagination?

I hate being unable to tell fiction from reality. The past few days have blended them together more often than in my entire life. It's odd how things which had once seemed unconnected have a way of coming together. I need to see Helena, to prove that I'm not as crazy as I think I am. If it turns out to be true, I'm doomed.

Maverick leads me to a building deep within the violet plants. They grow closer together here, and we slosh our way through the loose, mush black dirt. The air grows sweeter too, and I wonder if my brain is just so desperate for air not tainted with the scent of death that it's conjuring the smell of meadow flowers out of nothing.

Anything by comparison is an improvement.

This place is much smaller than all the other buildings I've been shown. This cottage with red siding and a white roof carries a style I don't remember seeing in any of the other Covens. Is that significant? When we open the door, I realize the decorative outside is just a faux pas. Helena's home looks remarkably similar to the cell I had been locked in yesterday. It's furnished, of course, and there's more room and light, but the walls, floor, and everything else are gray, with the exception of red sheets on the bed and a matching rug on the middle of the floor.

Helena stands by an open window—the only window in the building—staring into the strange wilderness beyond. The corners of her lips turn up in a slight smile, and I recognize that wonder in her eyes. She's more like the Helena I grew up with than the depressed version who had taken over her after the Arcane Ceremony. After a bit of an internal debate, I decide she doesn't seem miserable with her housing situation, so I let it go.

"As requested," Maverick says with a sarcastic smirk, jolting me back to reality.

"Yeah, thanks," I retort, and only when Maverick finally leaves the room do I let my shoulders sag with relief and my true emotions craft the smallest of smiles on my lips. When Helena's eyes meet mine, I rush across the room to pull her into my arms.

The smell of death on her is fainter today, and I wonder briefly if that's because she's recovering or if my nose has already become so adjusted to the smell that I hardly notice it. When we break apart, she opens her mouth to speak, looking flustered when no sound comes out.

I pat her on the shoulder and offer a quick smile. "It's okay. Don't try to talk yet. You'll get there eventually."

Helena smiles back at me and tucks a strand of wild orange hair behind her ear. Her green eyes bore into mine, and I don't understand the excitement I see there. If I were her, newly resurrected from the dead, I don't think I'd be able to smile for a long time.

"She's recovering well," a voice says from the doorway, interrupting whatever it was Helena had been about to show me. I turn as Willow walks into the room, her long hair swinging with each step. After not seeing her for nearly half a day, she looks smaller somehow, more like a ghost than a human. "You are too."

I nod.

"She's eating again," Willow adds, gesturing to the empty bowl on Helena's gray nightstand.

Somehow, I overlooked it on my initial survey of the room, but I nod again, pleased for the update. Still, I wonder why she's talking about Helena as if she isn't here. She's mute, not deaf.

"Can you come with me for a little bit, Lilith?" she asks. "Helena has some exercises she needs to work on."

I draw my eyebrows together, protectively standing my ground between Helena and Willow. "I can help her with them."

Willow smiles. "I know you care about your friend, but if she's going to get better, she needs to work alone."

"But I just got here," I say, pinning her with my stare.

"I understand that too, but I can't have you blowing off Coven duties." She wraps a tendril of her long brown hair around her finger.

"I didn't realize I had those," I state. "According to Ambrossi, I'm supposed to do nothing until I'm healed."

"This isn't strenuous. And my word supersedes his." She winks, and I suppress a groan and that deep-seated urge to argue. What could possibly be so important that she won't let me have this one moment to myself? Why is she so desperate to pull me away from Helena? It makes me paranoid that Helena *is* just an illusion, one they can't maintain long. Why don't any of the Elementals understand how much I need to be around her right now?

Willow's your sister, a voice whispers. *She worries about you.*

I frown. The voice sounds like Helena's, but she hadn't moved her lips. When I make eye contact, she smiles at me pleasantly, but no thoughts come to the front of her mind. It isn't possible that Willow gave her the ability to read minds … is it? I glance at Willow, but her face remains stoically closed, giving no hint one way or the other.

I'm going insane.

"Come on," Willow says, her petite frame nearly dancing through the doorway.

I glance between them both again before my eyes land on Helena. "I'll be back," I promise her, even though I'm not sure Willow will let me make good on it. Once the door closes behind us, I ask Willow, "Where are we going?"

"I want to introduce you to a friend of mine," she says, leading us once again through the odd, purple-plant forest.

Interesting. Who can she trust enough to give the title of 'friend'? I haven't even found many witches to fill that niche, and I'm no one compared to her. "What made you change your mind? Maverick said you were too busy for me today."

"I was, but I moved some things around, and my day just opened up. I'm going to take you on the tour you should have had."

I don't care for Maverick, but her slightly bitter tone suggests someone will be punished over this; oddly enough, I feel bad thinking that someone may be him. "It's not his fault, you know. Maverick's. He kept me from doing something I'd regret. I... I saw him... *Sabre*. And I lost it."

"Stop," Willow says, raising a hand. "You don't have to explain yourself. Maverick informed me of the situation, and I understand why you did what you did."

I dip my head in appreciation. That makes one of us.

"But..." she continues.

I squeeze my eyes shut. Here it comes.

"That doesn't excuse anyone. You might be my sister, but I can't just condone that type of behavior. We all have our demons, and trust me, throttling Sabre will not make them go away."

"You don't know unless you try, right?" I ask with a soft chuckle.

Willow turns to glare at me, and I flinch. She's right, I know, but part of me still wants to make Sabre pay for what he's done. It's a childish reaction after everything I've been through, but the realization doesn't make the feeling go away.

I don't know what to say, and I wait for her to tell me my punishment. She doesn't. It feels like we're at an impasse, neither of us wanting to continue the conversation that's clearly not over. Our walk continues utterly silent as we surrender to our thoughts. Just Willow's light steps and my irregular ones stomping through the foliage keeps it from being too quiet.

"You really make people live all the way out here?" I ask, smacking a broad leaf out of my face. I thought it had been insane to keep me from everyone else in the same *building*, but apparently, I could've had it worse.

"I don't make anyone do anything they don't want to do," she says pointedly. "He *chooses* to be out here."

I blink and plod along, questions growing in number, until she stops at a pile of boulders. I glance around in confusion. There's no house, no tent, nothing to suggest anything *lives* here.

"Malcolm, I'd like you to meet my sister Lilith," Willow says without hesitation. I cringe, wondering if there are more invisible witches than just Grief.

I humor her and look to the rocks in the place she indicates just in time to see a fairy emerge. Red wings encase the tiny body, and when they open, I'm shocked to see the fairy's a *male*. A Gothic fairy had taken me by surprise when the Council recruited me, but that's *nothing* compared to my surprise in this moment. I hadn't thought male fairies existed. Fairies, after all, are believed to be immortal, but this singlehandedly shatters that idea; a male implies reproduction.

Malcolm smiles at me, all warmth and hospitality, oblivious to the chaos his very existence has created in my mind. "She… she looks j-just like you," he says to Willow, and in some strange way, I realize I've blown his mind just the same.

I smile at the stutter. It somehow makes him seem innocent and almost pacifies the situation. Almost.

"Yes. She's my sister, and she'll be staying here for a while. So, if I'm not around, I'll need you to look out for her, okay?"

Malcolm nods like an obedient child, and I blink in amusement. The relationship between Willow and her fairy is a lot different than the one I had had with Fern. Fern. Her name drops the smile right off my face. I haven't given her much thought, even though she and Clio should always remain at the front of my mind.

I still don't know how many of my Covenmates are still alive.

It's a scary thought. But it's exactly what I need to remember if we have any hope of winning this war. Sometimes, fear can be a good thing. By the time my mind returns to the present, Willow is saying her goodbyes to Malcolm. He disappears back into the rocks, and I stare at the spot, wondering how he fit through it with such ease.

We turn back through the plants, and my arsenal of questions begins to fire. "No offense, but Maverick said you'd be introducing me to your higher-ups."

Willow shrugs. "So maybe not the *exact* tour I instructed him to give you, but this is important just the same."

I don't see how, and I struggle to come up with a reasonable response as the silence consumes us once more. I don't know how Willow can stand it. Over the course of a day and a half, my world has been flipped upside-down, and in the silence, I hear the destruction. But she's smiling as if this is normal.

I have to remind myself that to her, it is. Her world might've gone through the same at one point in the past, but she righted it a long time ago, and I envy her for it.

"So how long have you known Malcolm? You seem... *close*..." I say, for lack of a better word.

She slows a bit to match my pace. "I found him when he was a baby."

I blink at that statement—at the word *baby*—and even a sarcastic comment fails me. First *male* fairies, and now *baby* ones too? I'm sure there are fairies in all five Covens, most likely ranging in age and gender, but I've never met them. I can only imagine how different each one could possibly be from those I've already met. Maybe somewhere out there in the Land of Five are more male fairies like Malcolm ... and his father. Whoever that might be.

It's a little too much.

"Where's his mother?"

Willow tenses.

"A-are you like his mother now?" I ask, watching the strange way she crawls in her own skin.

"Bonding with a fairy is hard to describe," Willow says, scratching her chin. "I guess it *is* like being a parent, you know? Especially when they're young like Malcolm."

I nod wistfully. "I was bonded to one back in Ignis."

"Fern?" she guesses.

I perk up instantly. "Yeah. How do you know Fern?"

"She's Malcolm's mother."

"What?" I ask, jaw open far too much for my liking. My legs fail me too, and I'm amazed I don't fall face-first into the muck under our feet.

"She's his mother," Willow repeats, as if we're talking about the weather.

"Then why isn't she here with him?" I ask once I've finally regained control of myself.

"Because I asked," Willow states, long hair swinging with each step as she moves forward once more.

I grab her arm to stop her mid-step. "I'm sorry. Is there a conversation I don't remember us having?"

Willow sighs, and her shoulders droop. "No, but there's a story I need to tell you. After our parents died, Fern helped me escape the battle."

"I was told the Council *recruited* you... as one of them. Not captured."

"They have a way of twisting the truth like that. I was never one of them. I was brought in to keep people from searching when I disappeared from my Coven. To keep them from asking questions. It's the same reason no one fought the decision to have me executed. I escaped once, and when I got away, I came here. I was safe... everyone was. But then I made a mistake. I left this place, the place Fern told me to never leave, and I was executed. After *I* died, I came back to recover. By then, she had given birth."

"And she just *chose* to leave her child?" I ask, wondering just how many people around here besides me and Willow have mommy issues.

Willow shrugs. "Fairies are complicated."

That's not limited to fairies. I push my lips into a straight line, and the haunted pain behind Willow's eyes contrasts the tiny smile on her lips. "It was for me, wasn't it?" I ask. "The reason you left?"

Willow opens her mouth, then closes it. "Yeah," she says finally. "I thought I could help you, and I couldn't. Fern knows how much you mean to me. She volunteered to find you, watch over you, and bring you back when the time was right."

"I guess that time never came," I say dryly, glaring at the base of the nearest purple plant. And now she might be dead because of me. Another waste.

Silence again. Now I'm really beginning to hate it.

"Where is she now? Is her disappearance all just part of your plan?"

Willow sighs wistfully. "I wish I could say it was. Right now, I don't know where she is or if she's safe, but I've got people who will find out the truth... one way or another."

A flutter of hope warms my chest, but I'm too afraid to acknowledge it. Hope is a dangerous thing. "You have people who can do that?"

Willow nods. "My people are capable of many things."

"Can... can you find someone for me? In Ignis?"

Willow's black eyes turn on me, and I see a sparkle—just a hint of interest. "Of course. Anything for my dear sister. Who is it?"

I swallow, feeling a blush creep into my cheeks as I think of the right way to pass the information to her. "His name is Clio. He's my..." I don't know how to finish that sentence. He's not my best friend—that title belongs to Helena—and he's certainly not just another acquaintance. He's my rival, my friend ... my *lifeline.*

"He's special to you?" Willow guesses.

At least she can make sense out of me swallowing my tongue, because I can't.

She fixes me with a fervent gaze. "I'll do my best to have him found."

Chapter Eleven

Meet and Greet

ILLOW'S WORDS LIFT me up and carry me through the night. There's a feeling deep in my chest that I dare to call hope. I have *faith* in Willow that, come Hell or high water, she will find Clio. The night brings handfuls of dreams about him, and when I wake for the last time in the morning, I'm clutching Kado like a giant teddy bear. He catches my gaze from the corner of his eye and rolls over to rasp his tongue across my cheek.

At least he doesn't mind.

Bright and early, Maverick comes for me to take me on the rest of yesterday's abandoned tour. The day follows almost the same routine as yesterday. The only difference? Kado walks right by our side this time, confident as he follows us out of the safety of my bedroom and into the halls beyond. Even though he's my dog, I watch him from the corner of my eye, not entirely sure what his reaction will be should we happen to cross paths with any of Willow's undead cats.

I'm learning quickly just how important regularity is around here. Witches hustle from room to room, chatter echoing up and down the halls that seemed so lifeless yesterday. Willow makes sure everyone has tasks, and somehow, she keeps up with it all. I'm impressed by my sister's attention to detail. The Elemental Coven might be an unconventional group, but they're the strongest-running Coven I've ever seen.

"So how do you like it here so far?" Maverick asks in an attempt at small talk, and we round the first bend in the corridor.

I furrow my brow and glare at him. The question seems odd, and I have the feeling that the silence bothers him more than it does me. "It's okay," I answer with a shrug. I haven't been here long enough to decide either way.

"I was hoping for a bit more enthusiasm than that."

"Really? Were you just leaping for joy when you were recruited?" I mutter.

"Yeah, I was. I was excited to join the Elementals."

I raise my eyebrow. "I thought everyone's here because of some tragedy."

Maverick shrugs. "For a lot of witches, yeah, that's the case."

"But not you?"

He shakes his head. "No. I learned early on that I was Equipped, even though I came from UnEquipped parents."

I tense as his sentence rings out into the still hall. I can relate to that—I've literally been in that exact position. "How'd you realize you weren't like them?"

"We had a pet—a cat—when I was real young. It was a pretty thing with stripes and all. I loved that cat, but whenever she tried to jump in my lap, she just immediately fell asleep. Like clockwork."

I shrug. "And? That's what cats do."

"She didn't do it for anyone else."

"How'd you figure out it was an ability?"

"Our neighbors had a dog. I could make him go out the same way," Maverick says, scratching the back of his neck.

"Ah."

He shoots me a sideways, agitated look. I assume he gets this reaction from everyone.

"I bet your parents were pretty surprised."

"I never told them. Just the thought of it terrified me. My parents had never been a real fan of the Equipped. Never knew anyone who was. So I kept it to myself."

"And no one ever noticed you could do this?"

He shakes his head.

I frown. When my powers had begun to develop, they were sporadic and wild. It hadn't mattered how much I wanted to keep them under control; they couldn't be contained. "You had help," I say. It's not a question simply because I don't need to ask.

"Yeah. Me and Sabre did. That's how we met."

"Who helped you?" At first, I assume the answer will be Willow, though I don't know why.

"A girl from Aquais. She had this power to calm even the worst of my temper."

That sounds familiar. I remember the girl with the pointy chin who poisoned Callista. Then I stiffen. *She's* an Elemental too, which means she's here, somewhere.

"She sensed how upset I was the day I realized I was Equipped, and she came to soothe me."

"But she had to cross the border to do that," I say. "That goes against the treaty."

He shrugs. "I didn't think about it at the time. I guess she didn't either. We were kids. She consoled me, was someone I could *confide* in. She said there was a Coven that takes in witches like me, that when I got old enough, I could join it."

"And you believed her? Just like that?"

"I was young, not stupid."

I shrug. "So you just pretended to be UnEquipped?"

"Yeah, and it worked."

He makes it sound so easy, like it took such little effort to fool every Coven, especially when they were all gathered together. "How did you trick the Arcane Ceremony?" I ask, genuinely curious. Even my most heartfelt prayers hadn't been enough to change *my* results.

"I didn't. I skipped mine. Disappeared the night before."

I stare at him, feeling a rock in my stomach when I suddenly remember just how much of Aens had been missing for mine. If I had to guess, I'd say Maverick's about my age, which means we should've been at the same ceremony. "That sounds about right, actually," I finally say.

Maverick stops walking and turns to me so suddenly that Kado lets out an anxious whine matching my feelings. He folds his hands together before his eyes meet mine. "I won't lie to you. Today will be stressful."

"More so than usual?" I ask, glancing at him from the corner of my eye as I lean down to pet Kado.

"Willow is introducing you to the entire Coven today."

I tighten my jaw, freezing instantly. Kado's black eyes search my face as I try to hide exactly how uneasy that statement leaves me. "That's good, right?"

Maverick starts walking again, and I have a feeling that this time, he does it to avoid eye contact. "All depends on how they receive you."

"That's comforting." Although my snarky comment sounds founded on confidence, it's not.

As we near the end of the hall, Willow's voice echoes down the corridor from a room I've yet to enter. Maverick gives me a long look before pushing open the double doors and gesturing for me to step inside. When I do, I feel my heart pounding.

Willow speaks from a platform in the middle of the room, looking much fiercer than I've acknowledged her to be.

My nervous eyes dart around the room, taking in rows and rows of benches all filled with Elementals, before finally landing on the empty chair on the platform beside Willow.

I know before Maverick says it that the chair is meant for me, and the blood leaves my face. Sitting next to Willow would be fine in any other situation, but for this one? It's the worst scenario possible. Scanning the faces present leaves me within a sea of strangers. My fate is sealed. Their first impression of me, the girl they risked life and limb to obtain, will be me limping across the room.

Not at all what I want them to see. Not in this moment ... not ever.

"Go," Maverick whispers.

I swallow and repress the urge to glare at him as the feeling slowly returns to my body, choosing instead to thrust my energy into my telekinesis. It blasts out strong for the next few steps but falters and dies. My magic is nowhere near ready to be tapped for as long as this walk will take, and I'm suddenly envious of Grief's ability.

I'm completely on my own.

"I can help," Maverick whispers again, a little gentler than before.

I smack his hand away, drawing attention from the nearest handful of Elementals. Doesn't he understand he's only making things worse? If there's one way to possibly make this situation any more dire, it would be depending on someone else for mobility. Kado lifts a paw, as if he's on the verge of attempting the same move. I narrow my eyes at him, and he sits down, tail wagging uncertainly.

Without another moment of hesitation, I move forward. The sound of my uneven footsteps draws more Elementals' eyes, all of them burning my skin like hot needles, but my gaze stays on the chair. Part of me fears that if I make eye contact with anyone along the way, it'll be the end of me—that they'll see *through* me and decide I'm as weak as I feel. That I don't belong here.

Their thoughts fire up around me, loud and critical, but I try not to notice that either. In a way, I feel like I'm taking my first steps all over again, except falling down here won't be met with condolences and encouragement to keep going. Their upturned noses and flat expressions make it obvious that their acceptance of me will be determined based solely on this moment. What feels like an eternity later, I reach the chair and plop into it as if my bones are made of clay. Willow gives me an energizing smile, and I try to return the gesture, but my face feels heavy too.

"Right on cue. This is my sister Lilith," she announces.

When all their eyes focus on me, it's just as tense as the walk. The moment is about me and only me. They scrutinize me from head to foot, whispering to one another with quick glances in my direction, as if they haven't gotten their fill from the initial stare. The image in their minds, the one built up from Willow's stories and words, is the complete opposite of what I really am. I can feel them piecing it together. They're learning how badly they've been tricked. I try to push it off, but it hurts, and before I know it, I'm glaring at them—*all* of them.

If Willow notices the tension in the air, she doesn't comment on it. Instead, she launches into a discussion of other Coven goings-on, leaving me to my thoughts. I should feel bad for glaring, for stooping to their level, but I don't. After all, it's not as if I'm the only one with hostility in my eyes, and I want them to know I'm not afraid of them. Not anymore.

Maverick is perhaps the only one who doesn't look ready to kill me, and I tell myself I have no right to be angry. I get where they're coming from; just as these people have left their mark on me, I've also sculpted them. Chastity had been captured and executed for *my* attempted abduction. Even though I hadn't lit the fire, I was her executioner just the same.

I suddenly understand the reason for the lack of tears at her execution. No one had mourned her there because that had been done *here*, in her true Coven. No doubt some of them may still be out for vengeance.

"Maverick will be seeing to her needs," Willow says when I finally come back to the present. "Any more questions?"

No one speaks, and I frown, temporarily mad at myself. What did I miss when I was in La-La land?

Maybe it's better not to know.

"All right, then!" Willow claps her hands together. "Remember, vigil is at 8:00 tonight. Meeting dismissed."

I stand quickly, desperate to prove a point of which I'm not even aware. All around me, the Elemental Coven grunts and groans as they stand and file out of the room. A few of them aren't shy about sharing their displeasure with having me here, whispering curses and insults so Willow won't hear. One even bumps me with his shoulder, and reading his thoughts lets me know he'd intended to knock me down.

When the room is nearly empty, Willow gives me a small smile and moves to pass me. I grasp her sleeve, holding her in place. She turns to me with a curious glance.

"How do I know they won't try to kill me when I'm sleeping?" I inquire, raising an eyebrow.

Willow sighs and runs her hand through her long brown hair. "You don't, really, but the thing is, neither do I. This is a big Coven, as you saw, and while I'd like to trust everyone with my life, I can't speak for them all. That's why I gave you Kado." I realize he's padded to my side. His tongue lolls from the corner of his mouth as Willow pets the side of his face. "He'll keep you safe. We can *both* trust him."

I nod, glancing down at the undead dog. Despite my initial fears, he's becoming my best ally here—perhaps the only one beside Willow herself. "Thank you, Willow."

"You're welcome," she replies, just as chipper as ever. Then her voice drops to a whisper. "If you ever feel your life is in danger from anyone here, come to me *immediately.*"

"Of course," I say, surprised by just how quickly the good cheer left her.

"Good," she says briskly, then resumes smiling at Kado. "He still needs breakfast?"

I nod again, and she tugs on his collar once, leading him away without hesitation. I stand in place, watching after them.

"You handled it well," Maverick says as he approaches me. "Didn't cut any throats."

"Yeah, well, I'm sure they wanted to cut mine."

He shrugs, and I take that as a yes. "We need to get you back in shape for training."

"Ambrossi told me not to do that," I remind him, staring at the nearest bench, torn between giving into my body's pain and fighting it.

"Well, it's a good thing he's not our only Healer," he says, stepping into my line of sight.

That catches my attention. "You have others?"

"Mm-hmm. We're going to see her now."

That statement both excites and worries me. Yesterday, he was on Ambrossi's side about me resting, and now he's encouraging my training? Why the change of heart? There must be something he knows that I don't, or maybe his Coven's hostility is as apparent to him as it is to me.

Chapter Twelve

The Lost Aquais

MAVERICK WALKS WITH confidence, but his mind seems torn, split between disobeying Willow's direct orders and making sure I get the training I need. He clearly battles with something, wincing occasionally and chewing on his lip. Since I feel the same way, I don't call him out on it. Instead, I let myself revel in the idea that I'm connected to someone else, even if it is temporary. It's been a long time since I've felt united in anything.

We turn a corner, and Maverick pauses. I follow suit, halting when I see a girl there. I study her from head to toe, struck by her familiarity. She has curly blue hair tucked into a bun on the top of her head, and her rosebud lips are pursed as she stares at us through focused tawny eyes.

I know her name like the back of my hand.

"Katrina," I breathe.

She blinks, narrowing her eyes to sharpen her glare on me, and for all her trying, she can't hide her confusion. "Do I know you?"

Of course she doesn't. We've never been introduced, but *I* know *her*, if only from seeing her in Crowe's mind. It's hard to forget that night, even after everything that's happened since. I can still see the heartbroken look in Crowe's eyes as he spilled everything to me in Lazarus' house. Discovering that Katrina had left Aquais to become an Elemental had devastated him so much, it had compromised his loyalty to the Council and everything he believes.

I've hardly given him much thought, but he might actually be an ally in all this. I don't even know what's become of him since the Battle of Ignis. Is he still torn on which way to go in this war? A frown finds its way to my face. One thing is for sure—he hasn't given up his place on the Council, if that's an indication of anything. If another member had disappeared, Willow surely would've told me, which leaves me to wonder why he's decided to stay with the Council. Is he using the position for his advantage, or has he given up all hope of a different—a better—life? Has he searched for me at all, or is he glad that I mysteriously disappeared, relieving him of his job in keeping me safe?

The sickening realization hits me that I don't know if he's my friend or my enemy.

"Hello?" Katrina snaps her fingers in my face.

"No, you don't," I say finally. "But I'm a friend, I promise."

She wrinkles her nose and looks at Maverick for confirmation.

He shrugs. "As well as any."

Katrina quirks her lip and folds her arms across her chest, indecision obviously still unresolved. "Where are you off to?"

"We're on our way to see Laura. I figure Lilith's due for a checkup," Maverick says. I barely hear him, still impossibly distracted by Katrina's presence. Otherwise, I might've been bothered to ask him who Laura is.

Katrina nods and meets my gaze before dipping her head toward me. The look tells me everything—she wants to ask me something, but whatever it is, she doesn't want to say it in front of Maverick. I stare into her eyes, a conversation without words, but I don't question it again as we continue our journey down the hall. When the time comes, I'm sure she'll let me in on whatever it is.

Beside the last door at the end of the hall, Maverick cracks it open. "Knock, knock," he calls. "Can we come in?"

"Of course!" a sweet voice replies.

Maverick opens the door the rest of the way, and we step into an eerily white room smelling briefly of healing herbs much different than those in Ambrossi's room. The girl who had spoken, a petite thing with a pointed face and tangled, light-brown hair, smiles at me as soon as we step into the room.

"Laura," Maverick greets, but I hardly notice the exchange.

Two hospital beds fill the room, one on either side of the girl. One is empty, but Helena sits on the bed to Laura's left. I rush to her side.

"I-is she okay?" I ask, glancing between Laura and Helena.

"Yes, of course," Laura replies, wringing her hands together. "My job is to assess how well she's recovering."

I let out the breath I hadn't realized I was holding and clutch the side of the bed for balance.

"I need you to check Lilith too, please," Maverick says.

I quirk an eyebrow. "She's a Healer?"

"Of sorts," Laura replies, tipping her head from side to side.

"What does that mean?" I ask.

93

"She cleanses auras," Maverick explains.

The girl grins, showing all her teeth. "While traditional Healers can manipulate the illnesses of a human body using herbs, I've learned to do it with magic."

I watch her for a moment, both skeptical and fascinated. Healers are different from other witches in that their ability *isn't* based on magic; it's learned and passed down from generation to generation. There isn't as big of a distinction between the Equipped and UnEquipped in the Alchemy Coven, because they can all be *taught* their gift.

I've never heard of magic-healing beyond Lynx's isolated incident of healing magical damage.

"Take a seat," Laura says, oblivious to my temporary distraction.

I know she means for me to sit in the empty bed, but I'm stubborn and insist Maverick helps me sit beside Helena. On instinct, I reach into the pocket of the simple outfit I'm wearing for Ambrossi's amulet, only to remember I no longer have it. "So, how does this work?"

"You just relax and leave the work to me," Laura says, smile still plastered to her face.

Maverick smirks and takes a step back, as if he's about to view something extraordinary, leaving my skin to prickle with anxiety.

"Auras can tell us quite a bit about someone, especially their health," Laura informs us.

Helena nods, looking more prepared than I am for what's about to happen. Then I realize she's *excited*, and I know exactly why. She can *see* her aura in Laura's mind. Mine too.

Helena... can you hear me? I think.

'Yes,' comes the soft reply.

I freeze, staring into the window of Laura's mind, unsure if I'm more amazed by the sight of the auras or by Helena's sudden ability. Helena's aura is impressive; she has Willow's signature white ring surrounding her, rising into a flare of blinding light. Unlike Willow's other projects that display a clean glow, Helena has flecks of black crackling through like fire and disappearing.

Judging by Laura's mind, that's a bad sign but also to be expected.

What it says about my aura is unclear, being that it's *all* black.

Laura's frustration is enough to bring out my own—the same frustration that's plagued me my entire life. Even if she can't figure out the reason for my confusing aura, I can. It's the same reason for my limp—my childhood "accident."

"Helena, you're improving," Laura finally says.

Helena nods and gives me a comforting smile, reaching over to squeeze my hand. I know she's too preoccupied with her brief mind-reading stunt to hear what Laura has to say. I set my hand on her thigh and turn to Laura. "What about me?"

"I... don't know," she admits, shoulders sagging in defeat.

Maverick frowns. "That bad, huh?"

"It's impossible to tell." Laura turns back to me with a frown. It doesn't suit her. She has a face made for positive expressions, like smiles and blushes. "How do you feel?"

I shrug. "I feel fine."

"Really?" She clicks her tongue, looking torn, and lets her eyes stray to Maverick for just a second. "Then I would say light training is fine. Just don't exert yourself, okay?"

Maverick and I nod at the same time. Those are terms to which we can both agree. Laura dismisses us, and despite Maverick's complaints about time, he agrees to come with me and take Helena back to her house.

As we round the distance to her yard, Kado pads out of the forest, yipping happily with his stump of a tail flopping. I look around for Willow but don't see her.

"So... mind reading, huh?" I ask Helena.

She nods but doesn't take her eyes off Kado.

I blink and find myself frowning. I recognize the tension in her shoulders and look to Maverick for answers.

"Come on," he says, gently grasping my elbow.

I follow him but glance over my shoulder once to see if Kado is following. The dog glances back at me, but then his eyes land on Helena, and I let it go. He senses her sadness the same as I do. If I can't make her feel better, I'm glad that at least Kado can.

Maverick leads the way to the training fields, a sparse lot of grass that stands out from the purple plants, and it feels like an eternity passes with us just staring at one another. "Show me exactly what you can do," he encourages.

After a light demonstration of my magic, I feel surprisingly weak, and Maverick can tell. He calls it quits and walks me back to my room, the journey taking longer than the last time I made it. Instead of his usual cold dismissal at the door, he studies me until my skin crawls.

"What?" I snap, hand resting on the doorknob as I decide whether or not to slam the door in his face.

"That's how I know you belong here," he says, oddly proud.

I scrunch my eyebrows, waiting for him to continue.

"Today must've been hard on you, but you don't show it. Instead, you tuck it all inside, keeping your head up the entire time. Strength like that must be genetic. You and Willow, you both have it."

I breathe out slowly, unsure how to respond.

"She has a lot of faith in you. We all do."

That makes the hair on the back of my neck rise. The last person who depended on me was Helena ... and she *died* for it.

"For both our sakes, let's hope I don't let you down."

***

IT SEEMS LIKE I barely have the chance to sit before someone knocks on my door. Kado—having returned shortly after me—jumps to his feet, alert to possible danger. I expect Willow to be on the other side of the door, so I'm taken aback by a flash of blue hair. As soon as the door cracks open, Katrina bursts inside my room like her pants are on fire, causing Kado to let out an uneasy yap as she barely avoids stepping on his paws.

"Um… hi," I greet, scrunching my forehead. For the life of me, I can't imagine why Katrina would want to visit *me* at this time of night, and all her earlier appeal vanishes.

"I'm sorry. It's late, I know," she says but plops down on my bed anyways, eyes glued to the wall.

I feel invisible in my own room. "It's okay," I reply, folding my arms across my chest. She's making me uncomfortable at this point, but I probably did the same to her earlier, so it's only fair of her to return the favor.

"You… know me. How?" she finally asks, turning her gaze on me.

"Crowe told me about you."

She squirms on the edge of the bed, her face lighting up. "He did?"

Her eagerness is just a bit unsettling. "Well, not in so many words, but… when he went to Aquais, he looked for you."

Katrina bites her lip. "And?"

"It *devastated* him that he couldn't find you. He tried to hide it… but he couldn't. How could you do that to him?"

"I didn't want to leave like I did, but I *had* to. I wanted to tell him goodbye, but… I never got the chance." She drops my gaze. "I hoped he'd understand, even though I knew he wouldn't."

I know she isn't lying. This is a girl very much in pain, wounded by the same heartache overwhelming Crowe—the pain that comes with being separated from the people one loves.

"Then why leave like you did without so much as a note?"

"Couldn't risk it. The Council was cracking down on Elementals after what Fleur did. Not to mention Iris' fiasco, and I knew it'd be just a matter of time before they found me."

I grit my teeth. It's hard not to mention the fact that an innocent fairy almost died from Fleur's pointless attack. I almost point that out but somehow manage to bite it back. I try to remind myself that I'm one of these people now.

So why don't I feel like it?

"I miss him, Lilith," Katrina says, looking up from twining her thumbs. "Perhaps my biggest regret in joining the Elementals is that he couldn't come with me."

I frown. "You should be worried about the fact that you're on opposite sides of this war. What happens if you have to face him in battle? If you run, you'll be labeled a traitor, and I don't think I have to mention what happens if you pick the other option."

"My plan is to capture him," she replies without missing a beat; she's obviously put thought into this. "That way, he'll be here, and he'll be *safe*... even if he doesn't want to be."

I rub my forehead, wondering if I should tell her how messed up that plan really is.

She turns her wide tawny eyes on me, suddenly less confident. "Promise me you'll do the same if it comes down to it."

"Katrina, he was my mentor. Believe me when I say I have no intention of hurting him." I pause, the words shocking even myself. It doesn't sound like me. When I first met Crowe, all I wanted to do was strangle him, but now, I can't imagine doing anything of the sort. Time passes, people change. I *care* about him, and I don't wait to see him injured in this senseless war—or worse. He was there for me at my lowest, and for that, I will always remember him fondly. And at the same time, I will always hate him. "If it helps, he's torn," I add to avoid answering her questions. "He told me so himself."

Katrina's eyes grow even wider. "I need to talk to him." She scrunches her eyebrows, then releases the tension. "If we could get a message to him, he could be rescued."

She sounds so optimistic, I can't help but nod in agreement, even though we both know the mere attempt to contact Crowe is a suicide mission.

Chapter Thirteen

The Vigil

KATRINA EVENTUALLY LEAVES, and I'm left alone with Kado to settle in for the night. Sleep, however, is surprisingly hard to come by after everything that's happened today. When a knock sounds on my door, I'm tempted to ignore it, thinking it's Katrina with some kind of plan to get in touch with Crowe. Kado grips the edge of my sleeve in his teeth, pulling gently to get my attention. I roll my head toward him without moving from the bed. He lets out a soft yip, which I recognize as his impatient whine.

"Fine. You win, traitor," I say and climb out of bed. After a luxurious stretch, I grumble, "This better be good."

Kado blinks back at me indifferently, tail wagging for having gotten his way.

"What's going on?" I ask as soon as I open the door, wiping the sleep from my eyes before I even clear my mind enough to focus on who's on the other side.

Kado stumbles to my side, looking just as worse for wear. Then I realize the reason for his impatience; it's not just *any* visitor at my door. It's Willow.

"Vigil. For the battle," Willow replies.

She's cloaked in a flowing black dress that looks almost like a poncho—in a regal sort of way, if that's possible—with heavy red scour marks on her porcelain face. My heart skips a beat, and I feel terrible for having forgotten all about it—not that I even intended to go in the first place. Now that I see the effect it has on her, it hurts to think I might have just made the entire thing worse for her with my atrocious memory.

"You're coming with me."

I blink and narrow my eyes, unsure if I heard her right. It's one thing if I choose not to go but another if she's made the decision for me. "Do you really think it's a good idea for me to go? I might make things worse for them. I hurt some of those witches." I pause, not wanting the words to leave my lips even when they do. "*Killed* a few."

Willow gives me a smile with all the fragility of ice. "That might be true, but you can't be so quick to forget that my warriors hurt you too. They know just as well all the pain you've gone through on their account. They aren't so dull that they don't know what happened to your Coven."

I swallow roughly. I've never been a coward, but this is something I absolutely do not want to do. My brain flies through possible escape attempts, ways to get myself out of this, but none of them will hold up. They're weak—hasty. I send a quick frown toward Kado as he climbs back onto the bed to settle down to sleep, partially blaming him for this situation in which I now find myself.

Willow catches the hesitation. "Look, I know it's hard, but I can't think of a better way to bond with your new Coven than by being there for them. Yes, you might be to blame for some of it, but you're also here to pick up the pieces, and that says something. You need to show your place here. More importantly, you need to show that you're not afraid."

"That's just it. I'm *not* afraid." I made a show of it earlier, or at least I thought I had. Witches on both sides feel hostile toward me; it's nothing new. If I'm afraid of anything at this point, it's failure. The times I've failed already have cost me so much, I'm not sure I can afford to be afraid ever again.

"Then you have no reason not to go," Willow counters.

"If you say so," I murmur, sentence punctuated by Willow thrusting a dress into my arms.

"Put this on."

I feel too exhausted by my previous attempt to try arguing again, so I sigh and pad to the bathroom. Willow plops down on the bed beside Kado to wait. I make quick work of changing and splash water on my face to try to bring a little life back to my complexion. I avoid looking at my reflection. I don't need to see my dead eyes to remind me just how bad the prospect of this evening makes me feel.

When I step back into my room, Willow is petting Kado, and for a fraction of a second, I catch her real emotion contorting her face before she realizes I'm there.

"Ready?" she asks, jumping to her feet with the fake smile plastered on once more.

I can say a thousand things right now, but I decide on silence. This evening will be hard on her too. Despite the sorrow I know must be weighing her down like rocks, she walks with her head held high and keeps it that way until we reach the meeting hall. That takes effort. I know from experience just how draining of a show that can be.

Maverick's words echo in my head again. *That strength. You and Willow both have it.*

The meeting room is dark aside from a few candles, as packed as it had been earlier. But the atmosphere is different, homier, like a real Coven. No tables divide witches from one another and there are barely any chairs, but it doesn't seem to matter. They huddle together in groups, forming an enormous mass in the middle of the room.

Willow breaks away to begin her rounds of consolation, and I keep my head down, desperate to avoid all eye contact. They believe me to be a monster. And maybe I am. After all, if enough people believe something, doesn't that make it true? Standing on the outside of the group makes me feel like an outsider, and I am. I still don't think I should be here, and if I were brave enough to look up, I'd probably see confirmation on *someone's* face. Either way, it doesn't matter. They're right, but so is Willow, and that means I stay. With effort, I manage to push my anxieties to the back of my mind and shuffle through the crowd as quietly as possible. Then I plop down in an empty chair at the back of the room.

Maverick makes his way through the crowd, nodding politely at me. When he catches the distant look in my eyes, he pauses. "You're thinking."

"Willow's such a strong witch," I state, looking up to catch his gaze through the darkness.

"You don't know the half of it. See that ring?" He gestures to a heavy silver band around Willow's middle finger.

I turn my gaze toward her, squinting until I find the glint of silver. "Yeah? What about it?"

"Don't let it trick you. It's special... just as she is. That ring connects her to this Coven in ways we can't even dream of. All the Reanimates are close to her because of it."

I pause at that. "Wait. *Other* Reanimates? Besides Willow and Helena?"

Maverick nods. "There are always a few Willow resuscitates after every battle. See the group over there?" He gestures to a gathering of witches slightly separated from the others and huddled close together, as if they're unsure of their place in the vigil, either. "There's a good deal of others too. Willow keeps them close in her mansion."

"*All* of them? Really?" I ask, jaw hanging in disbelief. I had never seen any of the others, so it takes me by surprise, though I know it shouldn't. Willow's mansion is huge. It's not surprising that I haven't crossed paths with them.

Maverick bobs his head.

I look at the witches. There are quite a few of them, and it makes me frown to think they live with Willow. It's such a noticeable separation of the Coven. The living members of the Elementals all have their own houses, even if they aren't built to the best standards. Helena is the only Reanimate with her own home. I realize now it's so she can stay close to Ambrossi, in case there's some kind of medical emergency during the night, and that makes her stand out from them as well. Do the other Reanimates care? Do they want their own homes too, or are they content where they are?

If I were one of them, I'd want my own house too, but then I frown. Even *alive,* I don't have my own home and don't feel the need for one. Living with Willow and her army of undead pets makes me feel safe, secure, and I can understand them in a way.

"They're all bonded," Maverick says by way of an explanation. "They want to be close to her. Willow's ring lets her know where her Reanimates are at all times, and it gives her the ability to control them if need be."

"No way," I gasp, eyes focused on the band again. Just when I thought she couldn't get any more fantastic, she proves me wrong.

My eyes shift from her finger to her face, and that's when I catch a glimpse of her real emotions. She's silent, but I can tell she's crying. Dewy tears glitter in the corners of her eyes, and her teeth gnaw her bottom lip until its red. I understand her pain. This situation feels no different to her than the decision about my parents must have. Maverick must see it too, because he goes to her, caressing her elbow and murmuring comforting words into her ear. She smiles, but it doesn't look real— at least not to me. But Maverick looks pleased for it.

I turn my attention away from them, just looking at the people around me. The witch who had killed my adopted parents isn't here, and that leaves me to wonder. Had I killed her when I bashed her head against the rock in Ignis and Willow had chosen not to bring her back? Or had *Willow* killed her for me?

I shiver and force the thought away. Willow's life must be hard—a constant battle. She had to *choose* which of her Covenmates to bring back, whose lives she valued more. Even though no one says anything of the sort, I'm sure the thought has crossed their minds at some point. All the witches she saved in the battle stand out, marked by their glowing white rings. Those who lost loved ones know Willow values their lives more than the fallen. I feel bad for them in a way. This isn't their fault either, but I'm sure they feel guilty just the same.

And maybe their comrades don't blame them at the moment, but in time, they may. After all, I blamed myself for Helena's death; it's certainly a pain no one deserves. I want to reach out to say something even remotely comforting to the Reanimates. Standing on shaky legs, I leave the safety of my chair, but when I make a move to approach the witches, I lock eyes with one of them, and my words instantly die. The pain is already there, and nothing can fix it. My mind goes blank, and I forget everything I planned to say.

"Just stop looking at us." One of the younger ones, a girl with a blue dress and brown pigtails, gnashes her teeth before springing to her feet and bolting from the room.

I turn to look at Willow, my face frozen with shock.

"We all handle it differently," she assures me with a soft smile. "Amelia's having some difficulty with it. I think she just needs time."

Amelia's reaction reminds me of my own when I found out I *wasn't* dead. If I'm right, she *is* going to need more time.

I'm not the only one whose life has been turned upside-down by the Battle of Ignis. Maybe Maverick's bitterness toward me has been well-placed. There *are* witches who have it worse than me, and I'm partly the reason for it.

None of the other Reanimates call after Amelia; they barely acknowledge her absence, as if they're not part of the world around them. Then I notice how far from the rest of the Elementals the Reanimates stay, almost as if there's some sort of division line between them. I never thought about the possibility of the Coven being split this way. Everyone seemed so joined together at the meeting, but perhaps it was their mutual hatred for me that made it seem so. An uncomfortable flutter blooms in my chest when I think of Helena. If Reanimated people are looked down on, what kind of life does that offer her?

I'm not sure what spurs it, but part of me decides to go after Amelia. Maybe it's the thought of Helena, but it could also be guilt. Either way, I hear her sobbing when I take two steps into the hall. She's sitting against the wall, head buried in her knees. I swallow. I'm at least partly to blame for this.

"Hey," I say, twining my fingers uncertainly.

Her head pops up, hair matted to her blotchy red cheeks. "What do you want?" she snarls.

I raise my hands, unsure of what to say. Usually in these situations, I'm the one who's out of control, irrational, or falling apart, so it's weird to be the one expected to reel in the situation.

"If I offended you, I'm sorry. I didn't mean to," I offer.

She sniffles and wipes her nose with the back of her hand. "But you were staring at me... like... like I'm some kind of freak."

"No, you're not. I'm sorry if I made you think that. It's just... you looked so sad, I wanted to reach out to you. You remind me of my friend Helena."

"R-really?" she asks, looking torn.

I nod. "I like your dress."

While dresses are the last thing I care about, it isn't a lie. Her blue and purple dress *is* pretty, and Amelia seems proud of it. With a twitch, I remember how similar it looks to the dress Regina made me for my Arcane Ceremony but push it away without a lingering thought.

It all seems like eons ago.

Focus on the now.

Amelia smiles and wipes her face with the back of her hand. "Thank you."

I force myself to smile, cautious of setting off another outburst. I hope I can get through to her, but people skills aren't my forte. "Come back in. You shouldn't miss the vigil…"

She wipes her face again and stares at the floor for a long moment before she sighs and grasps the end of her pigtail. "You're right." She stands with ease and makes her way back into the room with me trailing a few yards behind.

Inside, Amelia makes a beeline to her friends, and Willow approaches me. Rather than speaking, she sets a hand on my back and smiles. I know what she's thinking without her saying it; she and I are related, after all.

Chasing down Amelia is something *she* would do. Before today, I wouldn't have, but maybe this place is changing me. *Willow* is changing me. As the vigil progresses, any and all hostilities—toward myself, toward Willow, and even toward the Reanimates—have ceased. Everywhere I look, witches sob— witches who are part of one united family missing brothers and sisters to the same senselessness. They hug one another, literally crying on their friends' shoulders, and I stand in the center of it all, watching the effect ripple outward until everyone is consumed by grief. Silence reveals everything. My skin prickles, but I refuse to acknowledge it, to disrupt the moment. Maverick stands nearest to the door, and even though he's not as outward with his emotions as most of the witches, he bows his head in respect.

I lose sight of Willow in the crowd, and I'm about to move from my spot to track her down when a pair of arms wraps around my shoulders from behind. I startle but freeze when a strand of curly orange hair drifts into my vision— Helena. I pull away and turn to see tears in her eyes. The reaction confuses me for a moment, but just that.

The vigil isn't only for the fallen Elementals; it's in remembrance of Ignis as well. My Coven is gone. The only home I've ever known is destroyed. My knees threaten to give out at the realization, and somehow, Helena manages steady me. *This* is why Willow insisted I come. Not to appease the Elementals, not to prove some point about Coven rank, but to *mourn* for my parents' deaths, for the destruction of my home Coven, and for the very death of the person I was supposed to be.

In the moment of clarity, I lose sight of my hostilities too and dissolve into tears, just another witch in mourning.

Chapter Fourteen

The Battle of Mentis

*E*VEN BEFORE LAURA'S "clearance", I felt as if my wounds were healing well enough to focus on my magic. I can twist and turn without cracking the scabs, and even my bad leg hurts less—either that, or my outlook on life has improved to a state that makes me hardly notice. Even though heavy training goes against Willow's wishes, I practice my telekinesis in short bursts on simple tasks like opening the window and lifting the blanket, barely even disturbing Kado. My magic is nowhere near what it used to be, and I try not to let that fact discourage me. Simple spells leave me feeling weak, but I know it'll take time to work myself to full health. I just wish the process was faster. Despite this, I'm grateful to Maverick for his support. Without him, I wouldn't even be able to do this much.

It's good to be training again, and I stare up at the ceiling as if I expect it to add its agreement.

I hear footsteps pounding down the hall, and I hurry to get in bed, feigning sleep. Less than a minute later, Willow bursts into my room, panting. The panic from her rushed movements alone convinces me to drop the act, and I sit up in bed, staring at her through wide eyes. "What's wrong?"

"The Council... they blacked out Mentis," she says, swiping her frantic brown hair from her face.

I pause. In any other Coven, it wouldn't have made a difference. Most witches hate electricity and function just fine without it—with the exception of Mentis. It's the only Coven with any electricity; they *depend* on it for survival.

"Why would they do that?" I ask. First Ignis and now Mentis? Where does it end? The battle is against the Elementals, not the Covens, so why are they bringing innocent civilians into the crosshairs, tearing families apart in ways that can never be fixed?

"They... they got Larc." She swallows, but it doesn't stop a tear from trailing down her face. "And they scoped his mind."

Alarms go off in my head, but I don't know how to approach this situation. What she said is bad—no doubt about that—but *why*? Larc is a nobody, the scum of his Coven, from what I remember. What does it matter if they read his mind? It might actually hurt them more than it does him.

"So?" I finally ask.

Her features contort into an expression of pain and rage, like I've slapped her in the face, and it startles me. "He knows me. He knows you... He knows the *truth*," she says, and I can hear how much effort the words take. "He knows *everything*."

It clicks, and I feel that cold sting of betrayal sizzling deep in my gut. He knows everything? That means he knows far more of my life than I do, which also means there's more to this story than she's bothered to tell me. Of course there is.

Whatever the history, I can guess the future. "It's a trap, Willow," I say before I realize I've opened my mouth.

"Maybe, but I can't let this go without a fight," she says, tears brimming in her eyes. "There's no telling what they'll do to him. It's not right. This is my battle, not his. He shouldn't have to suffer any more on my account."

"But they've let him live in Mentis for how long? Why would they target him now?"

Willow wipes her eye with the back of a hand, and I close my mouth, wondering why I asked the question. I *know* why they're going after him now. The day he approached me in Mentis, there must have been witnesses—people who talked to the Council about what they saw, what they *heard*.

"I have to go."

Though it's broken, I recognize the stubbornness in her voice. This is do or die for her, if that's even possible for Reanimates. "Then I'm coming too."

"No. You're to stay here and heal. That's an order," she says, hands clenched into fists.

"Then why come to my room?" I ask, thrusting the cover aside to stand from the bed, stepping as close to her as I possibly can so she can't avoid looking at me. "Why tell me anything about what's going on if you don't want my help?"

"I'm looking for Maverick," she says in a voice so weak, I know she's lying. *She* doesn't even know the reasons behind her own actions.

Now, she's regretting it.

"He's not here, obviously, and you knew he wouldn't be. Don't try to change the subject. Willow, with all due respect, if there's a battle, I should be there on the front lines with you. This war is just as much mine as it is yours," I say, pausing to lick my lips. "The same fire fuels us both."

The mix of fear, desperation, and guilt behind her eyes breaks my heart when she glances at my side, as if she can see the damage there through my clothes. Despite her being a leader, she doesn't perform well when it comes to indecision. "Yes, but you're in no shape to fight, Lilith. If something happens to you, I can't be there to stop it. To save you. Here, you're safe… I can make sure you're protected. I can make sure I won't lose you again."

My nostrils flare. My entire life, I've been "protected," hidden away from everything, and I'm sick of it. With rage bubbling inside me, I feel as if I could take on this entire fight *myself.* "You can't honestly expect me to sit back and do nothing after pouring your heart out like that. Don't you get that I don't *want* to be protected anymore? That's been my entire life. While you've had to live yours fighting, I've done the opposite. It's my turn to do something *useful.* Our lives were *shaped* by this war. Damn it, Willow, we *are* this war! What's the point of hiding me from it?"

Willow eyes me for a long time, not blinking for such an eerily long time that the corners of her bloodshot eyes well with tears. "There's no stopping you, then, is there?"

I arch an eyebrow. The only way to stop me would've been to never tell me in the first place. "What do you think?"

There's no more arguing. Next thing I know, we're on the move, nightclothes and all. We dash through the labyrinthine halls, where more and more witches join us, all dressed in their own mixed variety of nightclothes and battle gear. The group is not quite as large as the one that gathered for the vigil, but it's impressive nonetheless. Toward the end of the maze, I find familiar faces. Maverick walks on one side of me and Katrina on the other. Even without me reading their minds, it's evident they each have different intentions for this battle—one to harm, and one to liberate.

Willow walks ahead of us all, leaving me uneasy. For not wanting to be protected, I've somehow ended up in the middle of the throng—the safest place—and I hate it. I know Willow has something to do with it, even though she hasn't spoken since we left the room. If I'm right and this battle turns out to be a trap, it's designed for her, and she's walking into it with her head held high.

I guess that's what makes her a great leader. She's fearless.

The group moves in a never-ending wave. For all I know, the purple plants go on forever. I eventually lag behind the group, the pain biting at my leg, but I don't want Willow to see, to demand that I stay behind. With a huff, I gnash my teeth and push out my telekinesis to move onward.

Then the group stops. Confused by the sudden halt, I shoulder my way to the front. Willow stands beside a large witch—a massive bulk of dark skin and muscles easily three times Willow's size. He has the same ethereal beauty, and then I notice the ring of white, the black eyes, and the thick ugly scar across his neck.

He's a Reanimate.

"Zane," Willow greets.

The hulking giant of a man salutes her with an easy smile. He doesn't ask what she needs, and she doesn't say. He reaches out a large hand to pat her head, tousling her brunette hair, before he pulls a tiny, curved tool from his pocket. It's as black as his eyes and shaped like a miniscule scythe.

I glance at the witches around me, unsure what to make of this display. They don't show any emotion one way or the other. Like Willow's undead pets, this is just another part of their everyday life.

The tool in Zane's hand glitters in the weak sunlight as he lifts it up then slings it downward, a deafening, tearing sound filling the air. Astonished, I watch the very air itself part, revealing a fuzzy layer of colors on the other side.

Unconsciously, I grasp Willow's wrist, and she turns to look at me with a small smile on her face. "What is this?" I ask.

"Teleportation," she says. "It's safe."

She grasps my arm to lunge with me through the portal before I can say another word. I hold my breath for a second before the strange ripple of air swallows me. I expect it to hurt, but it doesn't.

When we emerge on the other side, I recognize the sandy borders on the outer edge of Mentis. Before I know it, the land of sweet scents and purple plants lies behind us, and even though I asked to be here, my heart pounds in my chest with anticipation, and the others join us. I don't know how Willow keeps her fear at bay, then I realize it's because she has no other choice.

Too many people depend on her for this to go any other way.

Maverick dips his head to catch my gaze. "You okay?" he whispers in my ear as the portal seals behind us.

I nod—the best answer I can manage.

"You're sure you can fight?" His voice is sharper this time.

So I glare at him.

"Don't give me that. I just need to make sure, because we're almost there." Just as the words leave his mouth, an explosion fills the air.

I blink and cower, hands covering my ears against the intensity of the sound, and that's all the time it takes for my Covenmates to scatter. Dazed, I try to scope out the scene around me, standing alone where an army stood just a minute before. Screams echo through the air, bringing me back to focus, and the world spins as I try to process what's happening. This place looks nothing like what I remember of Mentis.

What had once been a tropical paradise is now a warzone.

The air smells of blood and ash, and for a moment, it's hard to tell the difference between what's happening now and the Battle that destroyed Ignis. Somewhere between panic and indecision, I find myself moving, and then the true devastation makes itself known. Injured witches from both sides of the war lie scattered across the sand, blood staining it in chunks of crimson crystals.

I do my best to walk past the wounded, trying to ignore their desperate moans of pain and pleas for help. One reaches toward me, and it takes all my effort to dodge him. I hear everything, and my heart breaks for each person I can't save. I close my eyes and try to scurry forward, squeezing my eyes to hold back the tears. It doesn't matter if I want to help; I can't, and I can't afford to waste the time trying. I've never had any real training, so my Healer skills are novice, if that, and these witches are not the reason I'm here. Laura or Ambrossi will see to them. I'm here for Willow and Larc. That's *my* mission, and I need to help my Coven pull through it.

The sooner, the better.

Half of Mentis has already been leveled. The sight of the few buildings left standing around the empty oasis shatters my heart. How many of their own people have the Council killed with their trap? As if to prove a point, another explosion spell hurtles through the air, landing directly in the center of the remaining buildings. The explosion sends me flying. Ears ringing, I taste sand and blood but somehow manage to climb back to my feet. A quick once-over shows a trickle of blood running down the back of my arm, but other than that, I'm okay. I look up and find myself staring at a familiar person lying in the nook of rubble.

"Lavina," I gasp, rushing to her side.

Lavina is—was—Mentis' Healer. I only met her once, the day Crowe and I traveled to Mentis. She told me there was something about my injuries that didn't add up. Maybe that's not such a special remark, considering how obvious it is to anyone who has ever paid attention to me, but the fact that she was willing to talk about something most others were not *is* important. I didn't know her well, but she doesn't deserve this.

No one does.

I drop to my knees beside the edge of her shimmering green robes, and with shaking fingers, I roll her over. A trickle of blood runs from the corner of her mouth, and her wide brown eyes stare at nothing. I can't see the wound that killed her, but I know she's gone all the same. There's no mistaking the emptiness in her eyes.

She's gone, just another casualty of war.

"You can't help her!" a familiar voice shouts at me.

I recoil, instantly whipping around, ready to fight as I search for the voice's owner. On his knees, and leaning his shoulder against the remains of what I assume is the rest of his house, is Quinn, brother to Council member Rayna. Like Lavina, I only met him once, but that doesn't stop my need to protect him. As quickly as I can manage, I make it to his side and look him over for the worst of the damage. The painful thought surges in my mind that if he can't walk, I can't save him.

"Quinn. Are you hurt? Can you walk?" I ask, silently begging for him to tell me yes.

Blood streams from his knee, and he clutches his awkwardly bent arm to his chest. He blinks back at me as if my questions have no meaning.

Slowly, I ask again, "Can you walk?"

He nods once and locks eyes on me. They're glazed with tears, but he seems mentally cooperative for what he's witnessed. Or at least I hope he is.

"Come on," I urge, trying to pull him to his feet.

He tries to obey, but when he lets out a scream of pain, I stop and look down to see a thick plank of wood protruding from his thigh. I stare at the situation unfolding before me, brain flailing to create the best plan of action. The most sensible option would be to remove the wood, but without the proper Healer skills, I'll cause more damage than good.

I look from the bloody mass of flesh on the side of his leg to his eyes. "I know this hurts, but we have to move," I say, my voice wavering. If there's one person who understands leg pains, it's me. "It's not safe here."

"It won't be safe where you take me, either," he spits, hints of tears bubbling in the corners of his eyes. "You're one of *them*. You did this."

"*I* didn't do this to you. The Elementals had no part of this. *The Council* did… *Rayna* did… and I'll promise you this. They won't help you."

"That's impossible! They're fighting *with* us!" he says, trying to lean toward me in anger before his face contorts once again in pain.

"Who took Larc?" I ask, fearing I may have just run into a dead end.

Quinn pauses. "What? Why?"

I close my eyes and take a deep breath through my nose. I know I'm confusing him, but I have neither the time nor the patience to deal with it. "Who was he last seen with?"

"Rayna… but—"

"This? The explosions? It was a trap. Long story short, mostly because I don't know it myself, they took Larc to draw us here. *They* bombed Mentis to get rid of us and didn't bother to pull you out of the way first."

"Rayna wouldn't do that," he says, sounding stronger than he looks.

"You just keep telling yourself that," I say and stand. I don't want to leave his side, but if he's made up his mind to stand by the Council after what they've done, there's nothing else I can do.

The fire in his eyes goes out, and he reaches his good hand toward me. "No, Lilith… please don't leave. I need your help."

"I know," I say, wrapping my hand under his forearm that's not mangled. "I have no intention of leaving you behind." Inside, I'm cursing him for the time this argument cost us, but I hide the bitterness.

He's going through enough as it is. Getting Quinn to his feet is the last real memory I have. One minute, we're shuffling across the sand, and the next is complete blackness.

Chapter Fifteen

Regrets

I'M HOME IN Ignis, Clio and Helena by my side. They're talking and laughing—another careless day in the desert Coven, the kind of day we used to have before everything went to shit. I hardly remember what it's like, to feel that blissful, that *normal*. It brings tears to my eyes, and I never want the moment to end. I try to reach out to them, to say something just to see their gazes on me, but something's wrong. They can't hear me.

When I move, even right into their direct line of sight, they fail to see it. With a painful twinge, I realize I'm dreaming only seconds before the image disintegrates, leaving me in nothingness. I don't know where I am or what this void really is, but it's powerful, forcing all my doubts and fears out of my subconscious and into the light, where I have no choice but to face them.

119

Willow's land feels far from home, and I know it'll take time to adjust to life here. Still, I'm stuck with nagging anxiety, the worry that it never will. Even if Ignis is destroyed, gone for good, I still want to be there. An ache in my heart *demands* it, and the fact I can't grant myself that favor only makes it worse. My chest physically hurts, as if the thoughts are direct poison in my blood, constricting my heart with each desperate beat.

I've moved so much the past few weeks that at this point, nowhere truly feels like home. I wonder if anywhere ever will again, or if I'll always be a drifter, hung up on longing and memories. I feel painfully nostalgic for places I can no longer return to, times that have long since come and gone, and for people to whom, for one reason or another, I can no longer speak.

Nothing I do can ease that pain short of forgetting everything entirely. I have to wait it out, like an earthquake, and deal with the aftermath alone.

"Is she okay? Please tell me she's okay." A voice breaks through the blackness, bringing consciousness with it. The voice is female and familiar, but the waver in it is hard to place. Fear? Sadness? Concern?

"She lost some blood but nothing too serious. Mainly, she's lost a lot of energy. I've given her some herbs, and she should come around soon."

The second voice is much easier to recognize— Ambrossi—and my finger twitches. I groan at the thought that he's here to see me at my lowest once again. Whenever something bad happens, why is he always the one to pick up the pieces? When my eyes are barely cracked, light filters into my vision, and I struggle to open them the rest of the way. The light is particularly blinding; I'm back in the white hospital room. The surreal glow makes it harder for my eyes to adjust, but when they do, I see the people gathered around my bed. The female I heard is Helena.

"What happened?" I groan, reaching up to touch the side of my head. I have a slight headache, and my skull radiates a dull ache to the touch, but other than that, I feel fine. So why am I back in the hospital? "Why am I here?"

"You were hurt," Ambrossi says.

I frown, remembering the battle, and check myself once, finding nothing more serious than a skinned elbow. It certainly doesn't seem hospital-worthy. Lavina's body flits through my mind, and I cringe. It can always, *always*, be worse. "Quinn!" I gasp and sit up so sharply, a zap of fresh pain runs through my head, making me squint. "Is he…"

A soft smile graces Helena's lips. "He's okay. He's healing as we speak."

For a moment, all I can do is stare. Seeing her mouth open and hearing words follow leaves me in awe. Such a normal movement shouldn't strike me like this, and I'm almost mad at myself for the reaction before I shoot it down. I have to enjoy the little things. They're all I have left, after all.

"You're talking again," I state stupidly.

Ambrossi nods, looking as pleased as I feel. Some good news, at least. "She's recovering well."

"What… what about Lavina?" I ask, the image of her bleeding body once again at the front of my mind. I catch a glimpse of Ambrossi's reaction and almost regret asking.

Helena frowns but doesn't share her partner's expression. "Who?"

"The Mentis Healer. Sh-she was dead… and… Willow can bring her back. Right?" I ask, glancing desperately between Helena and Ambrossi.

Ambrossi's regretful frown doesn't change much. "No, Lilith. I'm sorry."

"Why not?"

"Her body is still there, in Mentis… Quite a few are still there, actually. Recovery efforts take witches, and we can't risk sending anyone else out there."

I don't know what hurts more—knowing it's my fault Lavina's been left behind or that I hadn't been able to save her from her fate in the first place. Before I can think of the proper response, the door creaks open, and all three of us train our attention that way as Willow steps into the room. Her jaw is set, eyes clouded over by an emotion pinpointing into rage when she focuses on me, her hands clenched into fists at her sides. I know this is going to be bad. Something happened, and judging by that look, I'm somehow at fault.

"Give us a minute," she says to them, voice full of professionalism, though her eyes never leave mine. "I'd like to speak to my sister alone."

Helena pats Willow on the shoulder, giving me a parting glance as Ambrossi drags her from the room. She doesn't want to go, but she isn't being given a choice. I know what that's like all too well.

When the door closes behind them, Willow whirls on me, the clouds in her eyes clearing to reveal blind rage underneath. "I told you to stay here, Lilith," she says, bloodshot eyes boring into mine. "I knew you weren't ready for combat. Why'd you have to ignore that? To insist that you were fine?"

I struggle to sit up, to clear the fog in my mind. Anger is not what I had expected from her, and it confuses me. Running through the list of actions at the Battle leaves me with no clues as to what I've done wrong. Considering my head still rings from the blow that knocked me unconscious, that's no surprise.

"Larc's dead," Willow says, wiping the tears from her cheeks with the back of her hand. "Dead because I had to choose between him and you."

I flounder for words. I've never truly felt dumb before this, but I'm too confused to portray anything else. "What's the big deal? Can't you bring him back?"

Her black eyes turn to fire. "No. I can't just 'bring him back.' They have his body. Being that he was a criminal means they have the right to do whatever they want with him. Primarily cremation."

I clench my hands into fists at my sides and utter, "I-I'm sorry."

"You should've stayed here," she spits, and suddenly, the anger makes sense.

I draw my eyebrows together. There a lot of things that can be blamed on me, I'm sure, but this isn't one of them. "You think it's *my* fault? Are you joking? How in the *Hell* is this my fault?"

"I had to save you. When the final explosion spell was cast, you were there, and you needed help."

"And you could've moved right on by," I remind her.

Willow's lip pulls up into a snarl. "I couldn't leave my sister for dead."

"You could've saved him *then* come back for me," I point out.

"Then they would've taken you instead."

I want to sympathize with her, I do, but she's making it increasingly difficult. "You're better off without Larc anyway," I reply, lifting my chin with each word.

"You really think so, huh?" A dry chuckle leaves her lips, and she huffs. "You know, you think you know everything, but you don't. You don't know a damn thing. *Larc* was the one who took you from the battle that killed our parents. Didn't you know?"

I scoff in disbelief. She's grasping at straws … right? "There's no way he, of all witches, is involved in my past. I won't believe it."

Fury crosses Willow's face in a way I've never seen before. "Then you're dumber than I thought. You shouldn't speak ill of the dead," she says, voice suddenly cold for the anger it held only a minute prior.

"Why? He was a creep, from what I remember," I say, nearly trembling with my rage.

"Well, that *creep* was a hero, Miss Ungrateful. In the past, he saved your life, kept you safe, housed you, fed you... until the Council found out and took you away."

A tear slips from her eye, and I suddenly realize the mistake I've made. Larc *means* something to her. Apparently, he should also mean something to me. He had to *care* for me. For a time, he had been my guardian, which means he risked his life for me ... especially if the Council had been out for my blood. There was nothing for him to gain out of it; he had done it for Willow because he loved her and knew that above everything, she loved me. That she would want me to be safe.

Willow cared about him, possibly as much as I care for Clio, and on top of choosing me over him, I threw her decision in her face, leaving her feeling abandoned when she needs me more than ever.

"Because he valued your life more than his own," she says, "he was captured, stripped of his powers, and crippled for life. I'd think *you* of all people could appreciate that level of pain."

Crippled ... because of me. My face twists, and I feel guilty, as I know I should, but that's about it. What else *can* I do? I can't go back in time to save him or even tell him I appreciate his silent sacrifice, and all the apologizing in the world won't take back what I said. It's not like I mean it, anyway. Larc never even attempted to tell me what he did for me all those years ago. Instead, he used his one opportunity at communication to hit on me.

Like a bolt from the blue, the memory strikes me in a way it never has before. I stare at Willow, but all I see is that day in Mentis.

"Ivy was our mother... wasn't she?" I ask.

Willow narrows her eyes, looking like I've just punched her in the stomach. The anger is still there, of course, but the conversation tangent knocked the wind from her sails. "Yeah. Why?"

"It... was something Larc said. That I looked like her."

A painful smile bites her face. "You do," she says and storms out of the room before I can say anything else. Just before the door slams shut behind her, I hear a sob break loose. I stare after her in stunned silence, then Helena creeps back into the room, Ambrossi right behind her.

She glances over her shoulder before looking back at me. "That didn't go well, did it?"

I bite my lip and find it suddenly hard to look at my friend. "How much did you hear?"

"All of it." Her shoulders slump with guilt. "I really didn't mean to, I just—"

I shrug and look away without waiting for her to finish. Right now, I have no right to be mad at anyone. "She's right, though."

Awkward silence follows my statement, and I can tell by Ambrossi's thoughts that he's struggling to figure out the perfect thing to say.

You can't fix this one, buddy.

"Is Quinn okay?" I ask before they have another chance to push the topic of Willow. I don't know how much more of it I can take.

Helena nods. "You want to see him?"

I'm up on my feet without their help. My memory is still nothing but a black hole. I don't know who bothered to save Quinn—or me—in Mentis, but I'm glad they did. Part of me hopes he has the answers I don't.

"Careful, Lilith," Helena says, eyeing me before leading me out of the white room and into another, the space separated into cubicles surrounded by gray curtains. She pulls the first one aside to reveal Quinn, a series of bandages along one arm and across his forehead.

He looks relaxed, and I'm glad he's asleep; even though I wanted to see that he was okay, I'm not emotionally ready for a conversation. I doubt he is, either.

"Does he know where he is?" I ask, glancing at Helena from the corner of my eye.

Helena frowns. "He's been out the entire time, so I don't think so."

"Who brought him?"

She shrugs. "I don't know for sure who found him, but Willow brought him in to Ambrossi the same time you were brought."

I can imagine how they must've found us—curled together in the sand, bleeding and barely clinging to life. "I want to be here when he wakes up, if that's okay," I say.

When he wakes with the realization of where he is, of who he's with, he'll fight it just like I did. I don't want him to do that. Even if he doesn't know it yet, this place is his best chance of survival. His Coven, much like Ignis, is destroyed. If he decides to leave here, he'll be Covenless, and that's no life.

"I'll make sure you are," Helena replies, grasping my hand to give it a comforting squeeze.

Another set of footsteps comes down the hall, and I look up to see Maverick slip into the room. "Willow's called a meeting," he says.

No further explanation is required for my anxiety to kick into high gear. A flutter of panic runs through my heart as I ponder the possibilities. What could the meeting be about? Is it possible Willow wants to have me evicted from the Coven for what happened? Maverick shoots me a sideways glance, and I wonder if he's had the same thought. Helena offers me a smile upon departure but doesn't follow us, instead stepping to Quinn's side to check his vitals. I try to ignore the voice telling me that's a bad sign.

Maverick doesn't try to make conversation, which makes the walk seem direr than it really is. When we reach the meeting room, the scene is much the same as it was the first time I was here. The chair next to Willow is gone, however, and that leads me to two conclusions—one, this meeting isn't about me, or two, she wants me to suffer through it.

Maverick doesn't hesitate by the doors to give me time to decide either way. He steps down the open pathway, and I cling closer to him than I normally would. The Elementals' eyes scorch my skin, and I duck my head to take out some of the sting. Willow's eyes and cheeks are burned red from crying, but the fury is still there as she catches, and holds, each of their gazes in turn.

"That was a disaster," she says, hardened voice echoing through the room. "We are a Coven both strung together and torn apart by this war. We lost people today. Good people." Her gaze finally lands on me. "And that can't happen again."

I lower my head, filled with shame, wishing I could curl up so tightly on myself that I would disappear completely.

"We need to refocus our training efforts. After what happened, that *defeat*, the Council sees us as weak. Breakable. We can't have that."

Murmurs of agreement ring through the room. My voice is right there with theirs. I don't see how anyone could argue.

"Grief, Laura, Katrina, get on it," Willow says.

All three state, "Yes, ma'am," and leap to their feet to gather various Elementals.

For a moment, I wonder who will pick me before Maverick sets his hand on my shoulder. "Come on."

I arch an eyebrow.

"*Someone* needs to teach you," he says.

I nod, appreciating the gesture. He knows just the same as I do that none of the others will pick me. Not with Willow as angry as she is, anyway. Despite that fact, I somehow keep my head held high. Even if Willow has lost her faith in me, it's good to know that not *everyone* has.

Chapter Sixteen

In the Face of Danger

WITH EVERYONE IN their designated groups, leaving the building feels like a field trip. I lose sight of Willow in the chaos, but I guess she's somewhere toward the front of the herd. I consider asking Maverick, then decide to keep my mouth shut at least this once. This allows me to both avoid saying something potentially stupid and to gather time to hone my observation skills. Being the smallest group, Maverick and I stay toward the fringe of the band of witches, as if we're afraid of being trampled if we get too close.

Up ahead, I recognize the path Maverick took me down during the only opportunity I'd been given to train. Knowing I'll get the chance to do so again causes a flutter of excitement to run down my spine—the first positive thing I've felt in Gods only knows how long. Without realizing it, I move faster than

Maverick, pass him, and step onto the familiar stretch of grass to study the scene for a moment. This is the only one I can see not covered in sparkling purple plants. It's an anomaly, just like me.

Even without Healers here, we make a formidable group, even more so when those Healers do join us. As I gaze at the faces of the witches all around me, I'm struck by the fact that these people are the outcasts of the Land of Five, the people who haven't left enough of an impression on their homes to be missed.

People who ended up fugitives of the law simply for being down on their luck.

I suppose I'm the same. Maybe none of us truly *made* a decision to be here, instead having come to this place as a consequence of every other decision. I'm never the same person I was the day before, constantly adapting to tomorrow, and these witches are the same. I can see the changes in myself as clearly as if they were physical. All that growth can't be bad for a person— or at least I try to tell myself that. Even if a majority of these witches don't care for me, these are good people— unconventional yet reliable. These very witches are going to make history for bringing down the Council, and my job is to motivate them to reach that goal, whether it be for hatred or passion.

If only I can motivate myself first.

I glance to my left, and a familiar glint of green eyes in the crowd makes me pause. Why of all witches is *Helena* here? Seeing as how she isn't Equipped with any combat powers—as far as I know—I really don't like the thought of her out here. She's vulnerable; she can't fight, and she can't defend herself, either. She'll be thrown around like an empty sack, and the thought brings out the lioness in me. I want to take out the rage on the witches in Willow's group, to demand she answer my questions. Helena is still too frail for this—for *any* of this. She only just regained her ability to talk, and I fear if she's pushed too hard, she'll *lose* progress.

Do they even care if she gets hurt? I pause. Unless she's here to practice healing.

That makes me feel a little better, but if that's the case, Ambrossi or even Laura would need to be by her side to make sure she's using the accurate techniques. In the meeting room, Laura hadn't been gathering Healers; she picked soldiers, people who can hold their own in a fight. I want to believe they wouldn't leave Helena to work alone, whatever the case may be, but maybe this is what she needs to make her strong.

I blink, studying the halo of white glowing around her skin. Is it possible she's slipping through the cracks because she's a Reanimate? A quick survey shows how few of them have been chosen for this assignment.

Why?

It makes no sense. Undead soldiers seem like the perfect weapon. The Elementals, however, treat them like a burden, which is hard for me to comprehend. I don't want to accept the possibility that they're *hoping* she gets hurt. Maybe the goal is to see if she can develop more powers than mind-reading. I know from experience exactly how powerful of a motivator a stressful situation can be.

Either way, I need to have a heart-to-heart with Willow.

Her name alone brings the memory of that look in her eyes. Her rage is laced with pain, and that's more difficult to get rid of than just the anger. Is this her way of getting back at me for what happened with Larc? If I think it's petty, I know she must as well.

I watch Katrina lay her hand on Helena's shoulder and whisper something into her ear. I don't invade either of their minds, but for some reason, the scene brings me comfort. I trust Katrina. Though we haven't talked since the day she came to my room, I feel like we've bonded in a way that's hard to explain. I'm confident she'll look after my people, as she expects me to do for hers.

Grief, Laura, and Katrina go to work leading their groups to different parts of the field, and I look to Maverick to lead me somewhere that hasn't been claimed. Less than a minute later, spells fill the air. The entire Coven engages in their collective practice, and I'm amazed by how smoothly it goes. Witches of all different backgrounds and powers work side by side with seemingly no issues, dodging and moving in sync, as if they share one mind.

"They're strong," I say.

Maverick smiles, looking proud. "It's what happens when a Coven is truly bonded. Ready to give it a go?"

I blink at him as he paces a few feet away, and for half a second, a bittersweet smile lines my face. A one-on-one duel reminds me of all the times I dueled Clio—when lives weren't on the line.

Things are so different now.

I have no idea how to go toe-to-toe against someone like Maverick, but this isn't the first time I've faced an opponent with unconventional powers. Paralysis is impossible for me to counter, even if I was in pristine shape. Maverick moves faster than me, and before I know it, tingling starts in the tips of my fingers and toes, slowly bleeding upward. I can tell he's taking it easy, and it angers me a bit. I try to use that to my advantage. When I connect to my telekinetic powers, I concentrate, forcing what energy I have into my next move. When my power blasts out, I'm disappointed in it even before it hits Maverick. It doesn't move him an inch. The paralysis takes hold of the more vital parts of my body, and I collapse to my knees.

"Concentrate, Lilith!" Maverick calls, watching my struggle with a mix of concern and hope.

Instead of an attack this time, I put my effort into defense, but the result is the same—a failure. Maverick sighs at the effort and frowns, retracting his magic. Feeling returns all at once, and I stare down at the ground, disappointed in my lack of fight and the amount of sweat I produced to do it. My leg screams at me to sit down, to stop fighting, but no one else does, and I don't want to be the first to call it quits. I force myself back to my feet and catch sight of Sabre across the field. As if he feels my eyes on him, he looks up.

Then he makes an error in judgement.

He decides to *approach* me, and I tense, no longer hearing the list of commands Maverick rattles off to me. He doesn't exist in my world, and Sabre takes another step, closer and closer. I can hardly breathe, I'm so angry.

Teeth clenched, I find my words are hard to get out, but I don't let that stop me. "Get him away from me," I state, never looking away from Sabre.

"Lilith, calm down," Maverick says, holding his hands out as if he's unsure whether or not to grab me.

But I can't calm down. Not with the return of the all-consuming rage that accompanies Sabre's presence.

This time, I won't ignore it.

"Lilith," Sabre greets.

"Get him away!" I scream, rage exploding out of me as my words fade into the still air.

A second later, a blast of wind soars across the field, knocking down everyone in its path. The training stops instantly. Every pair of eyes on the field falls on me, from both those still standing and those who were affected by the attack. No one speaks, but they don't have to. Looking at the aftermath puts out the rage, as if a bucket of ice water has been dumped over my head. That was me ... I did this.

"Lilith... you have *that* power, too?" Maverick asks, neck craned to see me from his place on the ground.

"I-I..." I stutter but come to no coherent conclusion.

The Sage had told me there existed a possibility of me developing a power from every Coven, but I hadn't believed her. After so much time of being lied to, it's easy to dismiss just about everything without a second thought.

This isn't one of those things.

I can't ignore the fact that I now possess an *Aens* power. That's three out of five Covens now. Who knows how far this whole thing will go? For all I know, she *was* telling the truth when she said I'm meant to be the next Sage.

***

AFTER THE INCIDENT on the field, I don't know what I expected to happen, but it certainly isn't being sent to my room like a kid being punished. Pacing across the room helps my anxiety slightly but not much. A thousand scenarios of what can happen next run through my mind, none of them good. Maverick's emotions are usually reserved, but the walk back to my room had been tense.

Kado's eyes follow me back and forth from his place on the bed, but he doesn't intercept me. He whines once and sets his chin on his paws, as if even he's stumped. I pet him a few times every fourth or fifth lap, but I can't take my eyes off the door. No one told me to expect any company, but after that incident, I can't be left to believe I won't have *any*. Though it seems like an eternity has passed, I know it's only been a handful of minutes. Then someone knocks on my door. Kado leaps off the bed, and I spring to answer the door. Before I can make it across the room, Maverick peeks his head inside.

"Willow wants to see you," he says, emotions under wraps once again.

"I figured she would," I reply, wiping my sweaty palms on my dress. If nothing else, at least this will be a subject that isn't emotionally charged. "Wish me luck," I say to Kado and follow Maverick out into the hall. Kado stalks away to the depths of the room, as if he senses something big is about to go down.

Maverick leads me through the labyrinth of halls to a part of the building I've yet to be see, and Willow greets him as soon as we enter the nearest room. She's seated in a red-padded chair, a cup of tea clenched in her hand. She turns her nose up at me, and if I didn't know any better, we could be strangers.

"Your powers are developing well," she says in that same tone absent of any emotion.

I nod and take a small step toward her. "I told you I can fight. I want to protect this place... I want to protect *you*."

Her jaw clenches at that. "And the way you do that is by following orders, which, so far, you haven't been willing to do." She punctuates her statement by slamming her mug on the table. "That being the case, I might as well put you on the front lines. First, we need to develop every power you possess. Since you've just come into touch with your Aens powers, it follows that those are currently your weakest."

I bob my head; that makes sense.

The door creaks open, and a pointy face peeks in—a *very* familiar face.

"Lilith, I believe you've met Fleur," Willow says as the girl takes her place beside my sister.

"*Her?* You expect me to get along with *her?*" I ask, jerking my thumb toward Fleur.

This is the girl who poisoned the river. The girl who led me to believe the Elementals were evil. Because of *her*, Callista almost died. Close to the Council or not, she hadn't deserved what happened to her. And this girl didn't deserve the likely praise she got for it.

"You can't have a problem with *everyone* and expect to stay in my Coven," Willow says, tapping her foot.

I pull my lips tight into a bitter smirk, running my tongue along the inside of my bottom lip as I decide the best response that won't get me thrown out of the Coven on my ass. "I don't have a problem with *everyone*, just the ones who have problems with *me*. The ones who have no problem hurting innocent witches or fairies."

Willow sighs and taps her fingers on the chair's armrest. "Tensions are high. I get it. They've had to do some unforgiveable things, but *this is war.* And that's life. If you're really one of us, you need to be here body, mind, and soul. Your defiance isn't helping anything or anyone."

I glare at the floor to avoid aiming it at any particular witch, since really, they're all to blame for how I feel right now. When Willow called this meeting, I hadn't expected her to be happy, but I hadn't thought she'd be this angry, either. Fleur has caused so much harm, and now she's just a step away, watching me as if *I'm* the problem.

"She's here to help," Willow adds.

"With what? You're going to poison me?" I ask, fixing my gaze on Fleur as the door creaks open again.

"Seems you have enough venom for everyone," she says.

I clench my teeth, waiting for her to continue.

Fleur smiles stiffly. "There's your teacher now."

The door opens completely to reveal Sabre, and my heart pounds so hard, it hurts. If I were in a rational state of mind, I might've been worried about a heart attack, with my blood pressure through the roof. Instead, a dry chuckle falls from my lips. "You're joking, right?" I ask, looking at each of the faces in the room.

"No, Lilith. This isn't a game, and I don't appreciate you acting as such. You're my sister, and I love you. But I'm beginning to think you're using that against me, and it needs to stop. I'm taking charge now... like I should have before. I get that you don't like Sabre, but he's the one who brought these powers out of you, so you'll learn what he has to teach whether you like it or not. One of these days, your eyes will be opened to everything, and you'll understand why I'm doing this."

My hands clench into fists, and I'm ready to shout obscenities at Willow, Sabre, and even Maverick. Then I feel the anger leaking out of me like water from a broken pail. I know who's behind it; Fleur pulled the same thing the last time I encountered her. I was so wrapped up in my emotions, I hadn't bothered to prepare for her magic. And now it's too late to counter.

Willow uses my silence to continue. "Sabre is one of my best Aens warriors, and he's more than qualified to teach you proper air-manipulation techniques."

I scowl at him, but under Fleur's influence, it's the closest I can get to my true feelings. His expression doesn't change, and something about his lack of emotion makes my blood boil. After everything, how can he be so detached? The new surge of emotion runs straight to my telekinesis, which I quickly grasp a hold of and knock Fleur to the ground. Without her magic to stop me, the anger rises full-force, and I knock Sabre to his knees.

"I know all too well what you can do," I scream. "Look... look, you bastard!" I hike up my dress to show the scars dappled across my side. It doesn't occur to me that I'm flashing my underclothes until a blush blooms across Sabre's face.

"I've seen *plenty* now, thank you," he says, composing himself before he stands.

Willow jumps to her feet and stomps toward me. She grabs my elbow, fingers digging into the skin until I drop my dress back into place.

"You're hurting me," I say with a grimace.

"What the hell is wrong with you?" she hisses in my face, as if she either doesn't notice how tightly she's holding me or doesn't care.

I give an innocent shrug. If she wants to play this game, I can just as easily do the same.

"Honestly, do I need to put you back into the holding cell until you learn your place? Or are you capable of self-control?" she asks, flicking her wrist to push away my elbow with disgust and finally loosening her grip on me.

I flare my nostrils but take in a deep breath, buying time to think about my next move. Given Willow's current mood, I know how happy she'd be to toss me into a dark hole and throw away the key.

"No, I'll stop," I finally say.

Willow nods. "See that you do. Begin her training tomorrow," she tells Sabre, then turns to Maverick. "Oversee it."

Chapter Seventeen

The Wind Warrior

SLEEP'S HARD TO come by once night falls, but I'm not surprised. My day has been so packed with emotions that despite wanting to push it all away to the depths of my mind, I can't. I'll have to sort it all out and agonize over every crucial second before I can get any real rest. It's hard to do that when my mind repeatedly returns to one thing—I have Aens powers, and developing them means having to depend on a man who tried to kill me.

What's become of my life?

I find myself asking that question more and more often. A week ago, I would not have pictured my life going this way. Friends turned enemies, enemies turned friends—this is hard, much harder than I imagined adjusting could be. Even my transition into the Council had been easier than this. Why? What's so different about this place? Am I really so scared of disappointing Willow, my only living blood relative, that I can't let myself relax for even a moment?

'But you've already disappointed her,' Grief reminds me.

Yeah, thanks, I shoot back, wishing he'd show his face but also knowing he won't.

As mad as I am at Willow for assigning Sabre to me, she's right to do it, to push me, because no matter what, I *did* let her down at the battle. She needed my help, and instead, I became a liability.

Never again.

If I'm ever truly going to blend in, these people need to become *my* people, and I need to be willing to die for them just as I am for Helena and Clio.

'Easier said than done,' Grief points out.

You want to come say something to my face? I ask.

Silence.

Somehow, I fall asleep during my tireless thinking, and when I wake up, Maverick's ready to take me straight to Willow. I'm glad for it this time. Lately, downtime has *not* been my friend. The thought of seeing Willow's anger so early in the morning makes my stomach churn, but staying by myself didn't prove any less bothersome. As I follow Maverick down the hall, my brain works on creating some kind of excuse to get me out of this.

For all my brilliance, I find none.

When we enter the room, Sabre, Helena, and Laura are present already, lounging about as if they've been awake for a while. Willow sits in the biggest chair in the center of the room, an empty chair beside her. I glance at her, waiting to see if she'll bother to greet me, and she makes a point of avoiding eye contact even after kicking the chair towards me. I wonder why she didn't offer it to Maverick, but I don't ask.

Even angry, she still shows favoritism.

No wonder half the Coven hates me. I can see it from their point of view. If I were them, I'd hate me too.

Another glance around the room alerts me to Fleur's absence, and I blink at Willow. Does she really trust me to behave, or did she just forget? The latter seems unlikely. My gaze lands on Sabre and how close he stands to Helena. They're talking and smiling; he even has the audacity to put his hand on her shoulder, as if he hadn't murdered her in cold blood less than a month ago.

A low chuckle escapes my lips, but no one notices. "He should apologize to her," I say softly.

Willow blinks, and the conversation in the room dies instantly as all eyes turn to me. Willow voices their question. "What?"

"Sabre should apologize to Helena. After all, he *killed* her," I say, gesturing to the two, who step apart under the spotlight.

"He's fine, Lilith," Helena chimes in, a small smile on her face.

I stare at her, thinking I misheard her. "Excuse me?"

"I said it's fine, Lilith. No harm done."

"No ha—" I struggle for words and round on her. "How can you *say* that? What of your scars? You'll have them for the rest of your life!"

"I like my scars. They show I fight back," Helena replies, head held high.

I pause, unsure if I'm more caught off guard by the strength behind her words or the wisdom in them. I wish I could be as positive about what happened as she's trying to be, but there's no way to explain how it felt to watch her die. With a slight quiver of indecision, I project the memory toward her.

She stiffens on the other side of the room, but her voice still flows out sweet and lilting. "Yes, but I'm better now. I got what I wanted."

That extinguishes all my need to fight better than Fleur's magic. It had devastated Helena to acknowledge the fact that no matter how hard she worked, she was UnEquipped, doomed to a life without magic. Our friendship had almost been destroyed when my powers began to flourish. Even though I want to argue, I bite my tongue. I have no way to fight, and Helena just stares at me, the knowledge of her victory written across her face.

"Well, now that that's out of the way," Willow begins, clicking her tongue, "Laura and Helena are going to check you over really quick to see how well you're doing."

Laura goes first, combing through the void of my aura for some clue as to my health. She seems more confident than she was last time, smiling as she finds whatever it is she was looking for there. After she's finished, Helena inspects me physically, observing my scars and my leg, before giving me a few herbs to chew for the pain. In less than five minutes, I'm cleared for training, and the Healers depart, leaving me with Willow, Sabre, and Maverick.

Willow dismisses us, and Maverick urges Sabre to lead the way back to the training field. I try to cling to Maverick's side, but he hangs just a few steps back in an apparent attempt to get me to bond with Sabre. Problem is, he underestimates how petulant I can be. I play the middleman, walking halfway between both men the rest of the way to the field.

Once we arrive, we form a loose semi-circle, running through mock battle strategies and defensive moves.

"I'm going to take a step back," Maverick says, stepping into the shadows around the field as Sabre switches focus to discussing attacks. "But I won't be far. Lilith, play nice."

I give him a scathing look and turn back to Sabre. "How do Aens powers work?" I ask, staring at the ground and trying to forget the fact that my question is aimed at him.

"They're easy... like breathing," Sabre says, a hint of a smile on his face. "Take a breath. In and out. Feel that pressure... that *force* inside you? That's what it's like but a thousand times more freeing."

My brain splits again between a sarcastic comment and obedience, but I force myself to submit and follow his instructions. It won't help anyone if I start another fight. After all, Sabre's going out of his way to help me. If I want to earn back Willow's trust, I need to do as she asks—even if it makes me want to swallow mud.

"Relax," Sabre says, noticing the tension in my shoulders.

My eyes open to glare at him, but I breathe in through my nose. It relaxes me, and my irritation washes away despite my gut feeling that he can't be trusted, that I need to fight. After a few more breaths, I feel it—the slightest wiggle of energy in my core. Earlier, I had mistaken the flutter for irritation and thought no more of it. Is it possible that some of my other quirks are new powers trying to manifest themselves, and I've simply not noticed?

I don't realize I'm smiling until Sabre calls me on it.

"Feel it?" he asks, raising his eyebrows as he leans slightly toward me.

"I just push it out, right?" I ask. Logically, wind power and telekinesis shouldn't be *too* different.

Sabre laughs. "And hurt your teammates too?"

"Wait. What happened on the field… That was *wrong*?" I ask, narrowing my eyes. I didn't think it was possible to hate him more than I already do, but now I know anything is possible.

"Your summoning, no. But your delivery, yes. Wind is a powerful element, but to use it right, you have to learn to manipulate just the air around you that you want to use, not all of it at once. In battle, you would've doomed your team with a move like that."

"Manipulate them how?" I ask, my voice stiff, and ignore the sting of his criticism.

"Watch me." Sabre smiles and lifts his hand. His breathing evens out, and a moment later, he flicks his wrist. A jagged white line appears on the tree at the far end of the field—the product of one of his air knives I've come to know so well. "Like that."

I frown and remember Leo, the Aens Adept. He also used his hands to create a ball of energy. I hadn't thought much of it at the time, but now I understand; manipulation is key to properly utilizing Aens powers.

I lift my hands in the same way but pause, feeling out of place. Sheepishly, I ask, "How do I know what shape works best for me?"

"Practice," Sabre says, clicking his tongue. "Like any other skill."

I roll my eyes at the cliché answer but keep my hands up. I can do this; if I managed to use allegedly inaccessible Ignis powers, then I can do this. I steady my breathing, slow and calm as Sabre did, until the wiggle returns. With some effort, I try to slowly push the energy to my hands, but it's a draining process. For every inch it moves closer to my goal, the weaker I feel. When the power hits my wrists, I'm ready to collapse to my knees but somehow manage to remain standing.

The energy doesn't make it to my fingertips before it shoots ahead, blasting the air around me like it did on the field. The difference this time? Sabre is prepared. He blocks it easily with his own wind and looks at me for a long time. My mind picks up on him internally contemplating his next words.

"You did… *well*," he says.

I toss him a scathing look. "Did I?"

"Yes. It'll take time, but I think you're off to a good start."

"That may be, but time's something we just don't have right now," I point out. Sabre shrugs but doesn't speak, and I sigh, reaching up to scratch the back of my neck. "So, when your powers first developed, you knew what to do?"

Sabre's lips draw tightly together. "Yes and no. Of course, I knew about air manipulation from my Covenmates, but as you've seen, finding what works is a journey only you can take."

"So, why knives?"

Sabre runs his tongue along his teeth and looks down at the grass before looking back at me. "That's rather personal, Lilith. Why the sudden interest?"

I crinkle my nose in distaste for his tone, unsure if I'm more upset that he won't tell me or that he's cocky enough to give me attitude, knowing how I already feel about him. "You can either tell me, or I can find out myself."

Sabre laughs and runs a hand though his shaggy blond hair. "Fair enough. My family has a history of producing UnEquipped children every other generation. I fell on one of them, so my family made sure to keep me far away from my Equipped family members. But it was my dream to fight in the Aens Army, to protect my Coven and everything like it. So, I utilized what weapons I could. A bow and arrow, throwing knives… things of that nature."

"And when you learned you had powers?"

"The skills transferred over," he says, "and it saves me time not having to carry actual weapons."

"Good for you," I say, barely keeping the bitterness out of my tone. Everyone has such fantastic stories of discovering their powers except for me. I'm still trying to decide what my real powers *are*.

"Look at it this way. Life may not always go the way we want, but it doesn't have to be miserable, either."

He's right, but before I have the chance to acknowledge it, a familiar voice calls my name on the breeze. I pause, scrunching my eyebrows, and turn to see Helena darting across the field.

"What is it?" I ask, mentally steeling my nerves for bad news. If she's all the way out here, it can't be good.

Her face gives nothing away as she replies, "Quinn's regaining consciousness."

Chapter Eighteen

Missing Piece

QUINN IS FULLY awake when we make it back to his room in the hospital hall. He's sitting up and looking around, but even from the doorway, I can tell he's anything but relaxed. The look in his eyes isn't curiosity—it's fear. Like a trapped animal, he's searching for a way out, an escape, growing desperate with the realization that there is none. It's strange to watch someone go through what I did, *knowing* what thoughts are running through his brain even without probing his mind.

That animalistic fear is something I recognize well, though I doubt even my insight into the exact emotions will be enough to clear them away. I think about the situation, what I would've done if there had been someone to talk to me, someone who had gone through exactly the same thing. I would've cursed at them, I'm sure—denied every possible attempt they made to help me. Once fear is too strong, it doesn't matter what options come your way; they *all* seem like bad ideas.

That's when I notice the restraints holding him to the bed. Despite his broken arm, his other three limbs are securely held in place, and I feel sick. I didn't want this—for him to think he's a prisoner or to be treated like one.

Glancing around the room for some sign of a struggle, anything that could ease my mind into believing they're doing the right thing, I try to reassure myself that maybe they didn't have a choice. Maybe he already tried to make a break for it.

"Is this really necessary?" I ask at last when my search doesn't provide the results I want.

"He's scared, Lilith," Helena says in my ear.

And it's probably worse now. I want to say it, but I don't only because it's Helena.

Instead, I ignore the comment and approach Quinn. I don't want to think of him as a feral animal in the same way that I don't want him to see me as a prison guard. But the way I move says it all. His eyes slide from where they were focused on the wall and lock onto mine. His expression has settled into something torn between relief and his earlier panic.

After our initial eye contact, his eyes move to my hands, as if to search them for potentially hazardous items, before returning to my face once more. "Lilith, what is this place? Where am I?" he asks, tugging his good arm against the restraints.

I know the intent behind that movement; he's hoping I'll be the one with the key, that I'll offer to free him without him having to ask. As if I could. I bite my lip, finding myself suddenly wishing I would've prepared something to say before coming here, but it's too late to back out now. Whatever I say or do in this moment, he's always going to remember it. So will I. He's waiting for me to talk, to say *something*, but I hadn't considered how hard this conversation might actually be. Now that the time has come, I'm at a loss.

I frown. What did Rayna say his power was? I can't quite remember. I take in a breath and try to open my mind to him, but that doesn't provide me with results, so I stop. Then I remember—he's telekinetic, just like I am.

"You're safe," I answer finally, hoping my voice is as calming as Willow's as I set my hand on his knee. If I were him, the words would've pissed me off, but I hope he reacts differently.

And he does.

"Where's my sister? Where's Rayna?" he asks, and I hear the pain when he says her name, the grief of a fresh loss. He still wants to debate what I told him in Mentis—an expected reaction—but the true weakness of his desire to fight surprises me.

I glance at Helena for guidance. I have no idea how much he's already been told of his situation and how much I can tell him without making him feel any worse—if that's possible.

"Rayna's not here, but it's okay. You're okay," Helena assures him. She twines her thumbs, apparently just as uncomfortable with the situation as I am.

"Is she?" he asks.

Helena and I exchange an uncertain look. There's no way for either of us to know something like that unless we witnessed it directly. If a member of the Council had been injured—or captured—I'm sure Willow would've wasted no time in telling us the news and using it to further perpetuate the war.

"Is Rayna okay?" he repeats slowly.

"We don't know," I answer him, holding my eyes shut so I can avoid seeing his reaction. "But you don't need to worry about that right now. Focus on getting better. These witches will take care of you." I crack my eyes open just enough to peer at him.

Quinn squints and lifts his hand to hide his face. "How do I know that?"

"They saved your life. You were hurt in the battle, and instead of leaving you for dead, they treated your wounds and are now offering you a home. Give it some time. You'll be fine." There are many reasons why that's a potential lie, but that's a fact I keep to myself.

To my disappointment, he's anything but pacified when he looks up again. "I'm a prisoner then, aren't I?"

"No, no. I promise you're not. You're here under my word of protection." I'm not sure if that's true, but it sounds good, so I let it pass. "And the restraints are just to keep you from moving too fast and reinjuring yourself. As soon as you're well again, you're free to go, if that's what you choose."

I glance at Helena again for permission, and she nods once before I untie the bond on his non-broken arm.

"They captured you too, didn't they?" he asks, gazing at me in wonder as the silky band slips to the floor.

I pause at that. After everything, it's a strange thought. "A while ago, but they didn't do it in ill will. This place, these people... It might be hard to believe, but they're *good*. A lot of them were in our exact same position at some point, but once you get the hang of things, you'll fit right in." I gesture to Helena. "She's an example. Does she look miserable?"

Quinn considers this and shakes his head.

I take that as a good sign. I can only think of a few ways to try explaining this place in as simple a manner as possible, but I know I have to be the one to do it. He knows me, he's depending on me to keep him safe, and no one knows what he's feeling right now better than I do. Part of me knows what he needs most is time to digest his situation, to accept that his home and everything he ever loved is gone. All the pretty words in the world can't ease that pain, so I don't put any more effort into trying.

Quinn tries to sit up but instead lets out a hiss of pain and thumps back against the inclined bed. I set my hand helplessly on his knee again and turn to Helena for answers.

"Has he had anything to eat yet?" I ask.

She shakes her head, scattering her flowing red locks, before disappearing from the room. Even though Helena hasn't been involved in the conversation, the room suddenly feels awkward without her in it. I smile at Quinn in what I hope is a friendly manner, but by the skepticism behind his narrowed eyes, I don't think I've nailed my intended expression.

"You'll feel better when you get some food in your stomach," I say just to break the silence.

He looks as unsure as I feel, but I don't have time to think of anything else. When I hear the door creak open, I turn, expecting Helena, but tense when Willow's black eyes appear instead. Her icy gaze lingers on me, as if I've somehow caught her off guard as well. "We need to talk," she says, with no regard to Quinn's presence, and ducks back into the hall before I can ask what it is.

I mutter curses under my breath and stare at the ceiling, wondering what I possibly could've done wrong this time.

"Who was that?" Quinn asks, fingers uncertainly stroking the edge of his blanket.

"I'll be back," I say without even an attempt at an explanation, but I'm not sure about the truth in that answer, either. With the way Willow looked at me, she might murder me in the hallway.

When I step out of the confines of Quinn's room, I find Willow pacing a lap around the hallway, white gown flowing with every step. I can't even see her face, but I know she's anxious. That can't be good. "What's going on?" I ask, though I already know I don't really want the answer—not with her like this, anyway.

"We looked for Clio," she begins, searching my face for a sign of emotion.

My peripheral vision blackens, and she's all I can see. If she says the 'D' word, I'll literally lose my mind. "And?"

Willow's shoulders slump. "We can't find him."

"You can't… *find* him?" I echo, raising my eyebrows.

I had expected some news, certainty as to whether he's alive or dead, but the idea that he's *missing*, that she, with all her seemingly infinite knowledge and connections, has *no* idea what happened to him hits me like a fist to the gut. My mind is far too imaginative for something like this, and even worse, all the mindreading in the world can't give me a sense of peace if no one knows a thing about it.

"From what our spies have gathered, he hasn't been in Ignis. A missing Adept gathers quite a bit of attention. There have been searches both inside Ignis and without."

"How much of my Coven is even left at this point?" I force myself to ask. I haven't been back to Ignis since the Battle, and up to this point, I've lived under the assumption that it was wholly destroyed.

Willow shrugs. "I'd say a fourth is holding on strong. Rebuilding, actually."

That's better than I expected. "But Clio's not one of them?"

"No," she says.

Never would I have thought one word could be so heavy. I don't like it. "You're sure the Council doesn't have him held captive?"

Willow nods. "Positive. He vanished without a trace. If he had been captured, we have our ways of knowing." She pauses. "The Council seems just as stumped on this one."

I roll my bottom lip between my teeth. "What about Fern? Any word?"

Willow swipes a lock of brown hair from her eyes. "That's the thing… She's missing too."

"If you really have spies in Ignis, how can the Adept *and* Coven fairy just vanish without anyone knowing how or why?" I ask.

"From what I understand, Clio disappeared during the attack on Ignis, which isn't unusual. A lot of witches did."

A rock of guilt sinks in my stomach. Whatever happened to him happened because of *me*, because I needed help.

Willow frowns. "Don't take this the wrong way, Lilith, but how do you know he was fighting on our side?"

I shoot her a glare, almost glad for the rejuvenated anger behind which I to hide my sorrow.

"All I'm saying is you were fighting for *them* when he went missing," she continues. "How do you know he's not still doing the same under the assumption that you're being held here against your will?"

I consider that for a moment; it's a fair point. "How can anyone still fight for the Council after what they did to Ignis? To Mentis?" I ask at last. "They know it's wrong."

Willow shrugs. "Then you underestimate the power of fear. The Council has a lot of supporters standing behind their every move. Remember Tabitha? Every witch in the Land of Five has been brainwashed their entire life and has no clue."

Each word she says makes me feel more and more grim. The only way to win this war is for all the Covens to come together with the Elementals to destroy the treaty and the Council—to fight back before the Land of Five is destroyed forever. But if the Council can even control our *thoughts*, how can we possibly fight back?

After another minute of silence, she adds, "If Clio really is on their side, it's probably better for him to stay missing than to get mixed up in another battle."

"How can you say that?" I demand, thoughts of Tabitha dissolving away instantly. "You don't know what he means to me. Helena and Clio were *everything* to me growing up. You have *no* right to wish him dead."

Willow draws her eyebrows together. "I'm not wishing him dead. I'm simply saying you might be better off if he is. If he's involved and on the wrong side of the war, he'll be nothing but a distraction."

"Oh, is that right?" I ask, a bitter smirk on my face and the barely resisted urge to slap her buzzing through my skin.

"Yeah, it is. *I'm* your family, remember? Not them," she says, standing just a bit taller.

I snort and roll my eyes so hard, it hurts my head. "Forgive me, but I had to make my *own* family because *someone* decided to hide the truth of my own damn life from me for eighteen years!"

A flash of anger illuminates Willow's eyes then passes, leaving her looking suddenly weak. "You're right. You were alone when you needed me, when you were clueless, and I can't blame you for being angry at me because of it. But remember, this Coven didn't exist before me. It's not like I hid from you and twiddled my thumbs until the perfect time came along. I had to find and persuade these people. People like me. People like *us*. People who needed help themselves because of the Council, so that when I did come to get you, I could keep you safe. To… to make sure you didn't suffer the same fate as our parents."

"It's funny for you to argue in the name of family, seeing as you're the one ripping us apart now," I point out, folding my arms across my chest.

Willow's cheeks flush, but I can't tell if it's in anger or something else. "Let me give you a little analogy to help you put things into perspective. How did it make you feel when I told you we don't know what happened to Clio?"

"Upset…" I reply, angrier for the question. "What's your point?"

"And desperate, right?" Willow continues, ignoring my sarcasm. "Think of it like this. The way you feel for Clio is the way I felt for Larc. Knowing he's dead because of a choice *I* made is devastating… in ways I can't possibly tell you. And maybe it was wrong of me to lash out like I did. But if Clio's really dead, I almost guarantee you'll do the same to everyone around you."

All I can think of is the fact that Clio had walked into his fate—whatever that may be—because he wanted me to be safe. And what had I done? Nothing. I let him go, possibly to his death. It's hard not to bathe in self-loathing at the thought that I might never see him again.

"Are you okay?" Willow asks, brows creased in concern.

I want to say yes, to smile, to bury my problems into their usual compartment at the back of my mind and move on with my day, but I can't. This is too much weight, and I'm not strong enough to bear it anymore.

"No," I whisper, sounding as heartbroken as I feel.

Willow reaches out a hand, as if she's about to set it on my shoulder, but I don't wait to find out. I don't want any part of her or this situation. I spin on my heels and hurry down the corridor to get as far away from her as I can manage.

Chapter Nineteen

Astral Projection

A WEEK PASSES WITH the same routine as my Covenmates work to heal from the Battle of Mentis. Groups gathered at meals are smaller now, and it took me longer than it probably should have to learn how many witches we lost recently. Even though I didn't personally know any of the fallen, I remain solemn on the subject, and I know Willow is taking it hard. She hosts another vigil, similar to the one for Ignis, and this time, we go around the room and let everyone say a few words.

Unlike last time, however, I stand on the outside of the group, watching but having nothing to contribute myself. I've surprised even myself by attending, because also unlike last time, Willow didn't urge me to be here. I *chose* to be here.

Mentis was never my home. I didn't know any of the lost witches by name, with the exception of Larc and Lavina, but from the pictures Willow hangs up at the ceremony, I recognize a few of the Elementals who faced me in combat at some point. It's a shame that I never actually got to know them as anything other than my enemies, because now I never will.

It's odd how this place, which I once viewed as a prison, now feels like home, how the people who had been out for my blood now rely on me to help them. And how sad I feel for the recently deceased. There's no bitterness, no anger toward me, as if I've been here all along. I can hardly remember my life before the Council's intervention, and maybe that's for the best. Sometimes, maybe the best thing we can do is forget.

With the tension still lingering between me and Willow, these people are the closest thing I have to a family anymore, and if I'm being honest with no one but myself, I'm glad they're past the point of icing me out. That thought brings a strange trill down my spine, which I can't name as acceptance or disappointment. The Elementals don't hiss insults under their breath anymore, but there's still a coldness in their eyes whenever I'm near, and I'm unsure if it will ever truly go away.

They'll never fully trust me.

I try to distract myself by working alone on my new Aens powers. I've utilized the breathing techniques Sabre taught me, but manipulating the air still comes as a struggle. I haven't found a shape that works the best for me; my powers are strongest when I let them simply blast out of everywhere at once.

But Sabre said that's dangerous, and I agree.

With a sigh, I stare at the ceiling and raise my hands in the air before me. Kado lifts his head up off his paws and runs his tongue lazily over his lips, watching me. I sigh and bring my hands just a bit closer, staring at the empty space between them, concentrating all my energy into moving the air, sweeping it into a tiny ball—a miniature windstorm. Then, just as suddenly as it appears, it vanishes.

With an agitated groan, I drop my hands to my sides, then run them through my hair. I don't understand why others have so much faith in me when I can't summon any in myself. Maybe that's why most of the Coven hates me; they see what I see.

I try to push away my despair. Instead of viewing this situation as half-empty, as I normally would, I try to force myself to see it in a better light—I'm making progress in my Coven. Maybe if I keep my head and hopes high, that ice around my new Covenmates' hearts when they think of me will eventually melt, and they'll trust me as much as they do one another. I still don't know how far this place is from Ignis or if I'll actually go back there again to see what's left, but I'm strangely comfortable with the separation, even if I *am* alone here. Willow has gone out of her way to avoid me, but I can't pretend I haven't spent the last week doing the same. She can keep a stoic expression during meetings and training for as long as she wants, but she can't fool me. I understand what's she going through; really, we probably *all* do. It's grief in its rawest form and all the experiences that come with it.

Watching Willow struggle through Larc's loss gives me a bit of a clue on what not to do while dealing with Clio's disappearance. While everyone respects her too much to say a word to her face, I hear talk behind her back about her mistakes, and it stings. It's not her fault for feeling that way; if *anyone's* to blame, it's me. My heart goes out to Willow, it does, but I have to keep my wits about me through this situation. Willow thinks I'll become bitter and out of control, but that's my normal state. For all I know, I'm calm and collected under *that* much pressure. But thinking for even a second of the way I acted after Helena's death reminds me that's not true. Though it tears me up inside to think Clio might be dead, I won't let it affect the way I interact with these witches. After all the effort it's taken to claw my way to this position in the group, they're my last possible bridge to sanity, and I refuse to burn it.

Willow just needs time. A voice in the back of my mind tries to convince me she needs support too, but I can't bring myself to offer it. Not after our fight, anyway. Maybe she'll get over everything first and come to me on her own, but I can't find the energy to make the first move.

I shrug off those thoughts, grateful for Helena and Kado's company to fill the gaps in my days. Through the mess with the Council, I had forgotten what it's like to have Helena by my side, the way she used to be during our carefree days in Ignis. Afternoons spent with her are easy—dare I say *peaceful?* Despite everything, I'm glad she's here with me and not just another casualty of war.

I don't know how I would get through this time in my life without her. I'm emotionally drained; it doesn't matter how much I try to shift my thoughts away from Willow, Clio, and Fern. They stray right back like a stubborn puppy. Where could they have gone? If neither Clio nor Fern can be found, is it possible they escaped the battle *together* and are hiding out until they find the opportunity to come back? I swallow roughly at that possibility, and my whole body tingles with a surge of hope. I have to believe they're out there somewhere, that they're *choosing* to stay away.

The other option is just too painful to consider.

It's so easy to see Clio's green eyes in my mind, both when I'm awake and asleep. He's the last thing I see when I close my eyes for the night and the first when I enter a dream. Not a night goes by anymore where I *don't* dream of him, though this one *feels* different—more lucid. I'm searching for him in the ruins of Ignis. Anticipation fuels my blood, a desperate urge pushing me to keep seeking him out, that at any moment, he'll appear to me.

But he doesn't, and I don't know why I expected anything different. I'm left just as crushed as when the dream began, even worse for the images my mind has conjured of Ignis' fate.

When the dream fades, I feel sick before I even open my eyes, as if I actually traveled to the desert Coven and back—as if I actually spent countless hours searching for Clio in vain. Before I know it, I'm picturing the border of Ignis, *seeing* it as clear as day.

Then I'm in the center—the Coven's heart—in the smooth spiral of stairs surrounding the Coven altar. It's a place I know well, where I had spent many Ignis afternoons on Coven duties. My mentor Angel lives near here—Ambrossi too. My gaze flicks back and forth from the house on one side and the small, cave-like dwelling on the other. Before I know it, I'm wandering toward Ambrossi's old place, desperate to see what's become of it now that Ignis' Healer is gone.

When I step inside, the familiar scent of herbs smacks me in the face, causing me to pause. They're *fresh* herbs. Does Ignis have a new Healer? I'm at the back of the room before I even realize I've moved. Ambrossi's bedroom is back here. I know that only because of the house's simplistic design, and I'm right. There's a bed tucked into the tiny nook of the room, and I gasp with familiarity at the sight of the witch sleeping on it.

Angel, my Ignis mentor.

"It's safe to say you now have an *Alchemy* power." Maverick's voice barrels into my head.

My eyes shoot open, and only then do I realize I'm in bed with my eyes closed, that I'd been *asleep*—or at least I *thought* that was the case.

"Maverick?" I ask, my voice groggy as I struggle to open my eyes, turning my head to see if he's really there.

He is. The light streaming through my window highlights his black hair, illuminating its lighter streaks of brown, and I wonder just how long he's been standing there, watching me. Kado lifts his head and lets out a little whine, as if he's thinking the same thing.

"What do you mean?" I ask at last.

He ignores the question, eyebrows knitted together. "What did you dream about?"

I raise an eyebrow and sit up, confused by the concern. Kado leaps off the bed to stand beside Maverick, but I can't take my eyes off Maverick's face. He smirks in the way I've come to learn means he knows more than he's saying.

In this situation, the sight of it makes my heart pound, the uncertainty fresh fuel for my anxiety. "Why does it matter?"

"I'm curious," he says simply.

Now, I'm even more suspicious. He's a solider—not the curious type but rather straightforward. I have the feeling that the only way I'll get to the bottom of this is to play along. "Ignis," I say.

Maverick dips his chin slightly. "What *about* Ignis?"

I flare my nostrils and swipe a lock of black hair from my eyes. "Clio. Okay? I was looking for him."

"Well, I hope you found something, because you were really there," he says, the smirk growing into a full-blown smile.

I stare at him, dumbfounded. I don't get it. "No, it was a dream, and…"

His smile could split his face in half at this point.

"What? What is it?" I demand, clenching my hand into a fist around my blanket.

"Congratulations, Lilith. You have the power of astral projection," he says.

My jaw hangs open, and I want to hit him for lying to me. Even if he's telling the truth, I still wouldn't mind smacking him upside the head.

"No, I was asleep. It was a dream," I insist.

Maverick raises an eyebrow. "Not to sound like a creep, but I came in here to wake you up over an hour ago. Your eyes were *open,* so I watched you for a moment and realized you were whispering under your breath. Instructions to yourself, I think. Anyway, I didn't know if I should wake you or not, then there was this loud *whoosh,* a bright streak of light, *and* your eyes closed."

I swallow and look down at my hands, unsure of what to say, so I turn my insecurity toward him instead. "Are you sure?"

He nods. "That's outstanding."

"If you say so," I murmur. All I can think of are his words. I had *really* been in Ignis? If so, the devastation I saw there was *real*—that was an honest snapshot of what's left of my dear old home. I want to cry again at that thought, reminding me that for all my searching, I've still been unable to find a clue as to Clio's whereabouts.

Maverick frowns. "You don't look happy."

Slowly, I drag my eyes up to look at his face. "That's probably because I'm not."

He sighs and scratches behind his ear before he plops down on the bed beside me. Kado jumps a little to avoid Maverick's feet and comes to a rest beside me, eyeing the boy with silver eyes over my knee, as if he doesn't trust him so close to me. I pat the white fur on the top of his head in reassurance, too lost in my newest despair to focus on the old ones.

"What's on your mind?" Maverick asks.

"I *saw* Ignis. I thought it was just a dream, and it was hard to take then. But *that...* It's gone, isn't it?"

Maverick shrugs. "Not all of it." I'm sure he offers this as a form of comfort, but it doesn't help.

"The Covenmates I loved the most are all gone," I say.

I hardly even realize I'm speaking out loud anymore until Maverick says, "I'm sorry, Lilith."

Something about his tone cuts me deep. I blink, breaking my trance, and try to scold myself. Why am I doing this? His sympathy changes *nothing.* It won't help me; it won't help *him.* I grit my teeth, steeling myself as I ask, "So, you said it's an *Alchemy* power? I thought astral projection came from Mentis."

Maverick shakes his head. "No. It's common in Alchemy. They scope out the Land of Five for herbs, mostly."

I nod, feeling numb. The gleam in Maverick's eyes as he explains this to me makes it clear how excited about the whole thing he really is, but I don't share in it. I think this was a fluke, that whatever Maverick says he saw was either a hallucination or a flat-out lie—an attempt to lift my spirits.

"That's four out of the five, Lilith," he says. "Ignis, Mentis, Aens, and now Alchemy? Willow will be ecstatic to hear this!"

"Yeah… I'm sure she will," I say and stand so he won't catch the look on my face.

Maverick is silent for a minute before he does the same. "I get it. You two still aren't on good terms, but maybe it just takes something like this to fix it."

I shrug. "Maybe."

Maverick shakes his head. "Usually, witches celebrate the development of their powers. But you? You'd think someone died."

He's trying to make a joke—part of me knows this—but I don't find any of this amusing. "I can see that kind of thing… with this gift, can't I?"

Laughter gone, Maverick pulls his lips tight. "Yeah, I suppose you could. But *all* gifts have downsides. Why would you do that anyway?"

I shrug and glance at Kado. "What else can I do with it?"

"Help us," he says. "We *always* need people to help with surveillance. With your gift? Gods, I can't imagine what we can accomplish."

I close my eyes. That was the answer I feared. I don't want *that* much responsibility—any kind that will only hurt more witches if I fail. I don't want any more blood on my hands, not when they're already so stained as it is.

"You can see what others *can't,*" he adds in a softer tone, as if he suspects my thoughts.

"Yeah," I say at last. That doesn't mean it's a good thing.

Maverick sighs again and briefly glances from me to the door, then back again. I know perfectly well that I'm making him uncomfortable, but I can't find it in me to care. "I came to get you for battle training, but—"

"I'm not up for it today," I say flatly.

"I figured not," he says, holding out his hands. "I'll let Sabre know." He takes a step forward, then paces to look back at me. "Look, just take a breath, okay? I know you're tired… you're going to be. You *did* just discover your Aens power. Relax, and remember that Willow will *never* force you to do something you don't want to do."

His words bring a small smile to my face—a *real* one— and that makes him smile too before he turns and leaves the room, the click of the closing door announcing his departure.

Kado glances up at me, yipping as if he thinks I want to play, but I plop back down on my bed instead. "Astral projection," I mumble, testing the way the words feel in my mouth. I look down at my thumb, at the place I've already managed to pull a few layers of skin free in my sparing bouts of anxiety. I have no idea how the power works or if it's even something I can control.

Sighing, I think of Helena and get out of bed. Maverick's words run through my mind while I pull myself together. When I leave Willow's mansion to begin the long trek to Helena's, I dread the journey ahead of me.

WHEN I GET to the tiny building, I knock once and crack open the door. I hear Helena's voice; she's reading, clearly and easily, a story—not one I recognize. When I open the door the rest of the way, I see her sitting on her step, book open on her lap. On the floor before her is the girl from the vigil—Amelia. She sits cross-legged, a smile on her face while she listens, as if in a trance.

The sight warms my heart. Helena glances up at the sound of the door opening, but I smile sheepishly and wave her to continue, closing the door with a quiet click. Once it shuts, I stare at it. It turns out she's already busy today, and now I'm not sure *what* to do with myself. I think of my gift again, of Maverick's excited words, and turn to begin the voyage back home. Apprehension wiggles in my stomach at the thought of such a long walk so soon. I would have welcomed the opportunity to sit and rest for a bit at Helena's, but as she's focused on other things today, it would have only prolonged my journey back for no reason. With a resigned sigh, I think of my astral projection ability again, and even though I don't want to admit it, it *could* come in handy for situations like this. How nice it would be to check in on my friends without having to subject my leg to the torturous pain of the real journey.

WHEN I OPEN the door to my room, Kado trots up to me, stumpy tail wagging. I greet him and plop down on my bed with a relieved sigh. I glance at Kado, and he cocks his head, watching me. "Only one way to know for sure," I say, then curl up on my bed.

Since I have the time, I may as well put it toward something useful. Lying in the middle of the mattress, I fold my hands over my chest and close my eyes. I exhale slowly, and as the breath leaves my lungs, a calm, dreamlike sensation washes over me. Before I know it, I'm *outside* my body. Eyes wide, I look down at my hands. They seem as solid as my body on the bed, as my *dog* beside me. Fascinated horror gradually gives way to curiosity, and then I'm wandering through the labyrinthine halls, following Maverick on his journey to deliver Sabre today's updates. He steps into the purple plants outside, and I stay put, watching him go. With a gasp, I slam back into my body and stare up at the ceiling as if I've never seen it in my life.

"It's real," I tell Kado. "He wasn't lying."

The dog yips, jaws parting to reveal a floppy pink tongue. I take that as his way of congratulating me. With the smallest smile, I delve into my new ability, picking up my search for Clio and Fern in the exact same place I left it.

Chapter Twenty

Connections

WHEN MORNING COMES, I don't want to let go of my new ability. I want to stay here and keep searching. It's so easy to lose track of time like this, trapped between different planes of existence, but I know I can't stay.

I have obligations today, and I'm sure they noticed my absence yesterday. Helena no doubt would have. Frowning, I force myself out of bed and get dressed, ready for whatever today has in store, though in the back of my mind, I'm already excited for it to end, to use my ability once again.

I make my way to Helena's house and peek my head inside. I'm used to her walking aimlessly around the space of her tiny room any time I visit, so it takes me by surprise to see her sitting down, a heavy Alchemy tome open in her lap. I shouldn't be surprised—reading has always been her favorite pastime— but this puts me at a standstill. For just a moment, it's easy to believe things haven't changed so drastically, that they're the same as they've always been, and that they always will be. Reality can destroy that image pretty quickly, but it's good to know some things never change.

"Taking your Healer studies seriously, I see," I say, taking a few steps into the room.

She looks up at me through shining eyes. "This place has the most amazing library. It'd be a shame to throw away the opportunity to look into more advanced healing techniques. Ambrossi says I'm a natural at this, and I must be. I can't get enough."

"He has?" I ask, quirking an eyebrow.

A blush lines her cheeks, and her gaze drops sheepishly to her book. "Well, he hasn't actually *said* it, but he thought it a few times."

I laugh. "Using your powers for evil?"

"Not all the time." She beams at me, giving her best expression of innocence, which is hard to dispute.

My smile remains when I say, "Helena, if he hasn't bothered to shield his mind from you by now, it's because he *wants* you to read his thoughts."

She nods, a guilty grin plastered to her face, and I know she's already reached that conclusion on her own. The mentor/apprentice bond is one of the strongest. Considering how many times I've switched mentors, I know the feeling better than anyone.

"How's your Aens powers?" she asks.

I shrug. They don't seem important in the wake of my newest discovery. "I have Alchemy powers now, too."

Helena's face pales, her fingers loosening until she almost drops the book. "You what?"

"Astral projection. Apparently, I learned it two nights ago," I reply, gritting my teeth as I remember how the ability came to be. "Maverick told me what it was."

"Does Willow know?"

I shake my head with a bit of irritation. Why is it that anything I do must immediately be Willow's business? I force my lips to relax as I reply, "No. Unless Maverick told her."

"How did it happen?" she asks, looking at me through sparkling eyes, as if I'm telling her the story of when Clio and I kissed. "I had a dream. Or, at least what I *thought* was a dream," I admit and look back down at that missing patch of skin on my thumb again.

Helena frowns. "About Clio?" she guesses. And just as suddenly as the good vibes had appeared, they disappear with one question. "How do you think he's doing?"

I freeze. My whole body feels like it's been encased in ice, with the exception of my rapidly beating heart. I hear my blood pounding in my ears, and I almost wish I would faint just for the brief bit of peace it would give me. It takes everything to filter thoughts of Clio out of my mind, and just like that, he's all I can think about. Both memories and fears of his possible fate intertwine, like a sickening web, impossible to unravel the logical from the insane.

Helena reads either my blank expression or my churning thoughts, because she stares at me for the longest moment without a word. Then she sets her book aside and comes up to me, wrapping me in one of the tightest hugs I've had in a while.

"I... I'm sorry to ask, Li. I miss him too, you know. I hope he's okay," she says.

It helps knowing her words are honest, sincere, but at the same time, I feel almost dead inside. Our purpose, our reason for *being*, is to scour every inch of this planet for that specific person. The one who can resuscitate us, bring us back from the darkness, and remind us why the light is good.

Clio is that person for me, but if he's gone, so is a part of myself, and I'll never get it back.

"I know you do," I reply finally, sighing into her ginger hair before she lets go. With her here, I can almost imagine that he is too, in a sense.

"If anyone can persevere in a situation like that, it's him," she says. She wanders with dejected steps back to her seat.

I want to say something comforting, but of course nothing comes to mind. How can I make someone else feel better when I'm nowhere near fine?

"Knock, knock!" Maverick calls from the door, saving me from the responsibility. "Lilith, you in here?"

"Yep," I reply, wiping my face with the back of my hand just in case a few tears have found their way free. Then I turn to him and flash an impossibly fake smile. "I'll be back later," I tell Helena.

She nods and looks all too grateful for the chance to return to her book. It's hard to ignore the thoughts flitting through her brain. She's far too worried that I'm upset with her, and while I want to be, I'm not. I can't hate her for feeling the same pain, for acknowledging that it exists rather than bottling it away. I leave her to her solitude and follow Maverick to the training grounds. With my current mood, some battle training will do me good, and I can only hope Helena finds peace of mind in the pages of her book.

"Where were you yesterday?" he asks.

I shrug, not wanting to go into detail.

"Well, you seem better today," he observes.

I look away. I don't know what he bases conclusion on, but it's wrong. "Have you told Willow yet?" I blurt out.

He smirks. "So, you admit you have it now?" I cut him a sideways glare, and he adds, "No, I haven't. I'll leave it to you, whether or not you want to tell her."

"I appreciate it," I say coldly and fall silent.

All attempts at conversation after that are ignored, so much so that I'm actually *glad* to see Sabre in the distance. He's already at the training fields, waiting for us to arrive. I nod at him as we approach—my small sign of respect. I hate to admit it, but Sabre is a good teacher. Even Maverick agrees, and for some reason, I've come to trust his judgement despite his ornery nature. Maverick reminds me of myself in a way, not to mention the fact that I like the way he looks out for Willow—especially since I've been slacking on that responsibility for some time now. Maverick cares for all of us in his own strange way, and I respect the hell out of him for it. Being Willow's second in command can't be using, earning and maintaining everyone's admiration, but he does it. I could learn a thing or two from him.

Maverick nods to Sabre. "I'll leave you two to it. I've got a supply run to make today, and Willow's expecting me back before sunset."

"Good luck," I tell him.

He glances at Sabre as if he means to say he won't need as much luck as my teacher. Sabre returns the gaze, and Maverick departs without so much as another glance in our direction. I watch him go, training my eyes stubbornly on his back as he disappears from the field. This is the first time he—or anyone else, for that matter—has left me entirely alone with Sabre, and I don't know what to think of that. I'm a grown woman, an adult, and I definitely don't need a babysitter. But I still have an incredible desire to wring Sabre's neck the first chance I get. Adult or not, it's not a passing desire.

Skimming his mind tells me the situation makes him feel just as awkward.

"So, I don't think I told you how much I like your underwear," he jokes, nudging me with his elbow.

Scoffing, I turn my nose up to gaze at the clouds. I have a feeling that if I look at him, I'll be tempted to attack him just for that comment alone. I never realized how much of a buffer Maverick's been, but I'm deeply feeling his absence now. I wish I could lie down right where I stand, letting the sunlight wash over my skin to disconnect my soul from the rest of my body and get as far away from here as possible.

"Oh, come on. It was a joke." Sabre pauses and tilts his head. "All right, I figured it out. It's not the joke... You still haven't gotten over what happened, have you?"

I let out a very unladylike snort and whirl on him. "Of course I haven't! Helena is a forgiving person, but she also doesn't have to live with the memory of what you did. *I* do. I carry my wounds *and* hers. Why the Hell would you think it'd be that easy to get over?"

"If it helps, I'm sorry," Sabre says. He opens his mouth but closes it again, either in frustration or lack of words.

I flare my nostrils and glare at him, waiting to see what else he has to say for himself. His apology doesn't help, but I need to learn to get along with him. That's easy with a chaperone steering me away from any potentially stupid moves, but to actually get to a state where I don't want to split him between the eyes on my own is going to be the hardest thing I ever do.

Without Maverick to encourage me, I realize just how off-putting the idea of battle training is right now. Sabre and I give it our all but the tension between us does not make us good sparring partners. Our moves are off-balance or too rough for training, and neither of us are willing to apologize or back down.

Sabre must feel the same, because he calls it quits around lunch—much sooner than the other sessions. I don't argue. I take the freedom, leaving the field without so much as a goodbye. Inside the warmth of the Community Villa, the voices are loud enough to drown out my thoughts, and for a moment, I'm grateful for it. But the feeling doesn't last long. Even surrounded by these witches, I feel alone. They might be all I have left, but for all my convincing, they *aren't* my family. If they were, I wouldn't have this gaping hole where my heart should be.

I gather a meager plate of food for myself, not really out of hunger so much as for show, and leave the cafeteria to look for somewhere I can be alone. I consider going back to Helena's, but I don't want to risk her saying something else about Clio. Not today.

Today, I prefer the solitude.

I take a bite of the sandwich I grabbed, gazing up at the conflicting blue sky against the purple plants as I wander into the wilderness beyond the Community Villa. This is a beautiful place, and I'm once again left wondering *where* it really is. If Zane has to transport us to the Land of Five, we could be *anywhere*. I sit on a mound of dirt, set the plate on my lap, and pluck a leaf from the nearest plant. Color aside, these leaves are nothing like anything I've ever seen.

I never thought anywhere within walking distance of the Covens would be livable. According to the Elders, The Land of Five had once been three times its size before the creation of the treaty. The war had been so brutal, the land itself had been deemed inhabitable for a number of factors. If the Land of New Life lies outside the Land of Five, can other livable lands beyond the borders possibly exist? My nose twitches at that. Can it be that the treaty was created on nothing more than another of the Council's lies?

"Hey, are you okay?" a small voice calls from the plants.

I jump at the sound and work to compose myself when I notice Malcolm peering at me. His red wings stand out amidst the plants, but other than that, he could've been completely camouflaged. There's no telling how long he's been watching my silent struggle. I shrug and set my sandwich on the plate, as if that thought doesn't bother me. I have no idea how to answer his question.

"I'm okay," I manage, picking at the sandwich's strip of brown crust.

"You and Willow still haven't made up, huh?" Malcolm asks, flitting to land beside my knee.

I feel myself sneering and tear the strip of crust free from the bread to hide my bitterness. "How'd you guess?"

"I'm a fairy. Sensing your emotions comes easy," he says, tilting his head in a way that reminds me of Fern. It hurts. "Plus, Willow hasn't seemed herself lately."

I nod. "That's the problem. She's still hurting over Larc, and I mean, I get it. It's my fault that he's gone, but to speak so evilly of Clio... It's just too much, you know?"

"She didn't have to let you go to that battle to begin with," Malcolm points out.

A hint of a smile touches my lips. At least Malcom is trying to come to my defense, even if he's wrong to do so. "I shouldn't have pushed her. She told me to stay. At first. That was what she wanted, and I changed her mind. I put her in a situation she was already uncomfortable with, and it cost her the love of her life. I wouldn't be surprised if she never wants to talk to me again."

"You're her *sister*. And Willow isn't like that. She's a strong person. She's just dealing with a lot right now."

"I know, and that's why I'm letting her be," I reply with a heavy sigh. I'm not sure whether that or cowardice is the true reason I haven't tried to fix things yet. Probably both. "Has she told you about Fern?"

Malcom offers a crestfallen nod. "I'm not worried, though. My Momma's strong. I have faith that she's all right. She has to be."

I stare at him, momentarily jealous. I wish I could have that much blind faith in something. Especially something *this* important. As much as I want to believe Clio is okay, I can't bring myself to actually find it true. I can't get rid of the nagging voice saying I'll never see him again.

"You were so little when she left... Do you miss her?" I ask.

Malcolm nods. "Every day."

I sigh and lick my teeth, the feeling of guilt prickling under my skin. Here is a child, hurting for his mother, and I'm the reason why. "Yeah, me too. I... I'm sorry for taking her away from you."

"Lilith, you didn't... *take* anyone away. She *chose* to go, just like Willow *chose* to bring you to Mentis. You can't blame yourself for the decisions others make."

"Right." I want to argue but know it won't do any good. I shift my gaze to the ground. It sure doesn't stop Willow from blaming me. "I hope Fern's okay."

"I hope Clio is too."

I pause. Of all the things that could've come out of his mouth, I hadn't expected this. How had word traveled to him about Clio? It seems pointless for Willow to tell him, but what do I know? Maybe she needs someone to console her more than I realized, if she's acting in the hopes of getting me to confront her.

"Lilith! Lilith!" Helena's voice rings around the field, interrupting us.

The panic in her voice has me on my feet before I even realize it. Malcolm disappears back into the foliage with a simple swish of his wings.

"What's wrong?" I ask.

"Quinn's gone!" Helena says, eyes wide as she finally catches sight of me. Red marks scour her cheeks; she hasn't spared herself a moment of self-scolding for losing him.

"What?" I can't help but wonder if I heard her right.

"Things were fine and dandy. He was in his room this morning. I went to get him breakfast, and when I came back, he was gone. Just like that."

"And no one's seen him?" I ask, wracking my brain for a possible explanation.

Helena shakes her head, scattering her hair in a blurry rush of red. "You don't think he went back to Mentis, do you?"

"Mentis? No." But I'm not sure about that answer. He hated it here, it's true, but would he really leave to go back to a Coven reduced to rubble? Another possibility I don't want to consider whispers in my ear—he could go to the source of our problems, the Council themselves, and spill everything to Rayna. Including where to find us.

I don't wait for Helena to say anything else before I take off through the purple plants. I trip but never fall. My leg screams at me to slow down, but I don't. I can't. Even if battle training had been short, it was fierce, and I'm feeling it now. I pant from the effort of ignoring the pain, focusing on *dragging* the dead weight of my useless leg when it can't handle the agony. There's no way Quinn could get very far; he's injured and paranoid. If anything, he'll end up running in circles until he collapses from exhaustion. I briefly marvel at who I've become when I realize I hope that to be true.

As if on cue, a bloodcurdling scream rings out from the direction of Willow's mansion, and as fast as I can manage, I hurry toward it with Helena on my heels, calling my name every time I stumble. I burst through the front doors and into the foyer to see Quinn backed into a corner by both Kado and one of Willow's undead tigers. At the sight of me, Kado wags his tail, less fierce for the show, but the tiger doesn't lose focus.

"Heel," I tell it.

It shifts its gaze to me, lifting the corner of its lip in an exasperated snarl before its large amber gaze leaves Quinn. It stalks away without another look back, and I rush to Quinn's side, checking him over for any possible injuries.

"Are you okay?" I ask, dropping to my knees beside him to create a barrier between him and my dog. Kado whines happily at my proximity and butts his head into my shoulder, completely oblivious to how uncomfortable he makes Quinn.

"What the fuck is wrong with these animals?" he asks, waving his good hand in Kado's direction.

"They're pets. My... my sister has the power of resurgence," I explain.

Quinn looks at me as if I just murdered his mother. "S... who?"

"Willow. The leader of this group. She has resurgence." I set my hand on the top of Kado's fuzzy head, hoping the display will show Quinn that, although these animals *look* scary, they're actually sweethearts.

"*The* Willow... the one from the legend?" he whispers.

With how tight-lipped the Council has been about Willow's existence, it impresses me that Quinn knows who she is. Then again, he is *related* to a Council member. Has he been told other secrets, too? Things I've never even *heard* of?

"The very same."

"Whoa," he says, slumping against the wall with a type of surprise I can't quite identify.

I nod and attempt an encouraging smile. "So, why the escape attempt, Quinn?"

"These people... are evil," he says, resting his hand on his sling, and glares accusingly at Kado.

"Who? Ambrossi and Helena? They saved your life. Am I evil too?" I ask, dipping my head to catch his attention. "I brought you here."

Quinn frowns. "That's not a fair question."

"But it is. If you're still considering the Council to be the good guys, just remember they *bombed* your Coven. All of us? The ones you're calling *evil*? We've worked nonstop, day and night, to save your life, expecting nothing for the effort but your well-being."

Quinn groans but shifts his gaze to the ground, blushing. He wants to argue but obviously knows I have a point. I give him time to search for his words. He's too entrenched in his despair for logic to matter much; his world is literally collapsing around him, and there's nothing he or anyone else can do to stop it. The Council has brainwashed him for Gods only know how long. This is only the beginning. Getting through that conditioning, to reach his logic underneath, will be the hardest part of this adjustment for him.

175

"We'll protect you," I assure him. "They can't hurt you here."

"Why? You're... you're..."

"What?" I ask, drawing my eyebrows together.

"You're supposed to be the enemies... the people we hate," he finishes, his voice strained.

"We're scapegoats," I state dryly. "The Council? *They're* your real enemy, and the worst part is, you never know until it's too late."

"Why would Rayna do this?" he asks, turning to me tears twinkling in his huge brown eyes. "She didn't even warn me that—" A sob escapes him before he can finish; the sound hurts me down to my bones. "She killed Lavina, and... and for what?"

I stare at him, rigid. I don't have an answer for that. Why does anyone do anything? Despite my inability to console people, I know I can't sit back and do *nothing*. Quinn's on a downward spiral of despair, and right now, I'm the only person who can keep him from drowning in it. I pull him into my arms, feeling his tears soak the shirt at my shoulder. I just hug him closer and let him cry it out for both of us.

Chapter Twenty-One

Addiction

I DON'T KNOW HOW long Quinn and I huddle together against the wall, but eventually, Willow, Maverick, Sabre, and Katrina stroll into the mansion. Their footsteps echo eerily around the empty foyer, amplified by the fact that none of them are speaking. I watch their approach, but Quinn keeps his face buried in my shoulder, as if he's ashamed to let them see him in this condition. His sobs run instantly silent, but his tears flow without interruption, having now soaked a large portion of my shirt.

Willow takes a few steps closer to me than the rest. She brandishes a long wooden stick, and I wonder if she's planning to strike me with it. "Lilith, we need you."

I look up at her through my lashes, doing my best to keep my face neutral even though I'm curious. She sounds only authoritative, in charge; she's set aside our fights, our emotions, our differences and leaving no room to argue.

I can respect that.

"Go find Helena, okay? She's worried sick," I say to Quinn, moving my shoulder slightly to prop him off of me.

He smiles, though I can tell how much effort it takes him, and wipes his reddened face with the back of his hand. He stands but doesn't look up from the floor as he pushes past Willow's entourage toward freedom.

"Go with him," Willow orders the others, never taking her eyes off me. "I need to talk to my sister alone."

The three witches behind her don't say a thing but move to surround Quinn like a protective barrier as he leaves the foyer. He stiffens at the speed of their movements but keeps his eyes trained ahead. I stare after him, knowing that kind of attention is the last thing he needs. I wish I could help, but even if I follow him, nothing I do can ease his pain.

Maybe they'll have better luck.

"What's going on?" I ask Willow, working to stand so I can talk with her at eye level. There's something degrading about her literally looking down her nose to speak to me.

Willow frowns at my struggle. "Here," she says, passing me the stick without anything close to an explanation.

I purse my lips, hand set to the wall for balance, and stare at her. "What the hell is that?"

"It's a walking stick. I had it made specifically for you," she says, inching it toward me as if the gesture couldn't possibly agitate me any further. I don't move to grab it, though it almost touches my arm.

Instead, my eyes run down the length of the stick, made of golden-hued wood, taking in all the elegant markings carved into almost every inch of it. They're pictures, a story, and I recognize the tale—the birth of Ignis.

I stare at the images, examining each one to pause the conversation at hand. In the beginning days of the Land of Five, before it *was* the Land of Five, there were no Covens, no distinctions between the Equipped and the UnEquipped. They all lived together in a society in which the Equipped's very existence was hidden behind the disbelief of the UnEquipped. They were outnumbered and crucified when the truth was revealed. As the society eventually collapsed under its own weight, the UnEquipped grew to trust the Equipped, depended on them for protection and shelter.

Many of the UnEquipped fell to disease, famine, and each other's the wrath, but the Equipped held strong, caring for themselves and the UnEquipped under their protection. After the ways of the Old World were forgotten, the living people remained strong, faithful in the Equipped to whom they had pledged their loyalty.

The witches themselves weren't much more organized until a young witch named Myalis took control of them. She was Equipped with telekinesis, and she was powerful—so powerful that many believed she also possessed the power to control minds. She was patient and calm and could manipulate the most logical person into carrying out her will, regardless of the circumstances. She was a great leader, except for her one major flaw—an obvious favoritism for witches like herself. Witches with mind powers.

They had the best houses, the best food, and were kept the safest from diseases and threats to which so many others had already succumbed. Needless to say, not everyone was happy under her governance. Igneous, a fire-Equipped witch, disliked Myalis and her method for treating witches different than herself. Young and hotheaded, he was convinced he would be a better leader. So he gathered other Equipped with fire conjuring, fire manipulation, and a range of other powers, and incited a battle from which neither faction emerged victorious.

The survivors agreed the best way to raise children of a certain ability would be to surround them with other witches of the same aptitudes and similar lifestyles. Myalis took her band of witches to the edge of the ocean, and Igneous, never wanting to see them again, went in the opposite direction to the best environment for his powers—the desert—leaving the rest of the witches to sort themselves out.

There's more to the story after that, but I can't focus on it. I keep comparing the rise of Ignis to the rise of the Elemental Coven. Willow faced a path quite similar to the one Igneous tread in his desperation to care for his people, and my heart wells in my chest. Hard to believe Willow and I were never from the Land of Fire, seeing as how we have so much in common with its founder.

"A… walking stick?" I finally ask, finding it difficult to decide if I've spoken in disgust or wonder.

"Yes, and I know you like to reject kindness," Willow replies. "But at least use it until you finish healing."

She's right; my instant reaction is to deny the gift. My pride demands it. I've never even considered a walking stick before. In all the years of dealing with my handicap, I never used tools and have always balked at the idea of help—with the exception of my telekinesis, of course. Even still, I can't push away the truth of how useful such a present would be.

Since the Battle of Ignis, my telekinesis has been undependable, and even when it does come, I don't trust it like I used to. Not in this place with witches who can lock it away like it never existed. I frown at that thought. Is it possible that the more powers I manifest, the weaker the others will become?

Only time will tell.

Either out of fleeting sanity or guilt, I take the walking stick. Willow clasps her hands in front of her with a hopeful smile as she watches me test it out. The wood is strong and smooth, perfect for my height, and the tip hardly makes a sound against the floor. Even without magic, it allows me to walk with ease. I stare at my sister for so long, tears well in my eyes and I hug her. Nothing matters more than her, and I wish I could make her understand just how much this gift means to me.

"Thank you," I say into her curly brown hair.

"I'd do anything for you, Lily. You're my family."

This shortening of my name almost breaks my heart; it's the first time she's called me by anything close to endearing. She tries to pull away, but I hold on just a bit tighter, just long enough to for the tears to stop. Then I finally let her put some space between us. Until this moment, I hadn't realized just how much I missed my sister, and it's fair to guess she feels the same.

"Did Maverick tell you about my newest power?" I ask uncertainly.

Willow tips her head to the side. "No, he didn't."

I take a second to let her words sink in. I need to take some time to thank him for being the only honest witch around here. "I have astral projection now," I reply, looking her in her dead eyes to see them spark with a bit of life.

"Really?"

"I went to Ignis," I say but don't tell her why. I have a feeling she knows anyway.

"Have you tried to travel anywhere else?"

I shake my head. I haven't wanted to *go* anywhere else. "Why?"

Willow tucks her lip between her teeth, and I stare at her. Despite the emotion in the air, something about how straight and tall Willow stands makes me feel as if she's here for more than a reunion.

"What is it? What's wrong?" I ask, forcing my blissful ease into a locked box at the back of my mind.

"I'm worried about Alchemy," she admits. "Even before you told me what you can do, I've suspected the Council may go after them next. They, uh... they found a replacement for you."

I feel sick, my heart threatening to give out completely. Clio. "Who is it?" I demand.

"His name is Colby. He's gifted with the power of earthquakes."

I blink at her, lost for words. "Earthquakes? Did you really say... *earthquakes*?"

Willow bobs her head. "He's dangerous, if anyone is."

"I bet," I murmur, but I'm thinking of Clio again. Even with Willow's bad news, I'm *relieved*. He's not there, filling the space I once occupied, and I have to hope he stays that way. "Why? Why attack *Healers*?" I ask, feeling the wind leave my lungs.

If they hadn't hurt my Coven already, I'd say *this* is the worst thing they could ever do. All the Healers I've ever met have been kind and compassionate; they aren't angry or violent. They're peacemakers, lovers, and maybe that's the problem. In this time of war, there is no place for kindness or understanding. Traits like that can be costly on the battlefield. Healers are the only witches allowed to cross between Covens, and Alchemy is the only Coven not bound by *all* the laws of the treaty.

The only threat to the Council right now is the one thing they offer—unity.

If everyone would come together to fight, there's no doubt in my mind we would win. But fear binds the remaining Covens, fear keeps them loyal; unfortunately, it also makes them vulnerable. The Council doesn't appreciate their sacrifices. They merely feel the need to rip away more, as much as they can possibly take, and do it with no hint of remorse.

Willow's jaw clenches when she says, "Hurt the Healers, hurt the chances of your enemy's recovery."

"That's not right," I mutter.

Willow puffs her lips in a pout, and I know before she says it what she's going to ask; it's the very thing I feared when Maverick first told me of my abilities. "Can you check on them?"

I swallow heavily, leaning on the new walking stick to give me a distraction, a reason to look down away from her hopeful eyes.

"What's wrong?" she asks immediately.

I look back sharply. "How can you trust me with something like that? How will I even know what to look for? When Crowe took me around the Land of Five, I was all but useless until your witches crawled out under my nose. What if I fail?"

Willow gives me a sweet smile. Not because I've said something touching but because she knows I have a point. "The only failing here would be to sit back and wait until it's too late to do anything."

Sighing heavily, I meet her gaze. "Okay. I'll do it."

Willow pulls me into her arms again. "Thank you."

I don't reply to that, and my sister laces her fingers through mine, leading me back to my room. Kado circles us happily as soon as we step through the doorframe. He's also immediately enamored with the walking stick. When I hobble into the room, he lunges for it, sinking his teeth into the wood as if he thinks I'm about to play tug o' war with him.

"No. No, Kado," I say, batting the edge of the stick playfully against his ribs. "Momma needs this to walk."

He yips in excitement but seems to understand my tone. He sniffs at the stick one more time but doesn't grab it again. Willow's attention turns to him as I settle on my bed. I stare up at the beams above my head, wondering how many more times I'll have to do something like this for her benefit.

"Just relax," Willow says.

I glance at her to see she's huddled beside Kado at the foot of my bed.

"Okay," I say and cross my hands over my chest like I did the last time. A moment later, I'm crossing through the barrier between reality and another realm, and I'm outside my body.

I stay in place for a long time, watching Willow and Kado, who have stopped to watch me. Even though I stand now beside Willow, she seems none the wiser, so I take a breath and continue through the building with ease. It seems as if no time at all passes before I'm in Alchemy. Though I've only ever set foot in this Coven once, things seem as they've always been. Lazarus is at home in front of his fireplace, instructing Flora and a witch I've never seen before on the proper ways to create some purple potion. It's relaxing to watch, *soothing*, even.

As I travel through the Coven, I pass the Coven alter—a boulder covered in a variety of moss and vines—and peek through windows, only occasionally drifting inside homes. The witches are content in their lives, cooking food and talking with their friends and family. None of them look evil; none of them look hurt. A twinge of panic grasps my heart as I remember Willow's words; the Council could be planning something. With that, I slam back into my body, gasping for air.

Willow's wide eyes turn to me, and she launches off the bed to her feet. "Are you okay?' she asks, coming to a rest beside my bed. "What'd you see?"

I blink the bleariness from my vision and turn to her. "Everything looked normal," I say.

Willow dips her head and straightens. I can't tell whether or not that's what she wanted to hear. She presses her lips tightly together, and I know what she wants but can't find the nerve to ask me.

"You want me to spy on the Council, don't you?" I ask for her.

She bites her lip. "No, I don't. The information you could obtain would be valuable, but… it's dangerous. I don't want to risk you like that."

"Would they even know?" I raise an eyebrow and think of all the other witches on whom I've already spied. I never really considered the fact that some of them might *know* I was watching them, but it's too late now.

Willow sighs. "I don't know. They might." She reaches down to pet Kado. "Don't worry about it, okay? I appreciate what you've done for me."

"Anytime," I say.

She stares at me for a long time, as if she wants to say something else, but she doesn't. Instead, she plasters a smile to her face that I'm sure is fake and turns to leave the room. Does anyone smile for real anymore?

Kado lets out a little whine as she disappears, as if he's disappointed she's gone. I sigh and relax back against the bed, lifting my hands to cover my face. I don't know what to think of what's just happened. Is she proud of me? Is she disappointed that I didn't do more?

What else could I do?

'You could scope out the Council,' Grief replies, his little voice burrowing into my head.

I growl at it. I don't want to go anywhere *near* the Council, but a feeling in my gut warns me this might be another one of those things about which I just don't have a choice.

You don't have to do a thing, Maverick had said.

He was wrong about that. When you love someone, truly love them, you *have* to do some things you don't want to do—some things that really make you uncomfortable.

And this is a perfect example.

Kado whines again and sets his giant paws on the edge of the bed, bringing his nose to the side of my face as if he senses my stress. I offer him a gentle smile before settling back into the bed and letting my spirit slip from my body once more.

Standing on the edge of the Grove, I find things just as I remember them.

I stare straight ahead at the shining glass walls of the Council's Headquarters, hardly able to believe I once *belonged* there. I take a few steps forward and freeze. This is hard—so much harder than my other travels—and that's when I realize my entire body feels sluggish, as if I've been wrapped in a web.

I take a step backward, and the feeling vanishes.

There are magical wards even in this realm. I make the attempt to move back to my own body, but the memory of a desecrated Ignis stops me.

Just because this trip to the Grove may be a failure doesn't mean I can't use the opportunity to also search for Clio. And that's what I do, taking in a deep breath as I prepare to see the carnage of my home Coven once again. The last time I was here, I purposefully avoided the areas I traveled the most. Now, those are the only places I want to go. I take another breath, then walk past the wreckage of what was my parents' home. It's been reduced to lifeless rubble, the blackened edges of one wall all that remains of the only home I ever knew. My stomach lurches, and I wish more than anything that I'd fought my way through the Council's wards around the Grove instead of this—coming here.

Now, it's too late. I've seen it, and I can't unsee it. So I indulge on my own pain and travel deeper through Ignis. I'm surprised to see Helena's house still standing, but I don't enter to see her parents. I don't need to witness their grief, the pain they don't need to feel because their daughter is alive.

I swallow, and in an instant, I'm at the oasis. My eyes drift to the lone tree Fern had called her home, but it's dark and empty. She hasn't been here in a while, just as Clio hasn't been back to his house in some time.

I rest my head against the tree, staring at the hole of Fern's home as if I expect her to appear from thin air. *Where are you?* I wonder at last. I stare out at the glittering darkness of the water, but the chance to sift through any more of those painful thoughts vanishes when I'm unexpectedly slammed back into my body.

I gasp and open my eyes to stare at the ceiling far above my head. I blink, confused. For a moment, I can't remember where I am. All I know is how dry my throat feels. I smack my lips, desperate for water. That's when I realize I'm not alone. Willow sits beside me on the mattress, a glass of water in her hand.

"Willow?" I ask, and my voice cracks.

"Drink," she says, holding the glass to my lips before I sit up.

The cool water runs effortlessly down my throat, and then I've grabbed the cup in my own hands, tipping it until it's empty. With a relieved sigh, I hand the glass back to Willow and sit up fully, gathering the blankets around me. Kado stands on the floor by Willow's legs, and when my eyes drift to him, he tilts his head. I wait for Willow to speak, to see *why* she's decided to visit me, why she decided to pull me from the freedom of the astral plane, but she doesn't say a word.

"Is something wrong?" I ask.

"Four days," she says, staring down at the empty glass.

I raise an eyebrow. "Huh?"

"You've been unconscious for four days." She drags the black pits of her eyes to meet my gaze.

I knit my eyebrows together, confused. "No, that can't be right... I..." I swallow again, the motion eased by the entire glass of water. I lift a hand to my forehead and glance around, as if something in the room will agree with me. "I just took a nap... " I frown again, not knowing what else to say.

"What did you dream about?" Willow asks softly, just a hint of concern in her voice and features.

"I did as you asked," I reply. "At first. They have wards. The Council." Willow nods but doesn't look surprised, like I expected. "Then I just... I don't know." It's too embarrassing to say I went back to Ignis, that I put *myself* through that level of torment.

"This isn't good," she says, putting a hand on my knee. "What you're doing isn't healthy."

"I was only doing what you *asked*," I say quickly.

Willow smiles, but I know it isn't out of happiness; it's sympathy. "All I asked was for a quick trip, sweetheart. I never wanted you to do more than that. You went to Ignis, didn't you? To search for Clio?"

I don't answer her, knowing there's no point in arguing. "What if I did? I'm not bothering you or anyone else. I'm handling my own business."

"But you're not really, are you?" she asks.

My vision blurs through the tears when I look at her, but I don't remember *when* I started crying. "Nightmares. Before this ability, all I had were nightmares. Every… single night. About Ignis and Clio and Fern… *everything*. This gives me *peace*. What's so wrong with that?"

Willow's face is drawn so tight that, for a long moment, I let myself believe she isn't going to speak. "Do you remember the last thing you've eaten?"

I don't. For all the thinking in the world, food seems eons away. "Moving is easy," I say softly. "There's no pain, no awkwardness, no…" I pause to swallow. "I'm *normal*." And that's the most striking part of this entire thing. As odd of an ability as it is, it's the only one leaving me feeling no different than everyone else. As if I don't *have* a handicap. "I don't need the walking stick there," I add. "I don't need *anything.*"

Willow pulls me into a hug the second I finish. "Oh, dear sister," she says.

I know that's all she *can* say.

"You can't keep doing this," she says into my ear. "You're *losing* yourself. You may think you're minding your own business, that you aren't bothering me, but you're wasting away from simple neglect. You think Clio would want you to do this to yourself in his name?"

No. No, he wouldn't. "He's not here," I snap, pulling myself from her arms.

"Exactly." She brushes the hair from my forehead. "For all the torture you're putting yourself through, you're no closer for the effort."

I want to hate her for those words. They cut me deep, and they hurt, but she's right. My eyes glaze over in more tears.

"Let's get you something to eat," Willow says.

THE ELEMENTAL COVEN

I don't object.

Chapter Twenty-Two

Battle of Alchemy

THE FOOD WILLOW serves me tastes as good as the water. At first, it's difficult to get more than a bite down, but as my stomach loosens, the hunger finds its way free. It grows easier and easier to shovel bite after bite of warm, savory food into my mouth. I adjust my walking stick, which I laid across my lap for easy access, and sit back a bit.

Willow seems more than happy to continually bring me plate after plate, drink after drink, until a pile of dirty dishes rises around me. When I plop the last bite of meat into my mouth, I groan in pleasure and sit fully back in my seat, holding my hand over my bloated stomach. I never knew I could eat that much in one sitting.

Just as I push away the last empty plate, Maverick strolls into the dining room, eyes widening as he catches sight of me. "You're awake!"

The enthusiasm in his voice is fake, I can tell, and that leaves me to wonder—had he been the one keeping tabs on me? The one to first notice I'd skipped meals and was absent during training?

"Yeah," I say simply, watching him take a glass of water from Willow and sit down beside her.

He bends toward her, whispering something in her ear. Willow's face transforms from calm to uncertain to horrified. She stands quickly, causing the chair to screech against the floor, and dashes from the room without another word.

I frown, watching the last of her long brown hair disappear through the door, then turn to Maverick. "What was that about?"

He sighs, tapping his fingers on the table beside him as if he's unsure of speaking. "One of our informants... has some news."

"What about?"

He shakes his head. "I'm not sure if Willow wants you involved. At least, not in your current state."

I grit my teeth. That's another concept they don't understand about living in the other realm; there's no one there to babysit me. No one to tell me what I can and cannot do or to assume that of which I may or may not be capable. "That doesn't mean I can't know."

Maverick ruffles his black hair before he stares down at the table, at the last sip of water in his glass. "From what I understand, the Council is planning a move on Alchemy next," he says at last.

I set my lips into a tight line. In the back of my mind, I vaguely remember Willow telling me the same thing and the quick trip to the Land of Healers. Nothing looked out of place there, but the fact I could barely get past the beautiful topiary garden in the Grove still serves suspicion.

"That's what Willow told me," I say.

"Did you see anything… when you were out?" he asks, glancing at me from the corner of his eye.

"Nothing in Alchemy to suspect the Council has even been there," I admit, blowing out a long breath of air. "But I couldn't even get close to Headquarters. They've got wards all over the Grove."

Maverick bobs his head. "Well, they've been busy since then."

I try to stand, stumbling as I push the heavy chair backward, and grip the table to right myself. "I can check," I say flatly.

Maverick's hand flashes out to grasp my wrist, his warm skin cushioned against mine as he holds my arm in place. "No. Willow wouldn't be very happy if you went back again so soon."

"I can help!"

He shakes his head and lets go of my arm. "Not this time. Not like that."

I glare at him, but before I can snap out a response, Willow reappears. "Maverick! We have to go!" There's no mistaking the urgency in her voice.

I catch her arm as she passes me. "Sister, what's going on?" I demand, wondering if she'll be as open with me as Maverick had been.

She breathes through her nose, flaring her nostrils in an attempt to calm her panic. "It doesn't concern you," she says at last, meeting Maverick's gaze as she tries to gently pull herself free of my grasp.

The dismissal angers me more than anything. "Alchemy. The Council's finally made their move, haven't they?" I demand.

She continues to avoid my eye, jaw clenching subtly, though she still holds Maverick's gaze. "Don't worry about it."

I narrow my eyes, gripping even tighter into her skin as she tries to pry open my fingers. *"Don't worry about it?* What happened to *needing* me? Remember when you *begged* me to help?" My voice is a choked whisper, and I'm not really sure why. "You can't cut me out now."

Willow sighs and glances at my fingers, then at Maverick, as if she's trying to gauge his reaction to the situation. His eyes widen slightly, but other than that, he's his calm, cool, collected self. "You're ill," she tells me.

I sneer. "What's your point? Wanting to astral project more than sit around here being useless means I should let them get away with this? I mean… they can't do this. It's not right!" The fingers of my other hand dig into the walking stick until my knuckles turn white.

"All the more reason to stop them," Willow replies, black eyes hardening to pieces of flint, as if she's battling her own mind just to make a decision.

I wonder why it's so hard for her to decide. Things are so much more different now than they were facing the Battle of Mentis. She's considering this, thinking of how far I've come since the mistake that cost her Larc.

"I can help," I say, pleading. What will it take to get her to agree?

She stares at me, sighs, then drops her rigid shoulders, as if her last will to fight has finally been broken. "Lilith, my dear, I *need* your help."

Those words fill my heart with warmth and confidence—I would've been willing to charge into battle for a lot less. She leads the way out of the foyer with a rejuvenated sense of purpose and through the purple-plant forest. Sabre and Katrina meet us by the Community Villa. I almost expect either of them to comment on my absence in the same way that Maverick did, but they don't. Their eyes carry both panic and strength; they're ready for battle. It's the only thing on their minds—the only thing they *let* into their minds. It's admirable, in a way. I wish I could be so straightforward with my thoughts, just for once, but I have no such luck. My thoughts jump and bob from Willow to my astral journey to the battle ahead of us to the witches on the Council.

I wish I could turn off my brain. It would make life so much easier. I try to stop my crowded head by focusing on my immediate senses and the world around me. Our group of battle witches grows as we walk through the Elementals' land. Witches seem to materialize from the shadows to join our army, many of them I have only seen a handful of times, and as we reach the border of our land, the group is formidable, though much smaller than the assembly that charged Mentis. I know why; most of the witches who went to Mentis hadn't returned. The thought makes me sick, but not as much as realizing a number of these witches will meet the same end.

Zane takes charge, tearing open the portal in the sky as if it's nothing, and one by one, we climb through it.

As Alchemy appears in the distance, I'm caught off guard for just a moment. In the back of my mind, all I can think of are the flashes of normalcy I witnessed during my astral travels. A chill of dread runs down my spine. What will I see now?

I'm willing to bet one thing; the peace I observed will be gone. I glance over my shoulder at the witches all around me. Their expressions do not waver from fierce determination; they're prepared for a battle proportional to those in Ignis and Mentis. These are *experienced* witches, and they know as well as I that going in with anything less than complete dedication can prove deadly.

I remember the screams and terror of the last two battles. I'm prepared for that same chaos of sound—my ears set to pick up the slightest whisper—so the silence when we reach the Alchemy border is the most unsettling thing I've experienced in a while. Has the battle already come and gone and we're simply too late to do a thing about it? Is it possible that Willow's informant had been *wrong*?

It's *too* calm, contrasting too much with the picture of carnage in my brain. I was so prepared for it that seeing nothing borders on disappointment. When I breathe, all I smell is fresh air and foliage—no ash, no blood. I blink stupidly and glance at Maverick, but his stoic expression gives nothing away. We shuffle a bit closer to the Coven's border, and the smell hits me—death.

"We're too late," Katrina says, and judging by my Covenmates' scowls and flared nostrils, they smell what I do.

Death is an unmistakable odor, especially to those who have experienced it before—like us.

"Split up and search for survivors!" Willow commands.

As soon as her barked order fades to silence, the crowd disperses into the shadows of the Alchemy trees like smoke. I don't know many Healers—aside from Ambrossi and Helena, of course—but the thought of finding them dead makes my stomach twist. Immediately, I think of Lazarus. He's a kind old man, the mentor to a large majority of Alchemy. His wisdom is unmatched by many witches, and I can't help but wonder if that will be his downfall. If the witches of Alchemy are dead, is he too?

Somehow, I get paired with Katrina, though I can't remember either of us saying a word on the subject. Despite this, I'm glad to be with her; she's smart and quick on her feet. If we get into trouble, I know I can depend on her to watch my back. In a way, we're almost parallels of one another—or we would be if I didn't have so many injuries slowing me down. My walking stick proves more of a burden here than an aide. After I manage to get myself stuck in roots, stumbling over twigs, Katrina darts between helping me onward and scoping out the area ahead of us.

Her blank face doesn't change, but I have a feeling she's slightly annoyed—either that, or she's so on edge she hardly has the mental energy to notice that annoyance. Either way, we comb through our assigned portion of the Coven, starting with the houses by the border, and work our way toward the center. The foliage we pass doesn't look trampled or ruined; it's healthy and flourishing as if this is just another day in Alchemy. The first house we enter is empty, clean, and silent as if the occupants have gone to bed for the night. But just because there's no visible sign of a struggle and no blood doesn't mean a thing.

The bad feeling in my gut is never wrong.

Whatever happened here was quiet but by no means less severe than the other battles. Katrina and I exchange a glance, as if we're thinking the same thing, and the sickening thought hits me that the Council sent assassins here to kill the Healers in their sleep. It's senseless, but so were the explosion spells they used against Mentis. They don't care about causalities. They want to win the war and will do anything in their power to achieve it.

As we trek through the darkness, a pit of foreboding yawns in my stomach. Since we arrived, we haven't seen any of the Alchemy witches. None mill about outside, and even the houses we've checked are vacant with no signs of life. The fact we haven't actually found a body yet—alive or dead—leaves me on edge.

Could all the Healers really be dead and their bodies destroyed?

How could the Council have carried out such a large massacre in the blink of an eye? If there *are* survivors, are they hiding under the impression that we're here to finish what the Council started? Anger flashes through me when I think of Quinn huddled against the wall, crying. He's broken and confused, trapped under the belief that *we* were at fault for tearing his life apart, not the Council. No doubt these witches will blame us too. I think of the first time I met Quinn back in Mentis.

That treaty, that godforsaken treaty, hurts us all in some way, he had said.

It certainly does, though I never would've imagined it could hurt us like this.

The fourth home we check I wish we never found. Death hangs heavy in the air outside, the way it does in Willow's throne room and the tiger pit. Except it's worse here.

It's ripe—*fresh*.

And the worst part? These corpses *aren't* reanimated. Lying sprawled on the living room carpet are two bodies. I can see them from where I stand beside the door, and I have to turn away to catch a lungful of clean air, hoping I don't hurl.

"What is it?" Katrina asks from behind me, her voice grim.

I point into the house without turning back toward the corpses, and Katrina passes me to step inside. Reluctantly returning my attention to the carnage, I watch her kneel beside the nearest body. Her face twists in disgust before settling into a neutral expression, making me wonder how often she's been in situations just like this. Her leadership eases me into taking a few steps into the shack, even though the closer I get, the harder it is to tear my eyes away from the bodies. Once I overcome the initial shock of seeing a fresh corpse, I realize the body on the left looks *familiar*. Her skin is purpled and swollen in some places, but there's no mistaking the hair and glasses.

"Flora…" I whisper. The Alchemy Adept. She was shy, sweet, and most importantly, *innocent*. "What happened?" I ask, scanning for battle wounds without focusing on any one part of her body for too long.

Katrina takes a deep breath, much to my surprise, and picks up Flora's tiny wrist. I couldn't be paid to touch these corpses, but Katrina doesn't seem to mind the contact. She strokes her thumb over the series of veins visible beneath Flora's pale skin and looks at me through narrowed eyes.

"She's been poisoned," she murmurs, letting Flora's arm fall back to the floor with a thump.

"H-how can you tell?"

"That sharpness in the air?" she says with an exaggerated sniff. "That's nightshade."

My eyes shift to the lifeless witch beside Flora—a boy about the same age as her, but I don't recognize him. "Him too?"

"Mm-hmm." Katrina gets up and crosses the room to the cubby shelves filled with herbs. She eyes them level by level before turning to me. "Nightshade isn't a plant she kept on file."

"I don't think *any* of the Healers do," I remind her. What reason would they have to keep such a potent poison lying around?

A light thump sounds from the back of the house, interrupting whatever Katrina was about to say, and we both freeze, petrified by the idea of another person's presence here. Is it one of us … or the Council coming back to ensure the Healers are really dead?

I brace myself for a fight and hear a pained moan instead. "Lilith?" a voice rasps.

My heart skips a beat and, dropping my guard, I rush toward the noise, all thoughts of possible danger swept from my mind.

It's Lazarus, and he's alive.

Chapter Twenty-Three

Take a Number

*T*HE WHITE WALLS of the hospital wing have become a second home to me, the strongest indication of many that my life has been in chaos for a while. This place even has Ambrossi and Helena—all the elements necessary for it to seem like Ignis. All that's really missing is Clio. A stab of pain finds its way through my heart, and the usual dark cloud of pessimism that accompanies thinking of him passes through my mind.

My hands clench into fists, but thankfully, the two Healers flanking me take no notice of the raging storm in my mind. We stare at Lazarus. He lies on the silver slate of a table as if he's already dead and gone. I forget how long we've stood completely motionless, as if the slightest movement will ruin whatever happens next. I'm not sure what it is I'm looking for—

what I *should* be looking for—but I'm too uncertain of breaking the strong silence to ask.

I crinkle my nose and blow a handful of black hair from my eyes. I don't see how the situation could get worse. Lazarus is deathly pale, and his breathing only slows even more as the seconds tick by. Even without the proper Healer training, I know he's losing his battle to the poison, and I wonder what Ambrossi and Helena are planning, if anything.

"Could you make him throw up?" I suggest, just to end the agonizing silence. I glance at my red-haired friend from the corner of my eye.

She shakes her head, parting her pouty lips. "He's too far gone for that to make a difference."

"His body has already absorbed a good deal of it," Ambrossi adds, his voice much colder than Helena's.

And somehow, I feel worse for asking. It just proves what I was already thinking—that I don't belong in here with the Healers. I have no way to help Lazarus, not even a faint inkling of *how* I could offer them any assistance.

I look at Lazarus again and shudder. It's unnerving, seeing a sick Healer, especially one as powerful as Lazarus who has healed half the witches in the Land of Five at some point. Death is inevitable for all of us, but a voice nags at me that this is wrong. He should be able to recover; he should be able to *make* himself recover.

Even after the Healers beside me move in a burst of sudden, synchronized motion, I stare at Lazarus, knowing it doesn't matter how many cures for illnesses a person knows when they've been poisoned. There are some things all the magic in the world can't fix.

To think, my handicap has taught me nothing.

Katrina sits on the other side of the room, a bowl resting on her lap in which she mixes herbs Ambrossi calls for Helena to gather from the line of cubbies embedded in the wall. The way they fall into teamwork amazes me, as if they grew up together, though they're all from different Covens. Fulfilling her obligations to Ambrossi, Helena turns to me, expecting the full story of the Alchemy situation. As I stare at the tears in the corners of her eyes, I find it impossible to lie to her. Still, I don't know how the truth could make it better in this case.

Helena joins Katrina in sifting through the leaf mixture, and my gaze falls back to Lazarus' face. His eyelids flutter, the movement causing my heart to pound, but other than that, he doesn't move. The faint whisper of my name back in Alchemy was the most he's said to anyone, and I wonder if the movement of his eyes is nothing more than an illusion brought on by the falsehood of hope. If so, I wish it would go away; it has no place here now. I don't want to be too late to make a difference, but with us gathered around him in this manner, it almost feels like he's dead already.

Ambrossi studies Katrina's mixture and mutters a string of unintelligible things under his breath, pacing across the room and running his hands through his red hair like a madman. I know what it feels like to believe I've been a failure in the face of the ones I love. Of all the patients he's ever had, most likely none of them have been closer to Ambrossi's heart than Lazarus, his own mentor. There's a good chance Lazarus won't make it. Ambrossi knows this too, of course, and I can only imagine his pain in trying to accept that fact.

"Is he going to die?" I finally ask, and the voices drop to silence as everyone here faces the elephant in the room.

Ambrossi stops pacing and turns to look at me. One heartbeat, two heartbeats, and finally, he says, "Right now, I'm not sure."

That's the expected response but not what I had hoped to hear.

"I will do what I can," he continues with a hint of a frown. "Don't you worry about that."

I'm not worried one bit. One glance down at my leg as he crosses the room toward Katrina and Helena reminds me that if there's one thing he's good at, it's not giving up. My eyes shift back to Lazarus' still form on the table, then I follow Ambrossi to stand beside Helena. "It's just wrong…" I add. "Why attack a Coven full of Healers?" I feel my face twisting in disgust. "They don't hurt anyone. It doesn't make sense."

Katrina scoffs. "Isn't it obvious? The Council will gain the upper hand that much quicker if they have Healers and we don't."

I remain silent, thinking of everything we have seen. It's classic war strategy—the Council took the Healers willing to bow to them and killed those who weren't. If they had slain every Healer in Alchemy the way they tried to take out Mentis, it would have hurt them just as much to be without any Healers beyond Lynx. It's a good plan, but at the same time, there are two important factors the Council didn't take into consideration—we have Healers on-hand, too, and witches, like Helena, always willing to learn how to do it in times of need. If push comes to shove, I'll pick up the skill as well.

The door bursts open, and everyone in the room pauses—battle stances assumed at the sudden intrusion—turning together to see Quinn standing in the doorway. He's panting, good hand clutched to the wall to keep his balance, his face as red as a tomato.

"Is it true?" he asks, eyes darting wildly from witch to witch.

I'm not sure what exactly his question is, so I don't say anything. Neither do Helena, Ambrossi, or Katrina. My eyes flick toward Lazarus lying on the table, and Quinn rushes to his side. He doesn't say anything for a minute, just stares at Lazarus with the same expression Ambrossi has used for the last half hour. The reaction stuns me as much as it does Katrina and Helena, judging from their wide-eyed surprise. I never knew there was a connection between Quin and Lazarus.

"And the whole Coven is like this?" he asks without turning around.

202

"Or worse," Katrina replies, shooting me a sideways glance from her place on the floor.

"I can't believe they would do this." Quinn clenches his free hand into a fist. "Rayna... *knew* Lazarus, and..."

It's crumbling again—his world—and I'm still clueless as to how I can help. "They aren't going to get away with this," I assure him, placing my hand on his shoulder.

Quinn turns to me, eyes red-rimmed and watery, but his face twists more in anger than sadness, as if I just slapped him instead of attempted to comfort him. "Are you kidding? Of course they will. Who's going to stop them? They're destroying entire *Covens* at a time, wiping out hundreds of innocent witches at a snap of the Sage's fingers. No one's stupid enough to say no to that. Isn't it obvious what they're trying to tell us?"

I clench my jaw and wait for him to finish speaking. His reaction is definitely *not* what I expected.

"Join them or die," he says, licking his lips like a rabid animal. "They'll take us all out if they have to."

"It's smart and no doubt effective," Katrina agrees. "After everything so far, who would refuse?" She rubs her chin to remove a spot of smashed green pulp that found its way free of the bowl.

I quirk my lip and look between them. "Us," I say, curling my hands into fists. "*We* will refuse or die trying. That's what this whole thing is about, right? We have to put an end to it. After everything, Aens and Aquais can't side with them."

"You're strong, Lilith, but not everyone is," Quinn says. "At this point, I don't see that they have a choice. Most of them will side with The Council out of fear. That's all it takes."

A tick appears in the side of Katrina's jaw, but she doesn't speak. She wants her people to be safe. If Ignis wasn't already destroyed, I'd want the same.

"Lilith..." a voice rasps, and it takes a minute for me to realize it came from *Lazarus*.

Without thinking, I shove Quinn out of the way to clutch the silver railing on the side of Lazarus' bed, leaning closer and desperate to absorb his every word. "I'm here, Lazarus. What is it?"

"Lynx... his powers..." Lazarus gasps, struggling against his own lungs to speak.

"What about his powers?" I frown, my mind flashing a variety of different warnings. Why would he be thinking of someone who isn't here—an *enemy*? I want to shake him for answers, frustrated by each and every second he spends coughing and choking on his own blood.

"His magic is special. It... it can heal... b-but it... comes at... a price," he rasps, followed by an immediate coughing fit.

"A price?" I ask, my eyes widening.

His glossy gaze focuses with burning intensity as he leans toward me. He opens his mouth, but instead of words, a horrific screech echoes up his throat. Then he collapses back to the table, his head lolling to the side as his hand thumps against the silver confines of his bed. I struggle to comprehend the situation, but before anything comes together, Helena grasps Lazarus' wrist. Her fingers probe his skin before she turns to look at me with wide green eyes.

"He's dead."

Chapter Twenty-Four

The Catless Witch

*H*ELENA HAS ALWAYS been smarter than me. This situation just gives her another opportunity to prove it. As soon as the knowledge of Lazarus' death sinks in, she bolts out the door like her clothes are on fire, leaving the rest of us to stare at each other, dumbfounded. I hardly remember how to breathe again before she reappears with Willow at her side. Maverick trails a moment behind, his face just as grim as the rest of ours, even though he was Gods knows where before now.

No one speaks, but their thoughts whisper a thousand words a minute, and I wish I could block it all out. At this point, they don't have to say anything. Helena's skin is so pale in contrast to her flaming hair, I'm surprised she hasn't passed out yet. But she holds it together well and she directs my sister to Lazarus' body.

Willow is the only one looking remotely calm. Amid the chaos, she is our rock. She has to be—for her and for us. She steps gracefully to Lazarus' table, her eyes never leaving his face. Her straight lips and barely visible frown make her look cold and unfeeling, but when I catch a glimpse of her eyes, I see a flicker of pain. This is by no means easy for her. Even with her gift, it grieves her to see someone die.

That strikes me deep.

"Everyone, step back," Maverick says, holding out his arms to make sure we all stand at a respectable distance.

I obey the command with little to no thought. We all do, but I wonder if it really makes a difference. Willow doesn't acknowledge our presence as we stand scattered around the edges of the room. She lifts her hands, rubbing them together before placing them on Lazarus' chest, as if she's about to press all her weight upon him. For a long moment, they stay like that—Willow's hands on his skin and patient, diligent nurturing softening her face. Nothing happens, and I wonder if maybe this case is beyond even her power.

I blink, and everything changes. The black pits of her irises flicker purple before burning into a bright white enveloping her skin. I stare at this woman, at my *sister*, as the electric energy flows from her and down her arms. When it connects with Lazarus' chest, a whisper rises not unlike the rush of voices I couldn't block moments before. Slowly, the light spreads through Lazarus' body, engulfing him in a veil quite similar to her own aura. I raise my hand to shield my eyes when the light grows brighter and brighter, swelling to engulf them both, leaving it impossible to distinguish one from the other.

When it covers Lazarus from head to toe, I hold my breath, my gaze volleying between Willow and Lazarus. The white light fades as suddenly as it appeared, but Willow does not move, so I watch Lazarus. What I'm expecting, I don't know, but I'm disappointed when nothing happens. His body remains still, just as pale as it was before he took his last breath. Willow's lack of response doesn't give away any clues either as she hovers over his body. When I finally make the decision to pick Willow's mind for information, Lazarus sits bolt upright, as if someone had poked him with something sharp.

Willow steps backward, and Lazarus gasps for air with such force, I feel as if he's taking my soul with him. He swivels his head from side to side, glazed eyes flickering about the room like he doesn't see any of us. And for all I know, maybe he *can't*.

Willow takes one more step away, a faint hint of the glow still rising from her skin. When the light fades from her eyes and her normal coloring returns, she collapses to the floor in a heap of blue dress and brown hair. Maverick and Helena rush to her side while Ambrossi whispers soothing words to Lazarus. Katrina and I remain in place, the odd ones out. When Katrina moves toward Lazarus, I take the cue to approach my sister.

"Is she okay?" I ask, dropping to my knees beside her.

Maverick wipes a strand of hair from her face and looks up at me. "She'll be fine. The process takes a toll on her."

Helena sits back on her haunches, looking as relieved as I feel. She stands to check Lazarus over, mumbling words of encouragement to him, then approaches me. Before she speaks, I see it—the exhaustion. Willow isn't the only one affected by healing.

Despite the look in her eyes, she lifts her chin. "Go get some fresh air, Lilith," Helena says. "We've got this."

I stare back at her, choosing not to speak. After all, who am I to argue?

***

IT TURNS OUT Healers *don't* always know what's best.

Fresh air doesn't help much at all as the seconds tick by, gradually turning to hours with no news. I don't feel any better after what I've witnessed. The scenes play a loop in my head, and for the life of me, I can't make it stop. I'm glad Lazarus will be okay, but I can't stop picturing Willow's crumpled form on the floor. If it's *that* exhausting, how long can she possibly manifest her gift? Could it even possibly, one day, end up *killing* her?

Can someone die if they're already dead? I ponder this, then pinch the bridge of my nose; I'm in no place to try solving that one.

I rest my chin on my knees and stare out across the field. I feel restless, but I don't know what to do with myself. I want to go back to the hospital wing, to help my sister, but without proper Healer training, I'd only be in the way. Kado barks excitedly and drops a stick at my feet. I smile at him and half-heartedly toss it again, watching him tear across the field to intercept it. I'm glad for the undead dog's company and the fact that I can always count on him to be here for me. It's too bad he can't talk. Several times, I've tried to pick his mind, but there's nothing to find.

"Hey, you all right?" Helena calls across the field.

I lift my chin to see her approach, not feeling even half as excited as I assumed I'd be. When she sits down beside me, I reply, "I'm fine. How are Willow and Lazarus?"

"Willow recovered about an hour ago, and Lazarus is to be expected."

I envision several possible meaning of this, but I don't bother to point that out. Instead, I purse my lips, nodding at her words.

"Lazarus will have to be kept in the hospital wing for at least a week now that he's... well, you know."

I open my mouth to speak but hesitate. Because of the Elementals and Willow's gift, the thought of death had such a different impact on me. Now it intrigues me, providing endless questions. All the people who matter to me the most are dead in some respect, yet I keep breathing. "What's it like?" I ask without realizing I've spoken.

Helena tilts her head. "Dying?"

I nod, biting my lip. I can still picture my parents' deaths. As much as I want to believe it was easy—that they didn't suffer—I can't be sure.

"Peaceful," Helena says with a bob of her head, and I wonder if that's the truth or if she can read my thoughts just by looking at me. "With any luck, Lazarus won't remember it even happened."

It's hard to believe anyone could forget their own *death*, but Willow mentioned something similar. "Hopefully," I finally reply as Kado pads toward us. He drops his stick and lets out a happy yip, tail wagging.

Helena's eyes glaze over as she reaches out to pet the fluffy fur on his head. "I miss my cat."

"Huh?" I ask, thrown off by the unforeseen change of topic.

"Lexi. My cat," Helena says, glancing at the ground. "I miss her."

I remember the silver and black furball who spent many nights curled up in my lap. That seems like ages ago, and the thought hurts. I clench my jaw, hearing the sadness in Helena's voice, the *brokenness*, as if she's ready to assume the worst of her possible situation. For all I know, she is, and I can't blame her. Something must have been really bothering her to make her finally mention Ignis.

"Maybe I can find her," she adds, tucking a strand of red hair behind her ear.

I don't want to say what I know has to be said. "Helena... you can't just go home."

The mask she wore in the hospital wing breaks. "I-I know I can't. I don't know why I said that. It's just... They think I'm dead, don't they?"

I nod stiffly. No need for words here, thankfully.

The rest of the day passes as roughly as it began. Willow pulls me from the field before I even get the chance to check on

Lazarus, to ask Quinn how he *knows* him. Willow's black eyes are enormous as she stares at me, and I feel as if they might suck me into their depths.

"Alchemy is gone," she says at last.

I know it already from the tiny portion Katrina and I scouted, but the words make it worse. Words *always* make it worse.

"How many dead?" I ask, wondering if her people keep track of such things.

"More than those who are missing," she replies.

I swallow heavily. "How many do you think followed the Council?" How many does she think avoided death?

"Less than half, I'd guess," she says. "Judging by… how many witches are still there."

I nod.

"Come on." Willow grasps my hand. "I need to hold a Coven meeting."

I follow her, but in the conference room, she doesn't make me sit in the chair beside her. She stands in the middle, completely alone, to deliver the newest wave of heartbreaking news. The announcement of another Coven's destruction doesn't seem to surprise the Elementals, but they mourn the news, the witches from Alchemy feeling the loss the hardest.

Willow gives them a moment of silence, then rounds up a volunteer group to gather any witches they can find. That brings me a bit of hope for Flora, that they'll be able to revive her, and she can live on as a Reanimate. I let that hope burn bright in my chest for the rest of the night, keeping me warm where I could otherwise easily freeze from despair.

Chapter Twenty-Five

Special Powers

I'VE GOTTEN USED to witches knocking on my door in the middle of the night. I don't know why they assume I don't need to sleep, but part of me also wonders if this is what happens when one is related to the group leader. Kado gets up for me, and I raise an eyebrow as I watch the dog jump up and use the side of his paw to turn the knob.

"Thank you, Kado," I call, using my telekinesis to pull open the door.

This time, Quinn stands in the hallway. He seems confused to find Kado there instead of a person, then he looks up and catches sight of me. "Lilith."

"Quinn." I sit up, gathering my blankets in my lap. "How are you feeling?" The last time I saw him, he was in tears. That seems like so long ago, I feel bad that I haven't taken the time to check up on him since.

"I was at the Coven meeting. Was Alchemy… It was as bad as Willow says, wasn't it?"

I nod grimly. "Yep. Probably worse, actually."

"Lazarus is pretty hurt by the whole thing," Quinn says, closing my door.

"Don't tell him too much right now. Let him heal first," I say.

"He was there, though, Lilith. He has a good idea already," Quinn says, looking at me through exhausted eyes.

I breathe out slowly. He has a point.

"You think it was Rayna or one of the other Council members who did this?"

"There's no way to know," I reply, then bite my lip.

"She's dead to me, you know. Rayna."

I don't know what to say to that, so I glance at the space on the bed beside me. "Need to sit down?"

"Yes, thank you." He ambles toward me, his hefty weight causing the bedframe to creak.

"How do you know Lazarus so well?" I ask, then catch his squinting eyes and wonder if I'm wrong for asking.

"Rayna," he says and nearly chokes on her name. "Lazarus would bring Lavina whatever herbs she needed every two weeks, and Ray—*she* would escort him."

"I'm sorry, Quinn. I know it hurts." I ball the blanket in my fists, wishing I could come up with something better to say.

"This is the pain you felt… when Crowe brought you to Mentis, isn't it? That sting of being betrayed," Quinn ventures.

I swallow heavily. "Yeah, pretty close to it."

"I can't believe my sister could hurt so many witches. Is it…" He stops to swallow as well. "Is it *wrong* that I hope she fails in one of her missions? That she experiences a portion of what she's put everyone else through?"

I pause, feeling useless. "No, it's not wrong. What she's done is wrong."

Quinn nods, his strong jaw jutting out as he clenches his teeth.

"One day, she'll pay for the pain she's caused. You can't put that much grief into the world and not expect some of it to find its way back to you."

"Yeah," Quinn says, but his voice is weak. "Harder for that to work when you're a cold-blooded bitch."

I gape at him.

He shrugs. "It's the truth. For her to not miss me? To not care whether or not I'm safe? I have no words."

He doesn't need any for me to understand.

He laughs softly and stands. "You're probably tired." I try to protest, to tell him to stay, but he waves a dismissive hand and flashes me a bitter smile. "It's okay, Lilith." Before I can say anything else, he's gone.

***

THE MAJORITY OF the next week passes in almost a blur. Willow sends a new recovery group to Alchemy every day, the previous group almost always unwilling to go back. They've only returned with a handful of witches so far, and I'm counting down the days until Flora is one of them.

I know what they're doing, picking out the witches who may have family in the Elementals first, and I can't imagine that Flora has anyone here who knows her—apart from Lazarus and me, of course. So I wait, filling the days with Aens and Alchemy training.

When Lazarus is cleared from healing, Helena informs me that he's been put in the same room of the hospital wing as Quinn, and I have a difficult time deciding if that's good or bad. I don't want them to think they're being *forced* to stay here, but with both of them lying in hospital beds in the same secluded space, I can't think of anything else.

When I walk into the room, both pairs of eyes flick to me in relief, as if they *hate* the idea of anyone else walking through the door. I smile at Quinn before looking at Lazarus. "How are you feeling? We haven't had a chance to talk since…" I'm completely unsure of the best way to say that.

Lazarus smiles and holds up a weathered hand.

My shoulders sag in relief for the lack of anger in his ancient eyes. Then I wonder if he *can* speak yet.

"Lilith," he says, answering my unspoken question. "I think we have a conversation to finish."

I blink at him stupidly, but then I remember—the information, the message he had tried to tell me before his passing. Lazarus asks Quinn for a moment alone, and Quinn obliges. Now it's just me and the elderly Healer in the tiny hospital room.

"You mentioned Lynx and his powers," I offer.

Lazarus sucks air in through his teeth and looks down at the bed on which he's perched. "He is the most powerful Healer I have come across," he begins, wiping his mouth. "But that much power is too *much* for just one witch."

"There are drawbacks?" I ask.

Lazarus bobs his head. "Severe drawbacks."

"You never told me about what happened… how Lynx learned he could do what he does."

Lazarus smiles up at me, ancient wisdom on his face and in his mind. "Consider it story time, then."

I don't breathe, don't *move*, just wait for him to continue.

"When Lynx was my apprentice, he was very quick with his hands and his mind. He could memorize the poultice recipes after just one glance at the formula. For a long time, I thought that was his power. I believe he thought so too."

"So what happened?"

"There was a fight. A boundary skirmish between Alchemy and Aquais. Some of the witches came into the heart of the Coven to steal herbs, I think. Well, Lynx's job is his life. He fought back just to keep every scrap of medicine he had. The witches backed off when they realized how much work it would be to get past him. They fled, but on their way out, they attacked every other witch they passed. The leader had *Aens* powers. It caught us all off guard. And Flora was one of the witches they attacked."

Hearing Flora's name, all I can see is her corpse, and I find myself wishing I sat down when I had the chance.

"She had to have been—"

"Young?" Lazarus guesses and bobs his head. "Lynx was overwrought. Here was this little girl, surrounded by Healers, and yet no one could do a thing to help her, because the damage had been done with magic. Lynx. If there's one thing I can say about him, it's that he doesn't give up. He rushed in when no one else would. Told her to hold on, to keep breathing. Even *I* was sure she was dead, but then… she wasn't. He just *touched* her, and the wound was healed. I couldn't believe it. None of us could."

I still can't. "That doesn't particularly sound like a fault."

Lazarus licks his lips. "Flora lost her powers."

I frown, remembering her display at the Arcane Ceremony. She hadn't seemed weak or uncertain. Her healing had been spot-on, and it's hard for me to wrap my mind around the fact that she had done all that completely *UnEquipped*.

I must look as confused as I feel, because he decides to explain more.

"She used to be able to make plants grow at her command. To *control* them. When Lynx healed her, that ability disappeared."

I feel sick, my stomach turning. I think of Larc. *Stripped him of his powers*, Willow had said.

Just how many gifts have the same awful consequences?

"She was still the Adept," I say in a dreamy voice, knowing how very unlike me it sounds.

215

"She studied so hard after... after she learned what had happened. No one had the heart to tell her to stop trying. She was brilliant. All the way up until... well, you know."

Yeah. I know. She worked her way up to Alchemy's Adept just to be brutally murdered. "It's not fair," I say, blinking back the tears.

Lazarus' smile was bitter. "That's the thing about it. Rarely ever do we actually get the things we deserve or desire. What's the old saying? Only the good die young."

I stare at him, realizing how *sad* he must be to say those words. His black eyes only strengthen that impression. If that was true, if only the good die young, what does it say about me, the only one of my friends who *hasn't* died?

The door opens, and behind it, Quinn looks at us with wide eyes. Helena stands beside him.

"The recovery team is back," she says.

I frown. What could that possibly mean?

"Flora is one of them," she says and dashes back out into the hall.

"I... I've got to go," I say, sharing an apologetic, parting glance with Quinn and Lazarus before I follow Helena, hobbling along as fast as I can.

I catch up with her as soon as she reaches the main door of the hospital wing, which leads to the room filled with the witches most in need of care. Inside are five beds and four bodies, but I only recognize two of them—Flora and the boy who had been laid out beside her. I lock eyes with Helena after studying Flora's body, and that's when Willow makes her appearance.

My sister's gaze runs over each of the bodies, not lingering longer on any one of them. It's not so easy for me to take my eyes off Flora. All I can think of is the fact that she was stripped of her powers—that no one outside Alchemy knows the truth about her.

"These are the ones from today's search, ma'am," Helena says politely.

Willow bobs her head once in acknowledgement. Her gaze darts around again, then stops to study the boy whom had died beside Flora.

"Willow," I say, and she looks up at me. I set my hand on the railing of Flora's bed. The girl in it looks so small there, as if she's merely an infant wrapped in swaddling blankets. "Can she be first?"

Willow's face softens, and she asks no questions as she takes her place beside me. That purple glow returns to her eyes. Even without instruction, I know to take a step back. Willow circles the bed until she stands before the shortest rail. The glowing strengthens behind her eyes, then she lays her hands on Flora's chest. Frozen, I watch the scene unfold, counting my every heartbeat. Helena stands on the other side of Flora's bed, her hands clasped in front of her chest, and I wonder if she's having flashbacks of her own.

When Willow collapses, I rush forward to catch her, cradling her off the ground. I glance up at Flora's bed, but from this angle, I don't see any movement. Shaking, I lay Willow gently on the ground and force myself to stand. Flora lies still, head slumped to the side. Her chest doesn't move, and when I place my fingers on her neck, I feel no pulse.

Even with a direct blast of Willow's power, she's still dead.

Helena's eyes are wide, but she remains just as silent. I stare at Flora, hoping I'm wrong and that, at any moment, she'll spring to life and prove it.

She doesn't.

I hear a groan from the floor and look at my sister. With a heavy swallow, I drop back to her side, and Helena takes a cautious step closer, eyes bouncing between Willow and Flora, as if she's not sure which issue to address first.

"Get Maverick," I order without really knowing why. Part of me feels as if he needs to be here, if for nothing more than to support and comfort Willow.

Helena nods and dashes off.

"Lily," Willow croaks, sounding as if she's just woken up. She sits upright and cradles her head in her hands.

Her very skull pulses in agony—I can feel it even without trying to—and now I understand the resurgence physically *hurts* her.

"It's okay," I whisper and try to help her stand.

She sways at first but grips my upper arms to steady herself. Then she catches sight of Flora, and her eyes grow wider than I've ever seen them. Her pale fingers drop from my arms to clutch the bed's silver railing with such intensity, the tips turn alarming shades of blue and white. "It didn't work," she whispers, her gaze growing distant.

I creep around the bed, waving my hand in front of her face. She doesn't respond.

"It didn't work!" she shouts, and her gaze flicks to me. I flinch at the unnatural power behind her stare, unsure what to do. "W-why?" she asks.

Just then, Helena re-enters, followed by a windswept Maverick. He fights to catch his breath, his face red from running, but when he notes the confused shock on Willow's face, he doesn't pause. He pulls her into his arms, and she lets him, releasing the bed. But her body remains rigid, her hands still held out before her as if she's ready to grab something else.

Maverick places a hand upon her brown hair. "Hey, hey," he murmurs, then looks at me and Flora. *What happened?* he mouths.

My eyes dart to Flora, then back to Willow, and his gaze follows, understanding dawning across his features.

"This… has never happened before," Willow says, her voice nearly devoid of any and all emotion. Then she turns and looks at Flora's bed as if she thinks the girl's playing games with her. "Why didn't it work?"

They're all clueless—Maverick, Helena, and Willow—but I feel an itch in the back of my mind and *hear* the story Lazarus told me.

"There's something I should probably tell you," I say at last.

All three pairs of eyes turn to me.

"Lazarus shared a secret with me... about Flora. She was UnEquipped when I met her, but... she wasn't always." Helena pales even more than usual, but no one says anything, so I continue. "You all have heard of Lynx's ability to heal magical damage?" Everyone nods. "Well, *she* was the one he saved. When he did... she lost her powers."

"You think that's why—" Maverick stops, choosing to look at Flora's body rather than say the words out loud.

I shrug. "It's a possibility. Lazarus said Lynx's magic was special. He healed her *heart.* There's no telling what the magic could've done."

Willow swallows and wipes her eyes, but I know this hasn't made her feel any better. "I suppose that makes sense," she says in an apparent attempt to sound strong. She knows that, as this Coven's leader, she needs to portray that strength at all times, but it's not possible. Not even for her. She sounds numb, *lost,* and I just want to pull her into a hug and hide her from all of it. Still, even if I do, it'll solve nothing. "I think I should be alone for a while." She moves toward the door, Maverick on her heels; he'll do what he can to comfort her in any way.

That brings me some peace. "Wait!" I call out, and Willow pauses to look at me.

Maverick groans and shoots me a bitter glance, as if he thinks I *enjoy* making my sister miserable.

"Can you try your magic on one more person before you go?" I ask.

"Lilith!" Maverick snaps.

Willow waves him off. Her expression belies her desperation to see if she still *can* bring anyone else back to life. "Who?"

I point at the boy. "Him. From what I remember, he *died* beside Flora. If anyone can help us understand this, it's him."

"Good idea," she says and approaches the boy's bed.

Maverick stands by the door, but his glare burns into the side of my face. I don't let it bother me. If this works, I have a feeling it'll be more cathartic for Willow than whatever he had planned. I back up to give her space, standing beside Maverick to watch her.

He huffs and folds his arms across his chest. "You don't know when to quit, do you?"

I shrug. "When I'm an optimist, you complain. When I'm a pessimist, you complain. How do I win?"

He smirks. "Smartass."

I smirk right back at him as the purple light flares to white in Willow's eyes. Now the boy glows with it, and Willow collapses again to the floor. This time, it worked; the boy gasps to life.

I turn to Helena again. "Get Lazarus."

Her tiny footsteps hardly make a sound as she dashes from the room.

Willow doesn't rouse herself from her second faint, and Maverick approaches her to scoop her tiny body into his arms. "I'll put her to bed," he says.

I nod, glad I had the impulse to summon him.

When Maverick exits the room with Willow, Helena enters with Lazarus. He looks so frail tottering behind her, and I eye him in concern. He doesn't notice me. His eyes focus only on the boy.

"Alpine," he says.

The boy stares at him for a long time, as if he's never seen the man before. I remember the extensive healing process

Helena went through, as did Lazarus, and I wonder if the boy can even speak.

"Lazarus," he manages.

These two witches, Flora and Alpine, have once again deviated completely from the stream of events I've categorized as normal. Alpine's eyes seem hazy, and I wonder if he's looking at the world through a watery gaze. That, at least, I can understand; it's what I saw when I first woke from Maverick's paralysis. Lazarus pulls the boy into a hug as if they're family, and I recognize entirely all the pain and loss behind that gesture—the same powerful embrace Helena gave me during the vigil for the witches lost in the Battle of Ignis.

When they pull apart, Alpine still holds onto the edge of Lazarus' robe. "Where am I?"

"You're safe," Lazarus says, using my typical, noncommittal approach to such a dangerous question.

Alpine presses his lips together as if he doesn't believe the man. "Flora?" he asks.

Lazarus is silent. We're *all* silent.

"They're all dead, aren't they?"

No one answers.

I frown and step closer, limping more than I should for the small distance. When Alpine looks at me, I find recognition behind his eyes. And why not? Half the Land of Five knew who I was when the Council brought me into the fold.

"What happened to Flora?" I ask softly.

He eyes seem to go even *darker*, if that's possible.

"It was horrible," he chokes out, swallowing as if the words hurt his throat. "The poison… didn't work on her. So, they… tortured her. Nothing they tried worked until…" The black pools of his eyes glitter as if he's about to cry. I have the feeling that if he was still alive, his face would already be soaked in tears. "They used telekinesis to… to keep the air out of her lungs until she…" A sob rises from his throat.

No one speaks. How *can* we? What is there to say when someone tells you something so terrible?

Lazarus sets a strong, reassuring hand on Alpine's shoulder, and Helena approaches them, grasping the bed's railing. "Come on.," Helena says. "Let's get you to your own room so you can get some rest."

She's careful to step directly into his line of sight, and I realize she does it to block the three bodies on the other beds he somehow hasn't seen yet. Lazarus catches on, and I just stand there, watching them push Alpine out of the room, shielding him to the best of their availability.

When I'm alone again, my eyes stray back to Flora. For just a fraction of a second, I envy Alpine. I wish there was someone to shield me from the carnage too.

Chapter Twenty-Six

'Til Death

A FUNERAL. HERE. IN the Land of New Life.

It's about as depressing as it sounds. All I can do is look at the tiny sheet, try not to picture the body of the girl wrapped inside it, and fail miserably.

Willow wears a long white gown, her dark tangles of hair pulled back into a simple ponytail, and she speaks from her place beside the open hole a few of the Elementals dug this morning—Flora's final resting place. I stare at it, but Willow looks neither at the pit nor at the girl beside it. Her back is to me, to *all* of it, and I'm glad. I don't want to see my sister's face. I know that, with or without looking, she's going to show the same amount of grief; either way, her failure remains at the forefront of her mind. If I know her as well as I think I do, it'll always be there to haunt her. Somehow, she manages to keep the sadness out of her voice as she addresses her Coven. I don't know how she can manage that dissociation of her feelings. Like a snake, she sheds away her emotions only to appear stronger for the struggle.

She's not.

"…but Alchemy will not be forgotten, and neither will Flora," she says when I tune back into the moment.

I glance across the field at the gathered Reanimates. There are three new faces in the group—Alpine, Cheryl, and Rosyln—and I avoid looking Alpine in the eyes. Instead, I turn my attention to his companions. Cheryl is an older woman in her forties with a hefty frame, an angular face, and layered red hair, while Rosyln, her opposite, is a petite teenager with a rounded face and sleek brunette hair. I haven't said a word to either of them. This is the first time I've gotten a good look at them, though Willow told me they're both Equipped. Cheryl can control plant growth, like Flora, and Rosyln has the ability to talk to animals. I'm impressed by them both.

I haven't heard what Alpine can do. I'm hesitant to ask for fear of Willow or Helena taking me to speak to him myself. I've somehow managed to avoid him since Willow brought him back, and life's easier that way. He will always have a tie to Flora in my mind, and judging by the curious look in some of the other Elementals' eyes, they're filled with the same thoughts.

In the middle of all this, I don't know what to do with myself. I've been to funerals before, but this one is not normal. Willow tried to comfort me before the ceremony by telling me they *have* indeed had funerals here—supported by the other graves around us—but I don't feel any better.

Maybe so, but there's no reason we should have to have *this* funeral. Flora was young, newly deceased; the formula had been perfect—not taking into account Lynx's miracle act, of course.

I can't approach the sheet covering Flora's body. Even after a few of the Reanimates lower her into the grave, I can't step forward. One at a time, each Elemental takes a handful of dirt, and only when the scattered earth has piled too high to make out a human form beneath do I approach and add my own handful. My hand shakes as the dirt slips through my fingers, and I feel as if I can *hear* every tiny grain hitting the body below. The other witches slowly disperse, but I stay here, staring into the pit.

"I'm sorry, Flora," I say and turn away, unable to look into the darkness any longer.

Chapter Twenty-Seven

The Informant

ETTING THROUGH THE rest of the day yesterday was hard. When I see Maverick and Helena beside my bed upon waking, I know today won't be any easier. I gasp, clearing the sleep from my eyes, and sit up quickly. "What's going on?"

"Just making sure you're okay," Maverick says.

I translate it to: *Just want to make sure you're not going to sleep the day away again.*

"I'm fine," I say, folding my arms across my chest.

"Let's get some breakfast." Helena sounds remarkably cheery.

That makes me feel even worse. Something about morning people upsets my stomach—especially after a funeral.

"Okay," I agree, and they help me to my feet.

Helena follows me into the bathroom, and Maverick waits outside with Kado. She helps me dress and brushes my hair, then we all head toward dining room in the Community Villa, Kado trailing closely behind. Willow is already there, a glamorous breakfast spread out on the table. Helena helps me into a chair before sitting beside me. We dig into the food, then Maverick excuses himself and follows Willow out of the room. I give them a fleeting glance, then look back at Helena. Both of our mouths are stuffed with breakfast.

"Is something going on?" I ask and swallow the huge mouthful.

"They're worried... about Ignis."

I frown, understanding now why Maverick came himself to wake me up today. He wanted to make sure I wasn't lost in the astral plane; he didn't want to risk the chance that I'd gone to Ignis ... for whatever reason. "Why? Ignis has already been hit. Shouldn't they focus on Aens and Aquais?"

Helena shrugs. "I don't actually know much about their reasoning for it. I've only read their fears."

My hands clench into fists, and I stare down at the remaining food on my plate, losing all interest in it. "If the Council knows Ignis is rebuilding, they might want to wipe out who's left. Just to make a point."

Helena bites her lip and looks at me from the corner of her eye. "If we ever get the chance to go back, wouldn't it be a good thing for them to know I'm alive?"

I've found myself once again in a delicate situation, even though I'm no good at handling these. How does this keep happening? "We don't know who made it out of that first battle, but you can't forget that some of them *saw* you die. Explaining how you came back means explaining *everything*, Willow and the Elementals included, and we can't afford that. I'm sorry."

Helena runs a hand through her long red hair before murmuring, "You're right."

I can't bring myself to look at her, to see the emotion behind her eyes. "It's dangerous, anyway. Not to mention how much it would hurt your family to know you're alive but that they can never see you again."

'If they're still alive,' she thinks, melancholy ringing just as loud as if she had spoken the words. I'm glad she didn't. Saying them in her head gives me more of a pass to pretend I didn't hear it, to ignore it. "How much of Ignis do you think is still standing?" she asks, as if she guesses I'm dodging her emotionally barbed thoughts.

The question makes me sick again. We were both taken before we could ever see what was left—or *who* was left—but my astral trips have given me clear enough glimpses. "I don't know," I lie. "I've been gone the same amount of time as you."

The light in her eyes dim as her gaze drops to the table, and I hate it. Does she know I'm lying? I'm so desperate for a distraction that, even though I don't mean to step into her mind, I do. And I only manage to make it worse. I see the admiration she has for me—heartwarming, to a point. She regards me in a much better light than I've ever thought of myself, and I wonder what I've done to deserve that.

"Do you think Lexi survived?" she asks hesitantly, as if she's scared of my answer.

I take a moment to consider my next words. I don't want to tear her down, to leave her bleak and cynical like myself, but it's hard. Honestly, I doubt her cat made it out of that battle when most of our fellow witches hadn't managed it. I don't even think Clio made it out alive, but I'm smart enough to know it won't make anything better to tell her any of that—not when she's still so fragile. If anything, Helena will know I'm holding back and read the thoughts herself.

Thankfully, I'm saved from answering by a voice. "Why don't we go *see* how bad Ignis is?" Willow says as she returns to the dining room

Helena's face draws tight, her eyes squinting slightly, and I know my face probably looks similar to hers.

Willow merely smiles. "My informant there has something we need to hear."

Maverick and Katrina emerge a moment behind her. I stare at Willow as she pops a bite of eggs into her mouth, studying how *emotionless* she seems.

"Who's the informant?" I ask.

"You'll see in a bit, but we need to move if we're going to make it before sundown," Willow replies, waving her Covenmates onward.

Maverick, Katrina, and Helena have no problem following her at once, but for the longest moment, I stay in my chair, staring after them. Helena finally helps me up, and my walking stick thumps against the floor as I move. I can't be the only one with reservations, can I? I scrunch my eyebrows, wondering why nighttime wouldn't be better to sneak into Ignis anyway. If the damage there is as extensive as I imagine, we'll be completely visible traveling across so much open ground in the daylight.

Willow casts a glance over her shoulder, peering at me through the gaps of her long brown hair. When I catch her gaze, I decide to keep the thought to myself. Helena and I look at each other but hurry to keep up with Willow just the same. She does not have to explain anything to me. I trust her judgement, and I know this is an important mission. It has to be if she's going to get the information herself. Willow walks with her chin held high, but it unsettles me that she seems to have no plan and no direction. She's moving on blind faith, and while that may be inspiring, it's not the best course of action.

"So, how does this work?" I blurt out once the silence becomes unbearable. "You think we can *all* step into Ignis unnoticed?"

"I send people all the time," Willow says over her shoulder.

That's different from her doing it herself.

But I don't tell her that, nodding instead and trying to remember that she's not only my sister but the leader of the Elemental Coven—powerful, in charge, and in complete control of her situation. She knows more about strategy than I can possibly imagine. Willow turns to issue commands to Maverick, and I fall back, skipping the next question before I blurt that one out too. Helena and I are the only ones new to this, the only ones who don't know what we're doing. Even if Willow's vision for our immediate future is skewed, Maverick and Katrina are reliable; they won't let us crash and burn.

The problem lies with me. I need to learn to trust in a world designed to make that impossible.

"This is huge," Helena whispers to me, her eyes wide. "What do you think they're going to tell us?"

I narrow my eyes to slits. She seems so small, so *innocent,* as she trots at my side, but she has that way about her. There's no telling what news the "informant" could have for us and why Willow wants *us* of all the Elementals to tag along and hear it. Does she believe it's information that could affect us directly? I think of Clio and clench my teeth. Surely, she would've mentioned it sooner if this had anything to do with him, right? Is it possible she's simply scared to *go* to Ignis?

If anything, Helena should be the one afraid of returning, considering the fact that they had to carry her corpse off the battlefield. Briefly, I prod into Helena's mind, searching for just an ounce of negativity. She's in the process of sorting through her memories of Ignis, both the good and the bad. Thoughts of the battle that killed her don't exist there right now; she's nothing but excited to go home again.

That leaves me to wonder how *I* should feel.

"No idea," I say, "but it'll be good to be home." I say. Or what's left, anyway.

"Yeah. It'll be even better when we find Lexi," she says, twitching her button nose.

My heart hurts at that. "How do we know your cat will be there? I mean, we don't even know if…" I stop, wanting to take it back, but Helena seems to have guessed what I was going to say.

"I need to know," she says firmly, her eyes on the path ahead.

I bob my head. *That* I can understand. In the back of my mind, I consider seeking out Clio's home to see if it's still standing in spite of the fires—and if it holds any clues to his disappearance.

Silence falls over our group as we zigzag through the purple plants, lost in our own memories of Ignis. I'm not sure if Helena read my thoughts of Clio or not, but if she did, she doesn't comment on it, and I appreciate her silence. Zane doesn't say anything today as he opens the portal, and none of the other witches even acknowledge him. Feeling guilty for their rudeness, I offer him a small smile, which he returns, before I follow the others through the strange, wavering air.

On the other side, water burbles from somewhere up ahead, and I recognize the creek leading into Mentis. I almost expect to take the same route on which Crowe led me—since Mentis and Ignis share a border—but Willow steps left to travel into the heart of the Coven of Fire, leaving me once again in a state of uncertainty.

Helena may be excited about seeing our old home again but I can't work up that energy. My heart thumps with expectation. I can't help but expect an ambush of powerful witches to leap from the shadows at any moment and slay us all. The last time I saw my home Coven in person was amidst the chaos of war—blood, death, and pain, with the bodies of my loved ones strewn everywhere like a nightmare from which I could never wake.

I feel sick every time Clio's face crosses my mind.

Helena's question from before we'd set out returns to me, ringing like an alarm in my head. *'How much of Ignis do you think is left?'*

I shiver in anticipation of the answer.

When I recognize some of our surroundings, I take a moment to study each member of our group in turn. How are they not effected by what lies on the horizon? The danger we face? Willow must have picked up on my mixed feelings, because in the fraction of a second, she freezes and turns to face us, gathering us into a haphazard circle.

"This isn't going to be easy," she says quickly. "And if we're going to be successful, we'll need to split up."

I pause. This is news. "I'm sorry. Did you say *split up?*"

Willow nods, her mouth grimly set.

"We came all this way, and we don't even get to hear what your informant has to say?" I ask, caught somewhere between hurt and disbelief.

"Tarj can't slip away for long, and if someone happens to notice his disappearance, they'll find us all. I can't risk that," she says. "If something *does* happen, we need a crew nearby who can swoop in and save us. And it's not like we won't let you know what's going on. The reason you're out here is because you're my most trusted witches. If I can't confide in you lot with this information, I can't trust anyone."

I blink, completely surprised, and forget where I even meant to aim my anger. Everything that's happened lately should've left me with an inability to surprised anymore. Unfortunately, that's not the case.

"*Tarj* is our spy?" My eyes grow wide, and I think for a minute I may have had a panic attack if I wasn't so baffled.

Willow nods, her eyes darkening as if she's unsure how much more information she should give.

"For how long?" I demand, irritated by the fact that no one, not even *Helena*, seems bothered by the surprise my sister just dropped on us.

"A while."

"What's a while? What about Iris? The attack on the Arcane Ceremony?"

Willow blinks, smiles, glances at Helena, then brings her gaze back to me. "Staged," she says at last.

"But Iris *died*," I say crossly, my hands clenching into fists. "Tarj was the executioner!"

Willow frowns and tosses a clump of brown hair over her shoulder. "I know, but all that *wasn't* the plan. You have to believe that."

"Did you bring her back?" I ask, staring at her blankly with the hope that she'll offer a deeper explanation. Maverick and Katrina look away, sensing the rising hostility. I have the feeling that if they could walk away right now to leave us alone, they would.

"No," she says softly, and her gaze drops to the ground.

"*No?*" My eyes have stretched so wide, it feels they may bulge from their sockets.

"The plan was for Tarj to let her go during the night, but Iris... Iris wanted something different. She wanted to leave an impression."

"She *chose* to be *killed?*" I ask, unable to believe what she's saying.

Willow's frown deepens. "She thought... she thought it would have the greatest impact."

"And Tarj was okay with that?" I whirl on the rest of our group, searching for anyone to speak up and agree with me. Every single one of them is oddly fascinated by the dirt right now.

"No. No he was not. But that's the nature of the beast. War can make you do some pretty ugly things. What happened with her got out of hand in the same way that your future did not go according to plan."

I huff. "*My* future? You had it planned, did you?"

"I never meant for you to join the Council," she admits. "But Tarj needed to step down, and after what happened with Iris, he was emotionally shot. To save him, another Ignis representative had to be chosen. We never expected you to jump in the way you did to save him. We hoped someone else would, someone who didn't matter to us as much. Once word of your bravery spread through the Land of Five, we couldn't pull the wool over everyone's eyes and steal you away in the night. Things got beyond our control for a while. For that, I apologize."

I swallow roughly, feeling the tears gather in the corners of my eyes. It seems as if every time I pull off a good deed—like saving Tarj's life—I live to regret it in some shape or form.

"Any more questions?" Willow asks, speaking calmly with a pleasant smile, though the bulging veins in her neck betray the stress put upon her by being shoved into the spotlight.

At my side, Helena remains calm, passive, but I can't manage the same. The knowledge that *Tarj* is our Coven spy pushes me over the edge. "How far does this thing go?" I demand, throwing my hands into the air.

"We have spies everywhere," Willows says, "but the Council has *numbers*. In a war, that matters."

I clench my teeth, unsure how to reply.

It's hard to miss the relief in Willow's eyes at my silence. "You and Helena scope out the outer edge of Ignis," she says, dismissing me as if this conversation never happened. "Try to find Helena's cat. Just take note of what you *do* see. Don't talk to anyone, stay out of sight, but keep close enough to help if we need you."

I stare at her, momentarily hurt, and wonder if she's still mad at me. This is a dangerous mission, and the first thing she tells me to do is to hunt down a *cat?* I turn to Helena, hoping for support, but when I see the worn determination creasing her brow, my rage melts away. This is important to *her*. Despite what I feel, Helena loves the cat, and I love her.

Sometimes, there are more important things in the world than pride.

Chapter Twenty-Eight

Everything that Glitters is *Not* Gold

HELENA LEADS THE way over Ignis' dry, cracked soil. We move away from Willow, Katrina, and Maverick undergoing their own search. I glance over my shoulder to see their fading shapes in the distance, wondering once again if this is really a good plan. The last time I split away from the people I care about was disastrous. I shiver in foreboding.

All around us, Ignis still bears the signs of battle—scorched trees, skeletons of houses, and the faintest hint of blood in the air. It's just as I imagined it would be, but it's worse now with the knowledge that this is *real* and not just part of my imagination. Deep inside, I want to curse Willow for bringing me here, for making me see this. I try to convince myself that it'll make me stronger but to no avail; if anything, it'll drown me in memories.

Helena slows ahead of me, and when I catch up to her, the corners of her lips are pulled into a slight frown. We see the same corpse of Ignis, but where it fills me with rage and itching wariness, it seems to only make her unbearably miserable. "This is hard," she whispers, blinking to keep at bay the tears she can never shed. "B-being here... seeing this."

"I know," I say. I'll never be able to understand anyone better than I understand her in this moment.

Her foot scuffs over a patch of bloody sand, and I can only stare at it. Based on what's left, there's no way to tell who's blood it is and whether or not it had come from a fatal wound. We have no idea just how many Ignis members died.

"My parents are just a half hour away, and I... I can't see them." Her black eyes stare at me, and I know if she could, she would cry. "I'm here. I can't... I can't reach out to anyone I love. I can't tell them I'm alive, that they don't have to mourn my death. It feels like someone just slapped me."

I put my hand on her back, struggling to think of comforting words. She turns and pulls me into a hug, burying her face in my shoulder. "I'm so glad you're still here for me," she admits, her hot breath sinking through my clothes.

My shoulders slump as I pet her bright-red hair, melting into the gesture. I don't want to imagine how bad my situation would really be right now without her. I squeeze her tighter, wishing I could take away her pain; I can hardly get past my own.

But she could be me. All of her loved ones could be dead.

She sniffles once we break apart, and I lead us onward. The back of my mind registers the familiar surroundings we've stumbled into, and I wonder if Helena does too or if her grief has dragged her into indifference. Either way, she doesn't say anything, and we keep walking. Then I catch sight of Clio's home lurking in the distance. My heart pounds in a new type of anxiety, caught between consoling Helena and rushing ahead to search every inch of his house for something I can use to find him.

Before I have to choose, a soft meow echoes through the silence, causing both of us to freeze. "Did you hear that?" I ask, not wanting to say *what* I heard until I'm one-hundred-percent sure I haven't lost my mind. Clio's house may be in Ignis, but it's *far* from Helena's old home, so it makes no sense to see a familiar, silver-and-black-striped cat running toward us from the line of shrubs on the side of Clio's house.

"Lexi?" Helena says in disbelief, dropping to her knees to coax her feline forward.

If physically capable, I probably would have done the same. The cat's pace slows, and it lifts a paw, hesitating to come closer, before its body begins to shimmer and shake, much in the same way as Crowe during a transformation. Helena's eyes stretch wide, but before we even know what to think, Lexi isn't a cat anymore. She's a *woman*.

I can't move. I forget how to even breathe. How do I react to this, to *her*? I have no clue. Do I attack? Run away? Simply wait to see what she does first?

The woman holds up a shaking hand, clearly as upset by the situation as we are. "Please, I mean you no harm. We are overdue a conversation. Helena, let me formally introduce myself. My name is Ivy. I'm so sorry to deceive you, but I am not a cat."

"You're a shifter," Helena finishes.

Ivy nods, scattering her long, curly black hair. "And a variety of other things."

I choke, it's been so long since I took a breath. Clueless but ever considerate, Helena doesn't hesitate to hand over her cloak to the naked, shivering woman, once again demonstrating her brain's superior ability to process the small details. My brain feels trapped in nothingness, on the verge of shutting down. Instead of responding, or even blinking, I feel my knees give out when I finally put two and two together. I hit the ground and hardly register the impact.

"Are you okay?" Ivy asks, running to my side. Her hands hover helplessly in the air above me, as if she thinks she can somehow fix this.

"No," I choke out, studying her familiar blue eyes—*my* eyes.

She lets out a distressed moan that only serves to further irritate me.

"Li, who is this woman?" Helena asks, her gaze settling on me.

My fingers dig into the dirt, the answer gurgling in my stomach like bile. It doesn't feel right. I don't want to believe it's the truth, but I know it is. One look into Ivy's mind offers all the confirmation I need. "She's my mother."

Now *Helena* looks ready to collapse, staggering back as if I'd just hit her with one of my abilities. "*What?* Your parents... *died.*"

"They weren't my real parents. They adopted me," I say through clenched teeth, then look at Ivy. "Right? *She* knows the story." Even I hear the spite behind my words, drowning in forced sweetness.

She dips her head in acknowledgement, but I have the feeling it's also to avoid looking at me. "It is, but it's not safe to talk here," Ivy says, helping me back to my feet despite my snarls. "Follow me, and I'll explain everything."

I stand there, digging my boots into the dirt as I stare at her. There are multiple reasons why I don't want to follow her— multiple reasons for my gut to warn me of danger—but I want answers. If this woman knows something—*anything*—about me, what choice do we have but to obey? I glance around desperately for Willow, but her group is nowhere in sight. I wonder what Tarj has told them and whether they're on their way back through Ignis yet. Will Willow cross our path in time to see this—our *mother*?

Ivy ducks into the woods before either Helena or I reply, despite it being a straight shot to Clio's from here. Maybe she feels the trees are safer or simply doesn't trust the clearest route. I can't say I blame her; almost two decades of hiding is bound to leave an impact on anyone's psyche.

Helena shoots me a sideways glance before making up her mind and bounding to my side. She moves far slower now than she did before, but she manages to shadow me as I trail close behind Ivy. My *mother* leads the way into Clio's house, waiting in the shadows of the living room for us to join her before closing the door and submerging us in darkness and memories. On reflex, my eyes drift to Clio's favorite chair—empty now, of course—and it's next to impossible to push him to the back of my mind, especially with the lingering smell of him in the air.

With the fireplace out, there's no real light in the house but for what filters in from the windows. I take the moment to study Ivy from head to toe. Midnight-black hair curls midway down her back, swooping across her forehead in a light spread of bangs and concealing the hollow pits of her cheeks. My eyes catch hers, and I realize she'd thought to do the same.

"You've grown into a beautiful young woman, Lilith," she says, a bitter smile on her face as she sets a hand to my cheek.

My lip jerks upward but not into a smile; the reality of the situation has crafted my mouth into a sneer. I *barely* keep myself from slapping her. "All these years... you've been *alive?*"

Helena glances at me, and a glimpse into her mind shows me the memories of her and Lexi; she's now questioning the validity of every single one of them.

"You hid from me... You hid from Willow. We *needed* you, and all this time, you were hiding like a coward." Ivy bows her head in shame, but I haven't finished baring my teeth yet. "Why not come to us? Why stay with Helena and have her believe you were just a *cat?*"

240

"It was too risky to reveal myself. They would've killed me on sight. You have to understand, I wanted to tell you more than anything, but I couldn't just step into your house. Regina and Howard... they knew the truth. If I turned up there... Well, they had orders too."

I laugh. "Orders... orders! *Everyone* has orders, is that right? No one is capable of thinking for themselves? Life is just one big orchestrated event?"

"In a way," Ivy croaks.

"What were their orders?" I demand, folding my arms.

"Kill on sight," she says, pausing to swallow heavily. "And really, Lilith, who was I to interfere in your life? You were at peace there."

"Really? That's news to me," I huff. "Suddenly you know me well enough to say what makes me happy? What makes me peaceful? You can't know who I am. I don't even know myself anymore. But now your assumptions have turned us both into idiots."

"I thought you'd be UnEquipped. That you were somewhere you belonged. I thought you were *safe*."

"You were wrong," I snarl, undecided whether to beat her with my walking stick or storm out.

"I know that now, and I'm sorry. You have no idea *how* sorry." Her hand trembles as she lifts it again.

I cringe. "Don't. Just don't," I say, squeezing my eyes shut.

"Lilith, look at me. Please. Life works in mysterious ways. Maybe it's for the best that I came to you now and not a moment sooner."

"How can you say that? How can you think *anything* you did is fine? You left me with the people who crippled me for life. Look at me!" I wave my walking stick toward my bad leg. "*They* made me this!"

"They did what they thought was best," Ivy says, though her hand pressed to her temple betrays her false certainty.

"That's a lie," I say through gritted teeth. I *will* whack her if she decides to touch me again. "How can you defend what they've done if you claim to care about me?"

She falls silent. I just barely register Helena's wide eyes turning to me. Until then, I forgot she was even there.

I scoff. "You should've been from Ignis. Half the people there only care about their own self-interest. You'd fit right in."

Through my blinding rage, I can only give a second of awareness to new sound outside amid the silence. Helena looks toward the nearest window, and only when Ivy's eyes stretch wide do I realize we all hear the footsteps.

"We've been compromised," she hisses and ducks to the floor.

The window beside us bursts in a shower of glass, and I recognize the witches on the other side. The Council has found us. There's only enough time for Helena and Ivy to scream in unison before Clio's house fills with witches and spells. The battle is smaller than the others but by no means any less hazardous. I try to stay by Helena's side, try to keep her safe, but as the witches force their way inside and we try to back away, I lose sight of her in the fray. Witches both familiar and completely unknown aim their spells at me, and I do what I can to fight back. Then my opponent changes from a faceless surge of endless enemies to Crowe, and I freeze, all the fight in me held in reserve. My only thought is my promise to Katrina.

Even if I wanted to, I can't hurt him.

"Crowe," I say, my voice wavering just as much as my indecision.

For the slightest moment, he also seems unable to move or think; the fighting rages around us, and yet we're suspended together in this moment. I don't know how the spell is broken or by whom, but Crowe returns to the present before I do. He shifts, and I recognize the transformation into his bear form even before its complete. The scar up my left arm burns as I watch him. I've been here before. The only difference now is

Crowe no longer has any reason to stop—to hold back. Working side by side with him had really made me take his ability for granted, but opposing him now, I'm terrified; he's a formidable fighter, and we both know it.

The worst of it is that he already knows *all* my quirks.

No. Not all of them. With a tiny spark of hope, I drop the wall holding my powers at bay.

When Crowe charges at me this time, I let out a small ball of wind. In that critical moment, I blink, and he somehow dodges my spell and lands on me with the full force of his weight. His hot breath blows across my skin, and his jaws drops toward my throat. When the agony of his teeth ripping into my flesh doesn't come, I feel his weight lessening on my chest. I open my eyes again to see he's returned to his human shape. His face completely devoid of emotion, he shoves a silver pair of handcuffs around my wrists. The sight of them sends me into such despair, I only notice he's lifted me off the ground when I see the floor swaying beneath me at an odd angle. And then I'm hoisted over his shoulder.

I can't decide whether I should feel angry, ashamed, or just plain *hurt?*

The handcuffs feel so tight—*too* tight—and I realize it may be Crowe's way of making a point, of assuring me that we stand on opposing teams. I think the worst part is the fact that he actually took the time to retrieve my walking stick when he could have just left it in Clio's house. He swings it from side to side, as if he's taunting me. My bad leg flares in agony, and all I can think about is how much the thing would help me. He inches it just a bit farther away, as if I'd spoken that thought aloud, and I consider throwing my weight to the ground and refusing to take a step—to fully engage in this childish game of his.

I don't.

He keeps the walking stick out of reach and bends over to set me on the ground, urging me to move forward. I obey, too defeated to act on any of the spiteful thoughts racing through my head. I finally let go of my defenses, and nothing happens but that the entire world now looks different. Only now do I recognize the world for what it truly is—faulty, the odds stacked *against* me rather than in my favor, like a kick to the ribs when I'm already down. I'm not a criminal, and yet I'm still in handcuffs.

I'm finished. I jerk at the restraints again, despair only growing with the knowledge that it'll do no good. They won't come off, no matter what tricks I attempt. These cuffs are meant to hold a witch's magic at bay, no matter how powerful that witch may be. Though we fight on opposite sides, I can't help the overwhelming devastation of Crowe's actions. Though we fought most of my time on the Council, the fact that my *mentor* is the one to capture me, knowing it'll most likely end in my execution, hurts more than I could have ever imagined. Being led away as his prisoner seems more of a deep betrayal than I know I have the right to claim. Even if these people were once my allies, they're my enemies now. They're treating me exactly as I should have treated them. Instead, I showed my heart. I should hate them—not just for this but for all they've done to Mentis, to Ignis, to Alchemy. To *me*. But deep down, I don't hate them, and I can't force myself to do so.

AS WE PASS through the Council's beautiful topiary garden, seemingly untouched by the war they incited, I'm surprisingly numb and wonder if that's for the best. Crowe walks silently behind me. I want so badly to know what he's thinking in this moment. Does he feel any regret for his actions? Anything at all? I want to reach out and prod his mind, but I'm scared of the answers I'll find there.

Why did I listen to Katrina? The question makes me feel foolish all over again.

Beside Crowe, Rayna chatters on like usual—like things are how they've always been and the past ten minutes haven't changed any of it. Though I was never particularly close with Rayna, it stings to see her so careless, so seemingly happy to have me here in custody like all the other witches before their executions. She laughs at something, and I turn to look at her in disgust. She doesn't seem in the least upset by the Council's destruction of her home Coven. She doesn't seem to feel remorse of any kind. For this, I don't hesitate at all to dig into the centermost part of her mind. There are no thoughts of Quinn—nothing at all about his disappearance and possible death.

How can she not care about her own family?

I'm broken from my thoughts when Crowe passes me to Hyacinth—walking stick still in his hand—and mutters something about the Sage before disappearing into the depths of Headquarters. I watch him for a moment, once again resisting the urge to prod his mind, before my gaze rests on Hyacinth. I'm in severe pain at this point and know that, for all my trying, I won't be able to hide it from her.

Hyacinth has always been the most sympathetic of the Council members, but now, her face screws up in a hybrid of indecipherable emotions.

'Why would you do this, Lilith? Why leave us?' Her question fills my head.

Why stay? I shoot back. *With every horrible thing you guys are doing… how can you think this is right? Witches are hurting—dead—because of you!*

'You want to know why I'm on this side, Lilith? Why I support the Council and the treaty and everything it stands for?'

I blink but urge her onward with my mind.

'I've read their thoughts. All their thoughts. It's chaos. Without the treaty, there'd be anarchy. Mayhem. Murder. Is that what you want?'

"That's because of *you*, you bitch!" I screech. "Families are being torn apart because of this senseless war!"

Hyacinth flinches, her skin drained even paler, but she doesn't speak again as Crowe reappears from the Sage's room.

"Come on," he says simply, urging me to follow him by tapping me on the arm with my walking stick.

There's only one place I can imagine he's leading me—to my death.

Chapter Twenty-Nine

Friends Turned Enemies

"**W**HERE ARE WE going?" I demand, forgetting about Hyacinth and my outburst so quickly, I don't even have time to wonder if I should be sorry for it.

Crowe doesn't answer, only pulling harder on the handcuffs, as if he doesn't think me worthy of the answer.

Arrogant prick.

I try to dig my heels into the ground, doing anything I can think of to buy myself just a few more seconds—maybe even minutes. The handcuffs may prevent me from using my magic, but they don't stop my physical protests in the least. Crowe sighs and stops, turning to look at me to figure out exactly how to get me to move again. The Common Room is empty, and he knows just as well as I do that he won't be able to summon help quickly. He'll have to deal with me for a while first. His hand slides down my arm, his fingers stroking my wrist, but he doesn't try to pull again, as if he knows this won't be an easy process—like trying to bathe a cat.

Around the Elemental Coven, I had come to a weird kind of peace with the thought of death. With most of my loved ones being Reanimates and the knowledge that I'll most likely become one too, it's easy to imagine. But out here, with living witches threatening my life, I feel on the verge of a breakdown. If I'm going to be honest with no one but myself, I don't want to die; I'm not ready for it. After surviving everything so far, it seems a cruel twist of fate that I should die now as just another public spectacle.

Crowe tries to drag me again, but I'm tired. It's been such a long day; I know my energy is close to running out. I can't fight forever.

Maybe he's already guessed that.

Crowe looks at me, and I catch the sympathy in his eyes. "I'm sorry, okay? But, uh… the Sage wants me to keep you on the Grove. And by the look on her face when she said it, I think she wants you in the holding cells."

He turns away after saying those words, hiding his emotions—if he even has any—and tugs on my arm again. With a sigh, I give in. I'm only delaying the inevitable, after all. If Crowe can't get me where the Sage wants me to be, she'll send others to do the job, I'm sure. With the handcuffs still locked securely in place, I can't even fight *one* witch, let alone *all* of them.

I swallow roughly. I didn't even know the Council *has* holding cells let alone uses them on a regular basis. Iris was locked in a dog cage the night before her death, and I realize now it must have been to humiliate her. If they find me dangerous enough to utilize their cells, they must have more in store for me—worse, probably.

"Can't I just have a dog cage?" I try to joke.

I expected the jest to fall flat, and it does. Crowe's eyes dart toward me.

"Where are we going?" I ask, trying to keep a firm tone but failing miserably. I'm not ashamed to admit I'm scared; details of my upcoming death only make it more real, more concrete, more *certain* that I won't be walking away.

Crowe's face hardly moves when he says, "Lilith, it's better to not ask questions at this point. Trust me. The Sage will explain everything when she gets here. Until then... maybe we shouldn't speak."

I look up at him through eyes just beginning to leak tears. "I... I don't understand. She wants to *talk* to me?"

Crowe nods and slides his hand from my wrist to my elbow to guide me out of Headquarters. My pace slows again, but Crowe doesn't argue.

"For what?" I ask in a breathy whisper. "Does this mean I won't be executed?"

The corner of his lip twitches as he fights his emotions into submission. "Please don't jump to conclusions," he says, keeping his eyes on the path ahead. "I don't want to say anything to give you false hope. That wouldn't be right."

I clench my jaw. The fact he could think of any of this as *right* is so wrong on its own, but I don't call him out on it. Hope has never been my friend. I signed up for this mission knowing perfectly well what the consequences would be if something went wrong—if I failed in *any* way—so I'm not surprised when the hope leaves me again while I wait to see what kind of cell the Council plans to cram me in.

I dip my head and obey Crowe's direction, though for the urgency of the situation, he doesn't seem to be in a hurry to bring us *anywhere*. That both surprises and confuses me. If I'm as dangerous as the Sage thinks, I should be locked in their prison by now. So why aren't they being more proactive to get it done?

"Why'd you do it?" Crowe asks suddenly as the darkness of the topiary garden swallows us.

I draw my eyebrows together, caught off guard by the question. "Huh?"

"The rumors? They're true, aren't they? That's why you were in Clio's house with *Ivy Paradox,* of all people."

I bristle at the sound of her name. "She's my mother," I retort before deciding if that was the best move I could've made.

Crowe's eyes grow wide for a moment before they glaze over.

"How do you know her?" I want to grab him and hold him in place, to *demand* that he tells me what he knows.

He doesn't seem to hear me, glossy eyes staring into nothing as he shambles through the dark across the garden. When he finally does speak, his voice is so quiet, I have lean toward him to hear it. "You're one of them."

I'm silent. The words are confrontational, but his tone is not. His fight is gone, too.

"Yeah," I say at last, seeing no reason to lie to him. "They rescued me from the Battle of Ignis." I won't add that they brutally injured me first in order to get me there. In the moment, it doesn't seem important.

"How can you do this now, after all the time you spent fighting on our side? That girl. *Chastity.* She died for you... you executed her!"

Every time she reenters my mind, it makes me sick all over again, but it doesn't bite as hard knowing Grief was the one who lit the fire. "You don't think that thought haunts me daily, Crowe?" I ask softly. Crowe doesn't know about Grief's part in it, and I don't want to tell him.

He shakes his head. "I don't know anything about you, apparently."

"But you know something about Ivy," I point out.

He looks away.

"What do you know about my mother?" I demand.

"It's a long story." Crowe lifts a hand to wipe his mouth before his gaze drops. "I spent time looking for you after you disappeared, you know. I didn't want to believe you would abandon us like that. I thought we were friends... I *defended* you... and—"

"I'm sorry," I interrupt. It's all I *can* say. I sympathize with who he is, just not what he's doing. "But they're right. The Elementals. The Council is going to collapse under the weight of its own power... It's just a matter of time."

He laughs at that, and my eyebrows shoot up in surprise at the sound. I didn't think it's particularly funny, but what do I know?

"We're *all* going to collapse. Don't you see that?"

I stubbornly shake my head. "No. One side of this war has to win."

"And how do you know it'll be yours?"

It's a good question. I don't know. Not really. I have a feeling in my gut, a sensation deep down in my intuition that comforts me, telling me I'm doing the right thing—even if it doesn't seem like it right now. "Where's my mother? Where's Helena?"

He turns to look at me, his green eyes watery pools. "I don't know. And dead." His voice falls completely flat.

A strangled sound makes it way up my throat, making me sick. Who's missing and who's dead? My head whirls trying to figure it out, to craft a scenario that won't destroy me with Crowe's words. With any luck, Helena could've slipped out unnoticed during my capture—Ivy, too, if she succeeded in shifting back to her cat form. Crowe hadn't mentioned seeing Helena in Clio's house with Ivy and me. Could he simply think she's *still* dead after the Battle of Ignis?

Crowe says nothing, and I open my mouth to speak before he turns toward his dormitory, and my sadness gives way to bewilderment. Wasn't he supposed to lead me to the holding cells? I follow him anyways, a shadow lost for words.

He opens the door to his room and pauses to glance apologetically over his shoulder. "Sorry. I know water isn't really your thing." Crowe splashes through the inch of water on the floor as he leads me inside. "But it was either this or the holding cell."

While the Elemental Coven treated me kindly in their holding cells, I know the Council won't show me the same courtesy. We both know what it means that I'm in Crowe's room and not locked up; I've been spared from torture, and he's the one I have to thank for it.

"This is fine, thank you," I say, hugging myself as I watch him close the door. "You don't *have* any holding cells," I point out. "Or I would've seen them when I lived here."

And Iris wouldn't have been in a cage.

Crowe shrugs as he walks past me. "Not necessarily."

My stomach flops with a new wave of nausea, and in the back of my mind, I pray Helena got away, that she's safe somewhere with Ivy. I'm not sure which is worse—being captured with the possibility of torture or hoping that my Coven doesn't care enough about me to attempt a rescue.

Finally, I release the respect I held for Crowe and decide to read his mind. If I'm going to die soon anyway, what does it matter? The effort turns out to be worthless; picking Crowe's mind gives me no insight into Helena's fate. If she *has* been captured, I hope that at least they're treating her as well as they are me. I can't imagine her in a dark, dirty cell.

Crowe sits on his bed, resting his head against the wall to stare up at the ceiling, looking somehow full of conflicting emotion even through his lack of expression.

"So you *do* have them?" I ask with a bit for hesitation.

He nods. "We have a lot of things you've never seen."

"Like what?"

Crowe frowns, and his gaze shifts past me toward the opposite wall. I glance over my shoulder too, wondering what could possibly be more entertaining than me. Finally, he drags his gaze back to meet mine. "I shouldn't tell you this, but really, I don't think it'll make a difference at this point."

I shiver in foreboding; this is the closest he's come to actually *saying* I'll be executed.

"The Headquarters are bigger than you think."

I wait for him to continue.

"What you see in the Grove is only a fraction of it. There's a door in the Sage's room. It leads to the staircase that stretches for miles beneath the earth. That's where the holding cells are. That's where *everything* is."

"Everything?" I echo.

"You can't honestly tell me you never wondered how five or six witches supply the entire Land of Five with all the food and water they need. All the protection? All the order?"

My shoulders slump beneath the weight of his words. "No..." Until I joined the Council, my worldview had been very simple. Equipped witches fight, the UnEquipped don't, and the Council keeps us fed. Now everything is jumbled. "Where *does* it all come from?"

Crowe smiles, but it seems more in bitterness than anything. "The Council is a Coven of its own."

I frown, taking the slightest step forward and watching the ripples move across the water on his floor. "Clarify, please."

"We show the world only one representative of each Coven. And the Sage. But the Council is a fully functional Coven with *hundreds* of witches."

If I didn't already feel nauseous and betrayed, I do now. "*Hundreds?*"

Crowe nods and runs his tongue along his teeth. "Yeah."

Hundreds of witches I've never seen before?

But I *have* seen them, haven't I? Sparingly, of course, but it *has* happened. Willow even told me about the Council's arsenal of witches when she mentioned Tabitha. Remembering my own Dedication Ceremony, I think of the girl who gave my Covenmates their crystals. I never met her—never even heard mention of her again after that. And the worst part is my own obliviousness; I hadn't even realized the girl was missing until now.

"Who are they?"

"Whenever a new Coven representative is chosen, the witches they replace are given a choice to either return home or work in the chambers. Of course, no one wants to go home after being here. It's the biggest demotion I know of."

I stare at him. When I was brought into the Council, Tarj had disappeared for a while and reappeared once again in Ignis. No one questioned it—at least, not that I know. Did anyone realize he was a spy? Or did something else happen and he just never got the chance to say? Still, I can't ask Crowe any of this; I don't want him to suspect Tarj of anything—if he doesn't already.

"You're saying the Council has *hundreds* of above-average witches at their disposal, hiding in a bunker underground?"

"Yep. The destruction of Mentis? That was the work of a single Council witch."

The thought of *one* witch with the power to cause that much devastation makes me sick. I can't help but wonder what the rest are capable of, and a new despair overwhelms me when I realize this war could go much longer than I originally assumed.

"That's why the war keeps going," he says, resting his head against the wall to stare past me again. "There are always more witches willing to fight and no one to stop them."

He's right, of course. While three Covens still remain from which the Council can pluck their new witches, the Elemental Coven will manage to maintain its current number of warriors, thanks to Willow's ability. Even when witches are killed or disappear, it's easy enough for both sides to replace them as if they never existed.

"Crowe, I know you're just following orders, but this isn't right... You wouldn't stand by them if they destroyed Aquais. I know you wouldn't. And they still might wipe out the rest of the Land of Five. Who knows? Executing me doesn't end this war. You know that. It's senseless, all of it, and going along with it just guarantees your death when the Council inevitably fails."

He doesn't react for a long moment, then finally asks, "Are either of us truly doing the right thing? We tell ourselves it's for a good cause, and sometimes, we even believe it. No, it doesn't solve anything, but in this situation, there *is* no answer. So who's to say what's right and wrong? People are going to die regardless of what *I* do… regardless of what *you* do."

"Maybe, but I don't have to die. Neither do you. You can let me go."

Crowe shakes his head just enough to scatter his red locks. "No. I can't. Or they'll execute *me*."

I expected that response. When it comes down to only one of us making it out alive, it doesn't surprise me that he's throwing me under the bus. "Then come with me," I whisper desperately.

"Let's say I did. What about my brother? My *mother*?" he whispers. "They strongly support the Council. All of Aquais supports the Council. I can't fight them. They're all I have left."

"Why do they continue to give that support, after everything that's happened?" I ask. "Why do you? Your parents *run* Aquais. They can influence their people in any way they choose. Why let them put their faith in something that will destroy them?"

"For that very reason. They don't want to lose their home, and neither do I."

"We can save it," I say, trying desperately now to convince him. "We can end this whole fight before it's too late."

Crowe closes his eyes, pretending he hasn't heard a word.

Grim silence falls over the room as I stare at his face, waiting for an answer that won't come. I glance between him on his bed and the door behind me. If I left now, would he even notice? Staying here means certain death, but what worse could an escape attempt do to me if I fail? The only two executions I've seen in my life have been of Iris and Chastity; that's all I need to know it's a painful way to die.

That's the point.

When I close my eyes, I picture myself on the pyre, tied to the stake. When I think hard enough, I can almost feel the burning torture of fire melting the very skin off my bones, can hear the cheers of the onlookers, their celebration of my deepening agony. Who will be the one to light the fire?

Who will be the one to end my life?

Chapter Thirty

For Life

TRY EVERYTHING I can think of to persuade Crowe to join me and the Elementals, to leave the Council behind, but his expression remains as bleak as it was ten minutes ago. I have a feeling it's because he's just as much of a mess inside as I am; he's on the verge of cracking, and that's why he ignored my pleas to escape.

He's tempted, I realize. He wants to escape, but he's afraid.

I scrunch up my face at the thought but shake it away and look at my mentor again. I can see the undertones of fear and hesitation creasing his eyes, behind the tight lines of his mouth, and I know exactly what I can say to push him over the edge. "I met Katrina." The sentence leaves my lips strong and unfaltering.

These are in fact the magic words. Crowe's eyes snap open, and he sits bolt upright, as if someone has sent a shock of electricity through his system. "You... what?"

"I met Katrina," I repeat, tilting my head as I look at him. "*Your* Katrina."

He shoots to his feet at once. "She's okay? Where is she? Can *I* talk to her?"

I raise my hands, a bit taken aback by the strength of his emotions. "She's an Elemental, just like you thought."

Crowe recoils as if I've slapped him. "She... she can't be," he says, lifting his hand to muss his disheveled red hair. "She's..."

"Crowe," I say, reaching out to put a hand on his shoulder; I change my mind when I catch his wild gaze, pulling my arm back instead.

"What?" he snaps, the tears that had glossed over his eyes now beginning to leak free.

"You remember when we toured the Land of Five looking for Elementals, and you first realized Katrina was missing?"

Crowe sniffs and stares at me, waiting for me to continue.

"You told me she's *smart*. That if she joined the Elementals, she would have her reasons. Trust me, she *does*. And you do too. You can be with her again. All you have to do is let me go. Come with me and leave this life behind."

Crowe lets out a loud sob, and my eyes stretch wide as he steps toward me to pull me into a hug. He presses his face to my shoulder and cries. I'm too stunned to move, listening for a long time to the pained, raspy wails the shapeshifter releases. I don't know what to say or do; mentioning Katrina seemed like a great plan five minutes ago. Now, I'm not so sure.

"What do I do?" he asks at last, his wet cheek brushing mine as he pulls back to look at me.

"Whatever you *want* to do," I reassure him, catching and holding his gaze.

He considers this. "Let's get the Hell out of here." Crowe wipes his face with the back of his hand like a kid crying from a skinned knee.

My heart feels lighter than air as the hope returns, filling it full to bursting until a sickening lurch grasps my stomach; we're not out yet. "Those are the best words I've heard in a while."

"Let's go," he says, setting his hand on my shoulder to lead me back out into the hallway.

My heart pounds in my chest. Crowe comes to an abrupt stop, and my stomach flips; I can't help wondering if he's on the verge of changing his mind again.

"There's a file," he says, turning to me in wonder.

"Huh?"

"There's a room with files on every witch who's lived and died since the Council was formed. There's one on Ivy."

I lick my lips quickly, feeling what few seconds we have to escape are ticking away on this pointless conversation. "Can't you just tell me what's in it?"

Crowe shakes his head.

So he's willing to switch warring sides at my word, yet he doesn't trust me enough to tell me about my own mother? "Why?"

"I don't know what it says," he admits lamely.

"But you're part of the Council," I say, astonished.

Crowe lets out a dry, raspy laugh. "You know that means nothing."

"Fair enough." A file on my mother means the truth of my origins, my *accident*, everything I've been searching for, and it's been hidden in the Council's bunker this entire time.

"Come on," Crowe says, setting his hand on my elbow to guide me as he had when I was his prisoner. Except now, everything is different. Now, we're allies united under the same goal.

The thought warms me until I realize he's leading me farther into Headquarters and not toward the doors that will take us outside. I swallow heavily, feeling the urge to dig my heels into the floor again. "Where are we going?"

"To get that file," he says with more determination that I expect.

If there's a file on Ivy—on my *real* mother—I want to read it. But it's a dangerous move. This may be our only chance to escape—the only opportunity to disappear before the Council realizes Crowe has deserted them.

It also may be the only chance to get the file.

Crowe doesn't appear to suffer from the same bout of indecision weighing on my mind. He chooses for me, his fingers digging into my skin as we approach the entrance to the Common Room.

"If anyone asks," he whispers, "you're my prisoner."

I nod sternly, knowing exactly how important it will be to play my role to perfection.

Crowe falls silent as we take the last echoing steps before the Common Room, and I have no choice but to move along with him. Inside, Hyacinth perches in her favorite chair, and I focus all my energy on trying to lock up my thoughts, to keep the clairvoyant from seeing our plan and getting us *both* arrested—if she doesn't already know what we intend.

At the sound of our footsteps, she looks up, and when she sees me, her eyes narrow and her lips purse. I don't have to read her mind to know she isn't happy to see me again. It's okay; I'm not happy to see her, either. Hyacinth lets out a disdainful humph and gets up to stroll out of the room, flipping her long straw-blonde hair over her shoulder. She passes us to leave Headquarters, and I pick up on her thought of heading to her dormitory to *get some real peace.*

Crowe sighs into my ear. "Irritation is better than curiosity."

I don't argue as we cross the Common Room. My eyes dart around, heart thudding in my chest as I wait to see any of the other Council members, wait for their questioning eyes and prodding interrogations. Thankfully, none of them make an appearance.

When we come to the end of the corridor and the door leading to the Sage's room, I turn to Crowe with wide eyes. "What are you doing? We can't just go in there."

"The door is the only way to the chambers," Crowe reminds me.

"What if she's *in* there?"

Crowe shrugs. "She wants me to bring you to the holding cells. For all she knows, that's what I'm doing."

I nod. Play the game. It makes sense, but at the same time, I feel more than a little uneasy. What if this whole thing is nothing but a trick—a way to get me into the holding cells without a fight? Swiveling my head slightly, I catch sight of Crowe's eyes—of the fear in them—and I know without a doubt that he's in this as much as I am. Crowe breathes in deep and lets the air out slowly before opening the door and leading the way into the shadows of the corridor on the other side. I don't want to go. Foreboding leaves goosebumps everywhere on my skin, but how can I argue at this point?

If he's not lying, he's doing this for *me*. He has nothing to gain himself by getting Iris' file.

"Breathe," he whispers to me a moment before we emerge into the Sage's room.

It's just as I remember it, cramped and smelling of a variety of flowers and herbs. The warmth I felt the last time I was here is gone, though I can't decide if that comes from the lack of a burbling cauldron or from my loss of respect for the Sage.

"She's not here," Crowe whispers.

I nod, and he lets go of my arm, moving across the floor to step behind her desk. I don't move as I watch him, too transfixed on what he's doing, as if I expect him to fall into a trap at any moment. Crowe moves with purpose, easily pulling the Sage's chair out of the way and bending down to disappear behind the desk. A moment later, I hear a loud clang. Alarmed, I harshly whisper his name, and his eyes peer over the rim of the desk.

"I'm okay, Lilith," he says. "Come on."

I'm not sure what exactly eases me onward, but I move one shaking step at a time. On the other side of the desk, Crowe is crouched beside a hole in the floor, the rug rumpled beside it. "This leads to the homes of hundreds of witches?" I ask, still entirely wary.

"It widens once you get inside," he tries to assure me, but I don't feel better for it. I stare at him, waiting, and after a moment, he adds, "You can trust me." He reaches up to ruffle his hair. "I'll prove it."

Before I can ask how, he grasps the edges of the hole in the floor and launches his body into the darkness. I stare at the hole with wide eyes, waiting for the repercussions of whatever is hidden in there. For a long moment, I hear nothing from the shadows, and that brings a new wave of panic. What if he misjudged his jump?

What if he's hurt?

"Crowe!" I hiss desperately, staring into the pit with the hope of catching any glimpse of him even though I know it will be impossible.

"Come on! It's safe!" his voice echoes from below.

I could collapse with relief if it weren't for the uncertainty of my imminent future. I eye the hole, judging the best way to do this. I already know I won't land on my feet. Even if I do, I won't be able to hold it. With the handcuffs, I won't be able to ease myself down, either.

How far is the fall?

"I'll catch you," Crowe promises.

I don't trust it, but again, what choice do I really have? I dangle the walking stick, feeling nothing but empty air, and let it fall to where it clanks on the floor below. Taking a deep breath, I sit down, swinging my feet into the gap before I let go of my fears and drop. I scream when the blackness consumes my vision, and less than ten seconds later, Crowe's arms catch me easily. He helps me back to my feet, and though I know he's still beside me once he removes his hands, I can't see him.

"Now what?" I ask.

"Hold onto me," he says, setting a hand on my elbow.

I don't argue, reaching out to grasp his arm. He leads the way again, as if we're going somewhere formal rather than the mysterious chambers below Headquarters. I strain to see anything at all and wonder how he can see as well as he apparently can. He must've been here before.

That thought alone comes with a myriad of questions, including why he would ever come here in the first place and how many times he's made this journey.

"There's a staircase coming up," Crowe says.

I jump at the unexpected sound of his voice. "Okay."

Without being able to tap into my telekinesis, the movement down the stairs is just as hard as I imagined it would be. Crowe does an excellent job of keeping me steady, and I would give him credit for that if I weren't so distracted. The deeper we go, the more light there is, contrary to my every belief. When we reach the landing, I realize why. Artificial light fills this place—the same kind that used to fill Mentis.

Crowe leans toward me, his dark eyes sparkling in the light. "It's popular here, too."

I only nod in acceptance with a fresh understanding of the attack on Mentis.

"I don't know if we'll see anyone or not," Crowe admits, "so from here on out, best performance from you, okay?"

I nod again. Those are terms to which I can definitely agree. Crowe offers me a gentle smile before setting his hand on my shoulder, staying behind me in the proper, guard-leading-a-prisoner form. He lets me keep the walking stick, and I wonder if I should remind him of it or not. I keep my head bowed, both to hide my awe at the sights around me and to appear ashamed. The first room we pass through is wide and airy. Heavy shelves line its walls, filled with a variety of Alchemy tools ranging from plants to cauldrons and bolines.

"This is Lynx's little workshop," Crowe explains quickly. "Though I don't think he spends much time down here. He says it's too creepy."

"And it's the *entire* first level?" I hiss.

Crowe nods. "Just about. Favoritism runs deep here."

I snort, but the sarcasm fades quickly. A breeze leaves goosebumps down my arm, and I shiver. I agree.

When we leave that room, we hear the first sounds of others' movement, and I freeze, the panic overwhelming me. Crowe doesn't say anything but simply squeezes my shoulder, and I move again, remembering the importance of our act. If one of us fails, we *both* fail. The next room contains several witches moving around to sort out a variety of bundled plants and vegetables.

This is where the distributors decide which Covens get what,' Crowe thinks clearly for my benefit.

"Hi, Crowe!" A slender girl with shoulder-length black hair and purple eyes approaches. "What're you up to?"

"Just a typical prisoner lockdown, Sabrina," Crowe says with a laugh; it seems to stem from nervousness.

"You're just all work and no play." The girl pouts, bending down to scoop a handful of plant bits from the container in front of her.

"You know me," Crowe calls back in an apparent attempt to sound playful. He shoves me forward and into the hallway as quickly as he can.

"Who was that?" I whisper.

"Sabrina? She's from Ignis. Though I doubt you've ever met her. She's been a member of the Council for about ten years."

"I don't think I know her. What's her power?"

"She causes earthquakes."

Wonderful.

Crowe leads me forward once more, and I realize Sabrina looks familiar, flinching when the reason why comes to me. She was the girl who gave Clio his piercing—the one who mysteriously disappeared after the Dedication Ceremony.

"The next floor will be easy—kitchens and prep stations for the witches who take care of the Council. There's also rooms for the Covenmembers themselves to eat."

I nod, remembering the extravagance of the Council's every meal.

"Next floor will be the heart of the Coven, if you will. It's got bedrooms and the Coven altar."

"Huh. I thought that would have been the topiary garden."

He shakes his head. "Too risky for that many old Council members to be seen aboveground at once."

"Can't have that," I scoff.

"The toughest part will be the floor after that. It has the file we want as well as the holding cells. It's also staffed with the witches responsible for the Council's security. These are topnotch witches, the ones who have found the most Elementals out of all of us."

I don't like the sound of that at all. "Wait. If the Council has this, why did the Sage send us around the Land of Five to scope things out?" I ask.

"Busy work, my dear."

I clench my jaw.

"There are three witches who work there for the most part, but two in particular worry me," Crowe admits, reaching up to scratch the back of his neck. "Sable and Caleb. They're twins."

I frown at his tone, surprised he doesn't mention Tabitha. If Willow's right, he probably doesn't know she exists. "Do I want to know what they do?"

"Probably not, but it's best you're prepared just the same. Caleb's magic is... *special*," Crowe says uncertainly. We take the first step down the stairs toward the next level. It strikes me as odd, reminding me of what Lazarus said about Lynx's power.

"Special how?"

"Special in that he can strip *other* witches of their powers. Those handcuffs you're wearing? His creation. It doesn't bind your powers inside you. It actually absorbs them so they become too weak to use."

This sounds eerily like what Lazarus told me about Lynx. Could he be related to Sable and Caleb? "Isn't that dangerous?" I ask, recoiling to twist my wrists in the bindings so as little of my skin as possible touches the bands.

"It can be."

"Oh, Gods. You were right. I was better off not knowing." I glance at him from the corner of my eye. "What does Sable do?"

"Sable? She knows whether or not you're telling the truth."

Chapter Thirty-One

The Plan

I STOP, TURNING TO Crowe with wide, shocked eyes. "She's going to know what we're doing," I gasp. "If you knew there was a witch like her down here, why would you expect this plan to work?"

"I've got another plan," he says quickly.

"What would that be?" He's wavering too much between hope and depression, and that leaves me with a bad feeling; there's no telling what else he's changing his mind about. He's risking a lot right for me—for both of us. He isn't foolish, he knows the consequences, but he also must know how easy it would be to change the story completely, to absolve himself of any responsibility if we do get caught.

My suspicion only grows to the point where I almost want our ruse to be discovered, just to see how deep his loyalty to me truly goes. It's selfish, I know, but I'm tired of being kept in the dark—tired of never having any peace of mind. That's a side effect of being a criminal, I remind myself. But have I ever truly been one, or have I just always been a prime example of what happens to those in the wrong place at the wrong time?

"The only way is to take you to the cells," he says. "If I'm really going to take you there, she won't pick up on a lie when we tell her where we're going."

That does it. I can't move another step. His fingers grip the top of my arm as he tries to urge me onward, but I don't move. His wide green eyes bore into me, searching my face with that battling flicker of emotions behind them. I'm sure all he can see is my suspicion. "This is all a trick, isn't it? I'm still under arrest. You're not going to help me. You're going to put me in that cell and walk away." I almost can't believe my own stupidity. Have I grown so desperate—so *careless*—that I believed in him more than myself?

Crowe sighs and stops tugging on my arm, bringing his face close to mine. "I know what you're thinking, but you *have* to trust me. Read my mind if you have to, but this is the only way."

I don't hesitate, plunging deep into his thoughts, sorting through the mechanics of his plan, and searching for anything he may be keeping under lock and key. For the first time since I've known him, I realize he's completely *open*.

He's not a hiding a thing.

"Better?" he asks, bringing me back to focus.

I nod, once again staring into his wide eyes. "I'm sorry I doubted you."

He turns his face away, and I know I've offended him. Still, I don't think an apology even matters to him at this point. He's still here, still trying to help me through this, and I have to believe that counts for something.

We pass the landing to the next level and continue to the Surveillance Floor. Once we hit the end of the stairs, the artificial light blinds me, and my steps grow even more uncertain. The light is so much stronger than on the other floors, and I realize that's because these rooms are constructed like the homes in

Mentis. The bright tiles reflect the light, making it seem impossibly bright as we cross the first section of the corridor. There are just a few chairs scattered around the edges, reminding me of the Headquarters' Common Room and their lush, throne-like chairs.

"Where's the file?" I dare myself to whisper. I don't know why I expect this part of the journey to be easy, as if after everything, it will just be sitting on a table in the middle of the room, waiting for me. My nose twitches in amusement; *that* would be a trap for sure.

"There's a room right beside the holding cells," Crowe informs me. "It's full of files. You'll see what I mean."

Those are the last words we can afford to speak as we sneak through that first room and into an even smaller second. Our footsteps echo, and I feel my confidence rise. If anyone were here, we'd definitely hear them. Crowe must've reached the same conclusion, because he picks up the pace, and that's when I hear the footsteps rounding the corner in the hallway behind us.

When I glance fearfully at Crowe, I realize he's looking back at me with the same reaction. We're still moving at this point, but just as quickly as Crowe was hurrying before, now he's slowed almost completely. I try to urge him forward, to avoid the footsteps behind us, but my gut warns me it's already too late for that.

They've already seen us.

"Crowe," a tired voice calls, echoing off the walls with the unearthly light. "What brings you to the Chambers today?"

He tenses, and I know without knowing that this is Sable. Crowe gives me a look before he turns slowly, hand tightening on my shoulder to make me turn as well. Sable looks a few years older than Ambrossi, her tousled black hair contrasting with her olive skin. She smiles at us, but I wouldn't by any means consider it friendly. It's sharp and bitter, reminding me of my adopted mother more than I care to admit.

"Miss Sable!" Crowe gushes with fake enthusiasm and extends his hand to briskly shake hers. "How good to see you."

"Mm-hmm," she replies with that tight-lipped smile, as if her skin is frozen like that. I wish more than anything that she would just stop that. It makes it worse, seeing how horrible such a pleasant expression can really be. "I don't believe you answered my question, dear."

"I've got a prisoner here," Crowe says with a sideways glance at me. "At the Sage's request, I'm taking her to the holding cells to await her trial. Unless there's been a change of plans I am not aware of?" Now *he* seems tight-lipped and bitter. I hold my breath, my eyes volleying between him and Sable. She merely stares him down, a subtle hint of disgust on her features, as if he's nothing more than dirt on her shoe.

I'd hate to see what she thinks of *me*.

"No, Mister Crowe, there hasn't," she says at last, raising her chin a bit to hide her embarrassment. "Carry on."

"Right," Crowe says.

Sable gives me a once-over, her eyes narrowing to slits as she catches sight of my walking stick. Then she turns away to walk back in the direction from which she came.

With a long, shuddering sigh, Crowe turns to look at me. "That was a close one."

"But your plan worked," I point out.

He nods. "Yeah, thankfully. Let's make this quick. I don't have another one."

I don't either. We resume our previously hurried pace, and after a few more minutes of traversing through similar rooms, we finally come to one that seems dimmer than the rest. It opens to reveal a line of three identical cells. From the doorway, I can't see inside any of them, and the anticipation gives me chills. Before this moment, I never stopped to consider the fact that the Coven could be holding *other* prisoners here.

Blinking, I glance at Crowe, but he doesn't even slow down as we approach the cells. Are the remaining Healers down here? I don't know why I expect the cells to be empty, but that expectation is shattered when I see a witch already imprisoned behind the second iron door.

A very *familiar* witch—Dawn, the Mentis Adept.

She doesn't stir at our approach, lying stiffly on the bed, as if it would kill her to move the slightest centimeter. My heart pounds quicker when I realize a *hospital* bed was wheeled into the tiny box of a cell, and upon closer inspection, I see why. Countless bandages are wrapped around her arms, and as far as I can tell, they swirl across her torso under the billowy blue gown she wears.

"The bombs," Crowe says by way of explanation when he catches me staring.

That's all he needs to say. I imagine the burns and shrapnel wounds that must have destroyed her skin, and I wish more than anything that I hadn't—that the images in Dawn's mind weren't so easy to pluck out of her.

"Why isn't she with your Healers?"

"She's a prisoner."

My eyes widen at that. "But she's the Mentis Adept."

"She gave that up. Gave up *all* her glory when she disappeared during the Battle of Mentis in an attempt to warn the Elementals rather than follow the instructions she was given." Crowe's voice is stiff as he explains this, but I still can't figure out how he truly feels about it. If this had happened to him, I can't imagine he would want to be left for dead in a dusty old cell. "She stopped him, the witch who bombed Mentis, and upset his timing… That's why the first explosion spell missed. This is her punishment."

"But she did the right thing. She doesn't deserve this. She's hurt," I say. "You can't just leave her here."

Crowe sighs and looks away again, as if ignoring her presence will hide the fact that she's injured, will take away the injustices she's already suffered since the battle. He doesn't offer more on the subject, and I have the feeling it's best not to ask.

Instead, he turns the corner, guiding me to do the same. I keep sending glances over my shoulder at Dawn, but I know we're running out of time. If I want that file, we can't waste what few minutes we do have, but I can't stop thinking of how to help her. Unable to help it, I whisk through Crowe's thoughts again. He doesn't think of Dawn at all as he presses onward; he's just as determined to finish *this* mission as I am.

"It's this way," he says.

I'm about the ask where before I see a slender entrance beyond the row of cells. Crowe glances subtly over his shoulder to be sure the coast is clear, then he pushes me gently ahead of him into the next room. Books and files line every inch of the three walls. It could take *weeks* to sift through this much paperwork, so I turn to look at Crowe with wide eyes.

"Where do we even start?" I ask quickly, trying not to let the despair seep into my voice.

"There's a section in here dedicated to dead witches," he says.

"She's not dead," I point out stubbornly.

He glances sharply at me. "I realize this, but until today, everyone believed she was."

"How do you know her file is still here? That they haven't already taken it?"

"Ivy got away… when I arrested you," he says, and the thought both angers and saddens me. Instead of trying to save me from my fate, she'd only thought to save herself.

I shouldn't be surprised. It's what she does best.

"Found it," Crowe announces with a victorious smile as he stands from beside a shelf. He holds the file up for me to see.

My heart flutters with excitement before it plunges right back down into the depths of my stomach.

"Crowe?" Sable calls, her voice echoing down the corridor.

"Shit!" Before I realize what's happening, he grabs me by the arm and shoves me into the nearest cell. My walking stick clatters to the floor beside the file room, and he slams the door shut with a clang.

I stumble into the cell and fall to my knees. "Crowe!" I shout.

He turns his back and heads straight for Sable. I can't hear what she says to him, but he doesn't even spare a final glance at me over his shoulder. I can't decide if I want to scream or cry. My knees roar in pain after having hit the stone floor, but over the pain in my chest, it's nothing. How could I have fallen for such an obvious trap?

I shakily remind myself to have faith; I saw the pure honesty of his thoughts when I'd searched through them. He can't possibly be hiding anything. But I don't feel any better. He's tricked Sable once already—the way he tricks *everyone* when he thinks it's necessary.

He *always* has something up his sleeve. I can't trust a single thing he says—or doesn't say.

Chapter Thirty-Two

Escape

IT DOESN'T TAKE long for Sable and Crowe's voices to fade into the distance, and that's when I let the first tear fall. I try to convince myself it's only a reaction to the pain in my leg, but I know better. It's from the pain in my *heart*. I trusted him—*really* trusted him—to get me out of this, but he used that trust against me.

And I fell for it.

I wanted so badly to believe in him—and to keep my promise to Katrina—that I was willing to believe anything. I'm beyond disappointed in myself. Groaning, I plop onto the ground, taking the weight off my knees. They're purple and black, instantly bruised from where I stumbled cross the cell floor, but I shrug it off. If I'm about to be executed, it doesn't matter much what they look like. With a small sniffle, I crawl toward the bed and pull myself up onto it.

I don't think about pulling on the bars, attempting an escape. It seems pointless. Even if I did somehow manage to slip out of this cell, without Crowe, there's no way I could get past all the witches on the floors above me—let alone traverse the stairs on my own just to get there. I curl up atop the white sheets on the stiff, uncomfortable bed, and stare straight into the gray pattern of the stone wall.

More tears leak from my eyes, as if I'm cutting onions, but I don't make a sound. I shiver instead and tuck my chin toward my chest, desperate to block out every aspect of my cell. This is where it ends, isn't it? I'll never find out what happened to Clio, never even see how the war ends. Staring into the face of death, I find my life seems so suddenly empty, so *meaningless.* I've lived for everyone but myself since the time of my Arcane Ceremony, and the realization dawns on me, threatening to choke me in my own tears. I do hear the footsteps echoing down the corridor, but they mean nothing now. Curled into a ball, I let myself sink into despair, wishing I could sleep just to make these last few hours pass by quicker.

"Lilith," someone hisses, and my eyes fly open to stare at the wall.

I don't move at first, but then I hear the bars rattling and realize how close this person actually is. When I sit up, I see Crowe pressed against the steel rods of the door.

"You came back?" I ask in disbelief.

His eyes are as wide as mine, and he gestures for me to be quiet.

I raise an eyebrow, ready to ask him why he'd do this, then I realize he's not alone. The Sage enters with graceful footsteps belonging to someone much younger. She doesn't hesitate for an instant, moving with purpose. I don't know why I expected anything less from her. She's the most powerful witch in all the land; she can do whatever she damn well pleases, and that includes traveling to a secret part of Headquarters with nothing but confidence. My fingers dig into the silver railing on the side of the bed as I steady myself, staring her over from head to toe. She's taller than I ever imagined. The few times I saw her, she only sat in her chair, hunched over her desk. She's much livelier outside her room, and it's unnerving.

Her eyes focus on me, and I catch no emotion whatsoever behind them. Her mind being the vault that it is, I have absolutely no way to guess what she has to say. By the time she stops beside Crowe, he's managed to pull himself behind an impassive mask again, although I still see a flicker of panic in his eyes.

"Crowe," the Sage says, turning her ancient face toward him, as if she can sense us having a conversation just by looking at each other. "Can you give us a minute?"

He swallows and without any other option turns to look at her. "Yes, of course, ma'am." He turns back to me, studying me for a long moment, then heads toward the corridor, only pausing briefly to look at the Sage. When his footsteps fade to silence, I have the Sage's complete attention—and she has mine.

"I never thought I'd see you in here, dear," she says with a wistful sigh.

I'm not sure *how* to respond, so I just sit up a little bit straighter and fold my arms across my chest.

"Why does it seem like, no matter what side of this war you're on, you're at the center of it?" she asks, an amused smile tugging at her lips.

I smirk, though I don't find any of her amusement in this situation. "Because this is *my* war. You said so yourself."

"We both know that's not the case, dear."

How can a simple statement sound both calming and threatening at the same time? "I'm a huge part of it though, right?" I say. "That's why no one wanted me to know the truth of my accident. Just like you didn't want me to know about Willow. Whenever something important happens, the Council makes sure to keep the knowledge away from the general public. All just part of the game, right?"

276

"Perhaps. And just like a game, there are multiple pieces, some more important than others. But ultimately, *all* are disposable. When you die, this war will continue," she says. "Just as if you never existed."

"But it doesn't have to keep going, and it won't. Nothing lasts forever, even if all the evidence points to the contrary. Let me go, and I can end this right now."

The Sage's ancient face draws tight, and I know I'm not going to like her next words. "Lilith, dear. You know I can't do that."

I expected that, but some part of me had stupidly hoped for different—positive—results. "W-what?"

"I can't do that," she repeats simply.

If I weren't wearing the handcuffs, I'm sure my magic would've manifested once again into a burst of wind, sending the bars flying. "But you *support* the Elementals. I'm supposed to replace you, remember? Wasn't that the plan?"

"At one time," she says. When she pauses, I glare at her until she continues. "I've done what I can. I let you go once, and you were caught, Lilith. You've determined your own fate."

"So that's it? You're going to let them *execute* me like Iris... like Chastity?"

"You've done well considering everything," she says, ignoring my question. "When you joined the Council, I had my doubts, but you've really shown yourself. I'm sorry things have to end like this."

"You're not sorry, or you'd let me go. Chalk it up to faulty handcuffs," I growl, rising slowly off the bed.

"You and I both know that would never work," the Sage replies. "Now, try to get some rest. I'll see you again before... well, you know."

"I'll tell," I seethe, gnashing my teeth as I take shaky steps toward the cell bars. "I'll tell *everyone* the truth. What you *really* are."

"Go ahead, my dear. You'll be just another radical Elemental. Remember what people thought of Iris? What *you* thought of Iris?"

I do, and my heart sinks. She's right. She set me up for failure, and now I've stepped in it. I'm her scapegoat—her failsafe. I always have been.

Just like Willow. The family legacy.

"When?"

The Sage raises her eyebrows.

I swallow heavily, trying to gauge how much emotion I can keep out of my words. "When am I going to die?"

The Sage looks at me for a long moment. It almost seems as if she's already regrets what she's about to say, but I know she doesn't. She can't if she's really still going through with this now, after everything. "At dawn," she says at last.

I open my mouth but close it again. What's the proper reply to news of my imminent demise?

Apparently, that bit of nothing suffices for the Sage. "Things will work out the way they're intended to," she says. "Have faith." Then she turns to leave without another word. She disappears down the corridor, her hobbling footsteps echoing behind her.

When I hear someone scoff, I jump and turn toward the sound just as Crowe appears in the doorway of the file room, dusting himself off after a fresh transformation. I glance at the door in confusion as he throws his clothes back on.

"I told you I was going to help you out of here," he says, buttoning his shirt, "and I meant it."

I nod with far less conviction than I would have liked. Even though he's here now, I still feel the sting of his betrayal. "How much did you hear?" I ask quietly, wondering if it'll make much of a difference.

"I heard enough," he says and digs into his pocket to pull out a handful of keys. "All of it. It isn't right. *This* isn't right."

I stare at him, my mouth gaping, and try to decide whether or not this is actually happening. And when was the last time I slept?

"You were right the whole time," he adds and slides the smallest key into the lock on my cell door.

I stand there, staring at him as if he's a complete stranger. I can tell he's in one of his moods, inspired most likely by the betrayal he feels himself. I don't know how long he's been a member of the Council, but the job clearly meant a lot to him; he loved his place.

I can't imagine the pain he must be feeling.

Yes, actually. I can.

Crowe pulls open the door, and instead of feeling any smugness over his acknowledging how right I was, I'm only relieved. "I'm sorry, Crowe," I murmur, uncertain if those are the right words for this situation.

"For so long, I kept her on a pedestal," he says, "holding her in the highest regard. I think it was because of how high I raised her—how high we all raised her—that I couldn't see her for what she is. Turns out my admiration only serves the show, the act, the *game* she's playing with all of us. With the entire Land of Five. Now that I see past it, *all* of it, it's clear. She's only poison masquerading as medicine."

Before I can respond, he snags the key hanging from around his neck and undoes the handcuffs binding me. They fall to the floor with a heavy clatter, and I rub the tender skin, looking up at him through teary eyes. For the rest of my life, I'll never be able to make up this debt to him.

"And she's using all of you to administer that poison," I add.

He only puts a guiding hand on my elbow to lead me through the barred door. When we pass Dawn's cell, I glance at her and dig my heels into the floor, lurching backward like a dog on a leash. "We can't just leave her here."

"She's wounded," Crowe reminds me.

"She'll be even worse off if we leave her," I remind him.

He bites his lip, then sighs and pulls out the handful of keys again, searching for the right one. As soon as he gets her door unlocked, I thrust it open, pushing by him so fast that I surprise us both. Dawn tries to sit up, to peer at me, before I drop to my knees by the edge of her bed.

"Lilith?" she asks in surprise.

I nod and look her over once, inspecting her for an idea of just how injured she really is. "Can you walk?"

Dawn peers slowly down at herself, looking so uncertain that I regret asking. What if she *can't*? What if she's just like me? When I examine the bandages on one of her legs, I realize in horror that part of her leg is *missing*.

"Crowe," I say, shooting him a desperate glance. He's looking over his own shoulder with wide, urgent eyes. "She needs help."

"I know," he says, looking one more time from Dawn and me to the empty corridor behind us, "but if I *carry* her, we won't be able to hide what we're up to. We'll never get out of here."

I want to argue with him, but I stop myself. There's nothing to dispute. He's right.

I turn to Dawn. "We can get you out," I tell her, noticing her chest rising and falling in quick, rapid breaths now.

"How?" she asks. I recognize the despair in her voice, the desperation, the pain that comes with knowing she's no longer capable of doing something that had once come so easily.

"You're going to have to work a bit," I admit. She stares at me. "The only way to get out of here without drawing attention is for you and me to look like prisoners," I tell her, then look to Crowe for confirmation.

He dips his head once, encouraging me to continue.

"Which means you'll have to try walking." She growls, but before she can even snap out a response, I add, "You can do it. *Trust me.*"

She holds my gaze for a long moment, and she either sees something in me she can trust or just decides to Hell with it. She sits up fully and leans toward me so I can help her to her feet. With her weight added to my own, I stumble, and Crowe rushes into the cell to steady both of us. Our progress is hard and slow—I lean on Crowe, and Dawn leans on me—but at last, we move. Crowe scoops up my walking stick on the way out, and I take it gratefully.

My leg hurts from the trek, but my senses are on such high alert with nerves that the pain isn't as bad as it could have been. We scurry toward the stairs, trying to get off the Surveillance Floor as quickly as possible. The next three floors of witches are just as eerily empty, and before we emerge back into the Sage's room, Crowe and I exchange a look. Something's wrong.

He jumps out first to pull Dawn through, then helps me out of the darkness of the hole in the Sage's floor. I'm grateful to be back onto familiar grounds. It doesn't last long; screaming in the distance makes sure of it. I piece the situation together instantly. Willow must have escaped from the second attack at Ignis.

And she must have come back for me.

Finally, we step outside the Headquarters building to see the devastation swept across the topiary garden, despite the darkness of night. A hint of smoke drifts in the air, and while I can't see any of the battle, I can hear it. I squeeze my eyes shut, momentarily wishing I was somewhere else. It's hard to forget this battle is for *me*—an attempt to save my life—but the price is too high.

If any of my Covenmates die, their blood will rest solely on   my   hands.

Chapter Thirty-Three

Clio

"**I**'M GOING TO take her somewhere safe," Crowe says, scooping Dawn into his arms and shooting me a determined glance. He nods once, and I don't have time to ask if he has another plan before he disappears into the night as fast as he can move.

This is a lot like the Battle of Ignis—direct, physical, and terrifying. I need to make a move. To either fight or run—*something*. Either way, I have a fighting chance now that Crowe took off the handcuffs.

There's a clamor behind me, rumbling up from the depths of Headquarters, and I scurry out of the way just a moment before dozens of witches flood from the building. I freeze in surprise, but none of them notice me as they hurry past me; no one knows I was the one walking with Crowe.

All at once, the tension erupts into full-blown war. Spells fill the air, and the cries only grow louder, more prominent, laced with both terror and pain. My heart thuds in my chest, but all the witches around me are unfamiliar. I don't know who to attack or with whom to stand, so I focus my effort instead into rushing across the field, desperate to find Crowe or Willow.

I should run *away* from the screams of agony, but some deep-seated, primitive thing inside me seeks revenge from these people who have brought so much torment into my life. Somehow, in my frenzy, I end up back inside Headquarters; it's complete chaos. The beautiful furniture in the Common Room is ripped, shredded, and destroyed. The alarm buzzes from the hallway, but no one cares. It's barely audible over the sounds of witches shouting at each other. Spells and magic fly everywhere, some aimed at me, but I don't engage.

Witches from Aens and Aquais are here, as well as the old Council members who lived in the bunker. They planned this, ready for the Elementals to attack Headquarters. My goal doesn't lie with any of them. I have to find Willow, to know if she's the one behind this, to confirm whether she escaped Ignis unscathed or whether this battle was planned in the event that she *didn't*. Then, the witches before me part, and familiar green eyes catch my attention, petrifying me where I stand.

Clio.

It's been so long since the last time I saw him that the moment doesn't feel real. I blink, tears in my eyes. Is this what it's like to see a mirage? It's cruel, so very torturous, and I wish the moment would stop. While the image may be fake, the hope it inspires is very real. I blink again, hoping the mirage will clear and everything will go back to the way I know it to be. When I open my eyes, he's still there.

For the first time, I realize my heart's smarter than my brain, despite the sight of him *here* at the Council's Headquarters hurting my head. He can't possibly be part of the Council … can he? Willow told me something about my replacement, but it makes more sense for the Adept to fill that void.

Please, Gods, don't let it be true. I'm already sure this prayer won't be answered.

He steps toward me, and I blink. It's Clio, but not as I remember him. His once clear, porcelain skin is now crossed with a variety of long, thick, ugly scars, the worst of which runs across the side of his neck—battle wounds. My heart sinks.

The Battle of Ignis. It's my fault.

I'm so overwhelmed by his sudden appearance, I happen to dodge Grail's ice attack by pure dumb luck, and I gasp as reality comes back to me. He could have killed me. If I don't get my act together, he will.

I pull my gaze away from Clio and turn to Grail, prepared for his next attack. I know he's a solid fighter—I remember his moves from my Arcane Ceremony—but there's a difference between watching and partaking. When he attacks again, it's easy enough to send up a shield.

I quickly learn that his ability isn't his only gift; his energy is out of this world.

Each shield I produce is weaker than the last, but his attacks don't lessen or weaken. Finally, my shield fails altogether, and I helplessly watch the icicles pass through it and into my leg before I feel the pain. When I hit the ground, it only registers for a moment that I'm lying in a pool of my own blood. The world spins, and the sounds of battle diminish. A blast of fire soars through the air, and when I glance at the floor, I see Grail lying a few feet away.

"Lilith!" Clio's voice fills my ears before I realize he's at my side, his arms wrapped around me.

Clio's closeness brings me back to simpler times, and all I want to do is bury my face in his chest and wish the world away. But I can't.

"Lilith, talk to me. Please," he cries.

I swallow raggedly and look up at him. "It hurts," I say, but I can't even manage a glance down at my legs to see the damage. It terrifies me to think that if I do, I'll lose what little will I have left to fight.

"I know, sweetheart." His voice is low, a little shaky, confirming he's already looked and wished he hadn't. He blasts away a few witches who stray too close, and I can see he's working up a plan.

I know what needs to happen. In such a confined space, the battle is bound to get remarkably worse before it ends. We need to get out, but the new pain in my leg makes me wonder how we'll ever manage it. Risking life and limb—literally—our only option is to move forward. Clio whispers encouraging words in my ear and somehow gets me up off the ground and kneeling on my bad leg, which is now conceivably more functional than the other.

"We have to go," he says. "Can... can you..."

I'm in far too much pain to do much more than nod and attempt to stand. The sudden weight of my own body makes me cry out in pain before I collapse again, and Clio freezes beside me, shielding me with his body, his eyes narrowed to attack. I don't look to see who he's hurting, because it doesn't matter either way. The sooner they're out of the picture, the sooner we can get away and I can rest my leg before my body shuts down completely. He tries to get me up again, but when that doesn't work, a frown overtakes his features. He defends us against hostile witches with ease, but the effort obviously exhausts him, his spells delivered at a decreased rate and his reaction time slower. He won't be able to keep it up forever.

He reaches for my waist—apparently to pick me up— but stops again to fend off another attack. This time, I do look at his opponent, glancing over his shoulder to catch sight of Crowe. "He's on our side!" I yell, desperately tightening my grip on Clio's arm. "He freed me."

Clio's hostility eases, and he looks at Crowe with a split-second of gratitude before the seriousness of battle returns, hardening his features.

"Aquais is here," Crowe groans.

My head swims with my own pain, but I clearly feel his too. He can't fight his loved ones, but he can't hurt us either, and my heart goes out to him.

Without warning, a blast of fire shoots toward him, but he dodges it with ease, turns to gauge the location of the attacker, and takes a step toward Clio and me.

"*Why* is Aquais here? Why is…" His gaze catches on something across the room, and I turn to see her too—Katrina, cradling the lifeless body of Crowe's mother Rena in her arms. Crowe races away from us so quickly, it takes me a minute to realize he's taken after them.

"Crowe!" I call, fighting to stand despite my useless legs.

"Let him go," Clio tells me, wrapping his arm around my shoulders. "We need to get you somewhere safe."

"I can't leave him," I say, gazing up into his emerald eyes. I can only think about how much Crowe risked for me. "He can't stay here. If he does, he'll die."

Clio's grip tightens, but he stops arguing with me and with himself. With a grunt, he scoops me into his arms before fighting his way to Katrina's side. She looks up at me through glazed tawny eyes, grief mixed with a surprise and horror when she catches sight of Crowe then the blood pouring from my legs and down over Clio's arms.

"We have to go," Katrina says. With me in his arms, Clio raises an awkward hand to blast fire at a pair of witches approaching us.

"Mother!" Crowe sobs, ignoring us all.

Katrina pulls his face toward her so he meets her steady, fervent gaze. "Crowe, listen to me. She's going to be fine, okay? We just need to get her out of here."

Crowe remains silent and motionless in shock. I can't say I blame him. When I first saw Helena broken and bleeding in battle, I'd forgotten how to *breathe*.

Katrina lifts Rena into her arms, staggering briefly under the woman's weight, then rushes out of Headquarters. I look down at Crowe still kneeling on the floor beside the pool of his mother's blood. I try to touch his shoulder, but I'm too far away in Clio's arms.

My hand remains outstretched, though, and Crowe takes it before standing. He stares after Katrina and her retreat with his mother's body, which snaps him back to the moment, and he finally moves again. Clio follows close behind.

"Dawn!" I shout, wondering where Crowe hid her.

He sniffs. "She's safe. We'll pass her on our way out."

Katrina's bun of blue hair acts like a beacon, making it easy for us to follow her through the screams and cries of battle. She doesn't slow down, and Crowe catches up with her as we stumble out of Headquarters. He hardly seems to notice any of the agony around him, his focus solely on his own.

Clio clutches me closer to his body as he runs, desperately trying to get me from the wreckage as quickly as possible, but every jostle is agonizing. His arm is dark with my blood, and though darkness threatens to cloud my vision, I force it away, staring up at the hazy, smoke-filled sky. By the time we get to the edge of the topiary garden, tears streak down my face, but all of us remain silent.

We don't need to say a word.

Chapter Thirty-Four

The Next Wave

*T*HE WITCHES WHO were once part of Aquais, as well as those with some kind of water powers, rush back inside the Council's burning Headquarters to put out the fires.

The topiary garden is studded with every witch from the depths—some standing, others lying in the dirt.

Every one of them carries the signs of the war, blood and bruises, and the Aquais witches are covered in soot from their firefighting efforts. Despite their work, the building crumbles, the pane of glass that served as one of the walls shattering with a haunting ring.

The witches can only stare. A few of them check on the Sage, examining her for potential injuries, but a lot more of them break down in tears. The current members of the Council—Lynx, Rayna, Hyacinth, and Colby—stare at the wreckage of Headquarters, of their home, and the few remaining Elementals scurrying over the border to disappear into the unknown of the woods beyond.

Rayna moves to follow, to fighting to the death if necessary, when Hyacinth stops her with a gentle hand on her arm.

"Stop. It's in his hands now," she whispers, gesturing to the shadowy figure of the witch emerging from the rubble.

KAYLA KRANTZ

About the Author

Kayla Krantz is fascinated by the dark and macabre. Stephen King is her all-time inspiration mixed in with a little bit of Eminem and some faint remnants of the works of Edgar Allen Poe. When she began writing, she started in horror but somehow drifted into thriller. She loves the 1988 movie Heathers. Kayla was born and raised in Michigan but traveled across the country to where she currently resides in Texas.

She has ideas for books in many genres which she hopes to write and publish in the future.

http://www.facebook.com/kaylakrantzwriter/
https://twitter.com/kaylathewriter9
https://authorkaylakrantz.com/

Other Works By This Author

Dead by Morning

(Rituals of the Night Book One)

Obsession is deadly.

No one learns that better than Luna Ketz, a pessimistic high
school senior. Caught between the intentions of her Muslim
father and business-minded mother, boys are the last thing on
Luna's mind, but this fact doesn't detour the mysterious Chance
Welfrey from trying to gain her affection.

Luna doesn't think twice about him until girls at their high school
begin to disappear. Girls who tended to hurt her. Girls she
wished would disappear. When she receives a call from a long-
lost friend, normalcy goes out the window as she's plunged into
the paranormal. There's a world beneath the surface of the

unconscious mind, and the killer knows how to navigate it. Luna is in danger and although she can avoid the killer in reality, she cannot avoid him in her dreams.

CPSIA information can be obtained
at www.ICGtesting.com
Printed in the USA
LVHW111924251120
672447LV00009B/147